FURTHER JOY

For Mary Helen Brandon & Mary Schneider

FURTHER JOY

Stories by

JOHN BRANDON

McSWEENEY'S

SAN FRANCISCO

STORIES

THE FAVORITE

Since Garner had been back, the only weather the town had offered was that familiar reedy glare that made everybody squint like they were in pain. Today Garner had on his darkest sunglasses, and his mother wore a big visor along with her paw-printed T-shirt of faded green. His mother's hair had reached that point where you couldn't tell if it was light or dark or mostly gray, but her eyes were still sharp as ever. Between plays she would look over at Garner with a sly, peaceful expression, grateful to be spending time with him again.

GCU. The Georgia Coastal Marsh Cats. Garner's mother liked to attend one game a year, to cheer the team in person, and the rest of the season she watched at home on a fifty-inch flat screen Garner had given her for her last birthday. The team was 4-0 and they were getting the upper hand again this afternoon. They'd done nothing but kick field goals but they had things under control. Garner didn't know what conference they were in anymore, but they were still running that same spread-to-run offense half the big teams were running now. They had a plow horse of a quarterback who never failed to convert a third and short.

Garner had been raised with football, but he'd always secretly looked forward to the day he'd be done with it. Even as a child he'd sensed, though he couldn't have put it into words back then, that the emphasis on sports in these parts was a key element of the small-town mediocrity he needed to escape. The public education system, from middle school on up, existed for no reason except to facilitate football games. A degree from Coastal saved you from driving a forklift at the factory but didn't get you any farther than an office in the same factory. These guys Garner and his mother were watching sweat and bleed down on the field would wind up middle-managing a fishery, rather than hauling up nets.

Garner hadn't been big enough to think about playing in college, even if he'd wanted to, but he'd played in high school, as was expected. People had been proud of Garner back then, and being an object of pride was something he'd learned to crave. His mother had taken tons of pictures of him in his uniform before the games and then beamed at him from the stands while he played. He'd had a way, on kick coverage, of getting lost in the scrum and then squirting out at the perfect moment and surprising the ball carrier. People loved it. They would compliment Garner's mother on his pluck at the grocery or the gas station. Still, Garner had felt relief when he'd stripped off his pads for the last time, when he'd done anything in this town for the last time, knowing that in a matter of months, weeks, days, he'd be in Atlanta using his brain to the utmost among total strangers.

And now he was living back here again, almost a decade later. Back in this string of sun-faded villages, all with the same seafood in the restaurants, each with one high school and a refurbished downtown of half a dozen shaded blocks. A few bored lawyers. A trickle of docile tourists. People raised in the area spoke with the accents of people who were stuck somewhere and didn't mind being stuck. Occasionally a chef got out, and once in a blue moon a musician.

Before halftime the Marsh Cats finally got into the end zone, on a fade pass to a lanky receiver named Forde. Garner asked his mother if she was hungry, then filed down out of the bleachers and made his way to the concession stand, which, besides the standard candy and chips, was offering a burger topped with boiled shrimp from a huge pot. Garner watched the man inside the stand pick up his coffee and sniff it, then drop the full cup into the trash. The man's mustache was neatly kept but he had a big belly and knobby knuckles. Garner ordered two burgers and the guy started getting the buns ready. He stopped and straightened up and said, "Ethel's boy."

Garner nodded. He waited as the man wiped his hands and offered to shake.

"I used to work with your mom at the carpet mill," the man told Garner. "She kept us in line. We used to call her the Vice Principal."

Garner chuckled, not completely falsely. Since he'd been back, his own gestures often felt odd to him, forced.

"I want to tell you I'm real happy to see you down here. For more than a weekend, I mean." The man asked if Garner's mother was in the stands, if that's who the other burger was for, and Garner told him she was. He made a succession of clicks in his cheek and leaned toward Garner, his eyebrows raised, an expression meant to warn Garner he was about to speak frankly.

"Buying her things is great, but coming down and spending your time—I'm real glad to see that."

Garner didn't know what to do but thank the man. He didn't see burgers anywhere, though he could smell them.

"It's not my place and I'm aware of that, but your mother deserved a good husband and didn't get one, and she deserves a good son and it'd be gratifying as hell if she did get that. I'm not trying to run down your father to you."

"No, you're right," Garner said. "She deserves good people."

The man slid a long-handled spatula out of a drawer. "Most guys with scratch like you got, they don't spend a whole lot of time buddying around with their old mom. Just thought somebody ought to say it to you."

"Appreciate that," said Garner.

The stadium loudspeakers were blaring on about some sale at a car dealership. The man slipped out the rear door of the stand, where there must've been a grill, and Garner stood alone.

*   *   *

Most mornings Garner rose before his mother and stared at the news on TV while hazy, fractured light swelled up behind the blinds. In the quiet dawns, Garner felt he could think, felt he could examine his circumstances calmly. The situation was that he was out of work. Almost six months. Just like every other loser who was out of work. He'd made it through a stifling Atlanta summer in a fog of denial. Finally, only a few weeks ago, he'd admitted the obvious to himself—without the income that had caused him to be rich, he was suddenly poor. That simple. He'd been a cash-burning go-getter for so long that it had become his identity, and now he had no cash. No one knew, and no one could. His mom couldn't know. The people in town couldn't. He'd been the kid who was too smart for these brackish burgs and had made it big on the outside, the kid who'd been good at everything he tried.

He could see now that he should've bailed out of his old life the day his income ceased. If he'd come home sooner, his finances wouldn't be such a mess now, but he'd been caught up in a fever, spending every penny he managed to scrounge up. He'd sold his patio furniture, his retro Cabriolet bed, but he'd kept paying every month for his loft, and then he'd had to pay still more when he broke the lease. He'd liquidated his car and a pricey scooter he'd never ridden, had *given* away his exotic fish to the only person he'd found who seemed like she'd take decent care of them, but then he'd signed up for a membership at the ritziest gym in the city. He paid an exorbitant penalty a few months later to cancel out early. He'd been carrying his own health insurance and had let that lapse just last week. And now he was living with his mother again—by choice, is what people assumed. They thought he was taking a break from the city grind, a working vacation of some sort, spending time with his mom because he was such a terrific guy.

Garner had brought a couple of his Italian suits down with him, he couldn't say why, and he had his phone working still. To cut off his phone would be to fully admit defeat. He had one last pack of Russian cigarettes out of a case he'd bought himself on a trip to Moscow back in January.

He smoked one every now and then but mostly he gave them away. He didn't like looking at the ornately decorated pack—it reminded him of all the exotic traveling he'd done for work. He remembered the view of that severe, windblown square out his hotel window. He remembered all the Russians walking around with ice cream cones even though it was freezing cold.

On Thursday, Garner frittered a midday hour away making small talk with his mother's friends while they constructed a quilt and monitored a tropical storm that was making its way up through the Caribbean. He listened to reports on all the women's children, one a kid named Lucas, now a *guy* named Lucas, whom Garner had been buddies with when they were younger. Lucas's mother had taken them to Atlanta once when they were little. They'd gone to the Coca-Cola Museum, the Professional Wrestling Museum. Lucas was around, his mother told Garner. She knew he'd love to get together. He was a tutor over at the college. They gave Lucas the important cases, the athletes and the exchange students. Lucas knew a little bit about everything, his mother said.

"Yeah, hopefully we'll get a chance to catch up," Garner told her, knowing he'd make no effort to make that happen. He really didn't care to be engaged in tales from the old days, or to hear about Lucas's band or whatever. He had a date that night to see Ainsley Thomas, and she was the only memory lane he wanted to walk down.

Garner accepted compliments from his mother's friends about his making time to come home for a nice long stay, endured their declarations that he was a fine young man. We know the area isn't real exciting for young folks, they told him. He managed to smile, though his face was hot and he was sweating under his clothes.

After a while he excused himself and retreated to his room. He put a decent shirt on and drove his mother's car downtown to a dim bistro that, as far as he knew, was the nicest restaurant in town. He was early. He picked through the car's consoles and compartments looking for gum or a mint, then gave up. He stayed in the car until he saw her walking toward the restaurant, and then hopped out to meet her before she went inside.

Ainsley Thomas. She and Garner had dated off and on through high school, and had somehow never had a bad breakup. When Garner had left to go to Atlanta, Ainsley insisted he do it a free man. She didn't want to hold him back, didn't want him to resent her, didn't want calling her to become a chore for him. And Garner hadn't put up much of a fight about parting ways. He'd wanted a clean break from the coast, from everything he knew.

Ainsley was wearing a simple sundress and flip-flops. Parts of her looked the same as ever. Her ankles. Her pointy chin that always made it seem like she knew more than she was saying. She looked clean somehow. She was a nurse now, Garner knew. She was divorced.

They sat at a small table next to a window. It was between mealtimes and the place was empty. They ordered croissants and some shrimp and Ainsley got a glass of wine and Garner a beer.

"You drink now?" Ainsley said. She was smirking at him, or at least it seemed like she was, because of her pinched little chin.

"Sure," Garner said.

"You never used to. In high school. You used to walk into parties with coffee. People thought you were weird."

"I'm still weird," Garner said.

"You were always lousy at vices."

"Self-destruction isn't my strong suit, I guess."

"Lousy at getting attached," Ainsley said.

She hid her face behind the bowl of her wine glass. She seemed calmer than before, either comfortable or resigned. Garner didn't want to have to talk about himself, didn't want to lie to Ainsley's face, so he asked her questions. He already knew most of what she told him, from second- and third-hand accounts his mother had provided. She'd gone to Coastal and held out as long as she could in graphic design before switching to nursing. She'd started dating a guy from one of the other marsh towns who played football at Coastal, a reserve linebacker. "He was slow," Ainsley said, "but nobody ever broke a tackle on him." After graduation she took a job at a rehab hospital a ways inland while the linebacker started a mortgage company. They'd gotten along well, had done small kind deeds for each other, had gotten married. For a time, the mortgage money had been rolling in. Then it stopped rolling.

"*You* broke a tackle on him," said Garner. "He had you and you slipped away."

Ainsley shrugged. "The short version is he couldn't stomach living off my income. 'Being kept,' he always said. I had no problem with it."

"You can't blame him for that," said Garner. "That's how they raise them around here. To make an honest living and support their women."

"Well, that wasn't the only problem. It's always more complicated than you can explain. Close to the end, we just quit trying. We'd hollered enough for a lifetime, so we just quit."

Ainsley swirled the last splash of her wine vacantly. She told Garner she'd been renting the third story of a house right out on the channel. In the mornings she watched the charters putter out toward the open water, or if she got up late, the real fishing boats coming back in.

The waiter came over offering more wine, which Ainsley accepted. Garner could see the wine was already getting to her; her neck and ears were flushed.

"And how's the nursing racket?" Garner asked her.

"I like the patients. My coworkers, not so much." Ainsley made a little sandwich out of a shrimp and a piece of croissant and bit it in half.

"Any interesting cases?"

"Interesting?" she said. "Let me see. A couple months ago we had a guy who fell out of a helicopter. Fell into water, so it wasn't as bad as it could've been. We had a lady who was delusional from dehydration. She kept calling me Delia and she thought we were in Texas. Never did figure out who Delia was. What else? A Coastal player got brought in this afternoon, if that's considered interesting. A fullback, I think they said." Ainsley stopped chewing and glanced behind her. "We're not supposed to tell people this stuff. HIPPA."

"What's HIPPA?"

"It's the rules. You can't go around talking about people you're treating. Everybody does, though."

Garner sipped his beer. It wasn't cold anymore. "What's wrong with the fullback?"

"Took too many pain pills and fell asleep in a drive-through. They started giving them to him last season because something was wrong with his shoulder. I guess he got a taste for them. We're going to hold him for a few days. The coaches are keeping it hush-hush. I don't know how they kept the cops from giving him a DUI, but they did. Oh, and down the hall from him we got this guy on vacation from Africa. Something's wrong with his stomach. He says he's a prince in his nation and women aren't permitted to look upon him disrobed. I guess it's not the dullest job, at least."

"Number 41? That's the fullback?"

"I don't know his number. Regular-looking white kid, except he has a mohawk."

"Huh," said Garner.

The waiter was back again. He didn't have any other tables. He dropped off a couple more napkins. Once he was gone, Ainsley reached across the table and took Garner's hand.

"I didn't know I was missing you until I saw you," she said, her voice placid but a touch raspy.

Garner's throat went dry. Sitting here with Ainsley was making him feel grateful, an unfamiliar feeling of late. He drank the better part of his beer and signaled for the bill. He made sure to put down the single credit card he had that wasn't maxed out. He could float this meal on credit and maybe a couple more, and then he'd be making a last stand with the cash he had left in the bank.

He and Ainsley left the bistro, pushing out into the salty, still air of the evening. He walked her to her car and she invited him to sit in the passenger seat. He started to say something and she interrupted him and said she just wanted to kiss him for a while, like back when kissing in a parked car was all they needed.

*   *   *

When Garner got home he went to his bedroom and shut his door and lay there in the dark, dozens of things wrestling in his head. He wondered, not for the first time, why he couldn't bring himself to come clean— why he couldn't sit his mother down and explain to her that he'd gone outside regulations to secure a big account and had gotten caught, that the rule he'd broken was one he'd broken a dozen times before, that everybody broke, but that this time the account had been lost and that this had caused problems. It wasn't a complicated story. There was the possibility that he wasn't really duping his mother at all, that his mother knew something was wrong and was giving him space to figure it out himself. He knew at least part of what was stopping him from telling the truth had nothing to do with her, anyway. It was the town—what this sincere, right-and-wrong hamlet thought of him. He couldn't tell whether he despised this place and couldn't stand the idea of being pitied by it, or whether he still needed the town to be proud of him. He thought of Ainsley, of course—her lips, her fingers in his hair. After all this time, she still wanted him. She'd wanted him back before his success. She'd wanted him, he knew, for his toughness. That he'd ever thought he was in her league to begin with, back when he was the scrawniest kid on the high school football team, said it all. He wasn't the type to give up, to be run off by long odds.

He was up from the bed and pacing now, arms crossed, pulling in whole breaths. There his suits were in the closet, dormant, dutiful. A fly was buzzing around over near the window, probably trapped behind the screen. What Ainsley had told Garner about the fullback was picking at him. It *was* number 41. He remembered the mohawk. He'd noticed the kid last Saturday, easily the best blocker on the team, one of those kids who had that innate knack for colliding squarely with another human. He was stout enough to lead inside and quick enough to pull wide on outside runs, and when the offense got stuck they'd sneak him out of the backfield and throw to him. Usually that type of offense didn't even use a fullback, but this kid was always out there. Several times Garner had even seen him directing traffic before the snap.

Garner sat down on the bed and plucked his phone from the nightstand. He looked up the lines and found that Coastal was favored by nineteen points that Saturday. Almost three touchdowns. They were on the road, at North Florida. Three touchdowns on the road. Their star fullback wouldn't be playing and nobody knew it yet.

Garner reclined stiffly onto his back, the fly in the window quiet now, gone or else resigned to its fate. He stared into the dark and must've slept an hour here and there, and in time, as it had to, the sour bluish light rose up into the world. He showered and dressed and drove his mother's Honda directly west on Route 8 until he came to a town two counties in where no one knew him. He had to wait fifteen minutes for the bank to open, and then he went in and withdrew everything he could from his checking without having to close the account—a little over two grand. He didn't love the idea of using cash, of using a live bookie, but that last credit card didn't have nearly enough room on it, so here he was, doing this the old-fashioned way. This was the way desperate people bet and he was desperate.

The teller asked if he needed anything else and he said he did. Garner had an old money market he'd opened with the commission from his first big deal. He'd never touched it, had planned to leave it be until he was older, when he'd be able to tell people it was the first score he'd ever made. Then he'd do something magnanimous with it, maybe gift it to some ambitious young man he would have begun to mentor.

It hadn't had time to accrue much interest; it was still around five thousand. Garner drew a steadying breath and told the teller he wanted to close the money market.

On the drive back to the coast, he felt a pang of contrition over the fact that he'd gotten the information for the bet he was about to make from Ainsley, information she wasn't supposed to have shared with him, but he told himself he was being ridiculous. No one would find out why he'd made the bet, and no one was getting cheated except the bookie. He'd make this one bet, and after he won he could figure out a better way to get some money coming in.

He pulled up behind Cuss Seafood, an ancient, tidy diner where everyone knew the owner took wagers. Garner had never been in the place. He poked his head into the storeroom and asked for Cuss and after a minute a wiry black man with one of his eyes askew walked out and accepted Garner's money like it was twenty bucks. Cuss reeked of harsh, outdated soap. It was hard to tell if he was looking at Garner or off into the live oaks. He peered at Garner's driver's license, scribbled in a little booklet, then slipped Garner's cash into a blue envelope stamped LOWER COUNTRY ENTERTAINMENT. "You sure this just for entertainment?" he said. "We a entertainment outfit."

Saturday morning Garner's mother's hot water heater crapped out. He insisted to her that he'd take care of it, having no clue how much a hot water heater cost. He wasn't going to look into it until after the game. A hot water heater would be the least of his worries if he lost the bet. He'd get to find out what rock bottom felt like.

He skipped a cold shower. Down at the end of the block he puffed away at one of his Russian cigarettes and when he got back to the house his mother's friends were appearing. They were putting hors d'oeuvres together for the game. They liked to watch it here, on the big TV.

Garner said his hellos and returned each woman's hug. The big woman who tottered around in high heels, the skinny one who always wore a ball cap. Lucas's mother was there again. Lucas's band was rehearsing, she said, or he would've come over. They were getting ready to record a demo, so they had to practice every chance they got. They always received terrific reviews in the local papers, Lucas's mother told Garner. He should go listen to them sometime.

"Sure," he said. "I just might do that."

He spent another couple minutes turning down the food the women offered him, then claimed he wasn't feeling well and retired to his room to watch the game on a tiny old TV set that normally stayed in the back of the closet. Garner didn't want to be around people for the game. He snuck out and fetched a beer from the fridge during the highlight show that aired during warm-ups, thinking the alcohol would dampen his nerves, but it tasted stale and he only got about half the bottle down.

He saw the opening kickoff, saw the spheroid spinning end over end against the sky, and then he watched in a trance as the first minutes proceeded exactly as he needed them to. One drive ended with a dropped pass, another on downs. Both teams were using the full play clock, like they wanted to get the game over with. The only scoring opportunity in the quarter was a North Florida field goal that sailed well wide. Everyone on the field was testy. A player on each side got whistled for a hit out of bounds, and then the Coastal tight end got ejected for throwing a punch at a North Florida safety. Both coaches stripped down to undershirts and kept yanking their headsets off to scream at the officials. The Coastal running back had no pop and wasn't falling forward like he usually did, mostly because, to everyone but Garner's surprise, Coastal's fullback had been a late scratch.

Everything was moving quickly, even the commercial breaks. The stands were half empty, Garner noticed. Bad shotgun snaps and booming punts. When Coastal finally hit a long post route to that receiver Forde, the play was called back for illegal procedure because the backup fullback had lined up wrong. And at that point, watching the Coastal players begin to celebrate and then stop celebrating and drop their heads at the sight of the yellow hanky on the ground, optimism filled Garner's guts.

At halftime, with the North Florida band forming itself into letters that would spell out AMBERJACKS, Garner was snapped out of his reverie by a rare call on his cell phone. It was Ainsley. She didn't so much invite him as she *told* him he was going to come over to her house for dinner Thursday, her night off. She was going to cook Indian. She'd already been to Savannah for the spices. She wasn't in the business of rushing things, she told Garner, but she also wasn't in the business of stalling.

"I thought you were in the business of kissing," Garner said.

"I am, but I'm thinking about expanding."

"High demand, huh?"

Ainsley scoffed. "Seven-thirty."

Garner was still holding his phone and staring at nothing when he noticed that the third quarter had begun. Coastal was pressing and suffered one pre-snap penalty after another. The offensive line was in disarray and one of the tackles came to the sideline and hurled his helmet into a fence. Afternoon was waning into early evening. Garner's appetite was returning, but he didn't want to leave the bedroom and break the spell.

He kept his eyes on the TV as all the scoring arrived in a fourth-quarter rush. Coastal managed a field goal and then North Florida ran back the ensuing kickoff and then Coastal, almost out of time, called that same simple dive play up the middle, a play that had been stuffed all day, and somehow none of the linebackers were home and a couple defensive backs got tangled up with each other trying to make the tackle. Sixty-yard touchdown. Kickoff. A couple doomed deep passes. The last seconds ticked off. Game over. The coaches were shaking hands. It was a three-point victory for Coastal. Garner had won his bet. He'd won it by a mile.

Garner showed up early at the diner Monday morning, walking around back with the delivery men dropping off the morning catch, and collected from Cuss, who said "The rich get richer" when he handed over Garner's winnings. Then Garner raced inland to the bank, again getting there before they opened, and dealt with that same teller. He drove back to the coast and paid off a lesser credit card, had his mother's new hot water heater installed, made sure he was paid up on his phone bill. He filled the Honda with gas and ran it through a car wash and bought a twelve-pack of imported beer for his mother's fridge. He had his strut back. He went for a jog and shaved, straightened up his room and ate an overstuffed roast beef sandwich. Then he went to a jewelry store on the edge of downtown, his blood humming, and picked out a restored rose-gold Baume & Mercier wristwatch for Ainsley, and he left it on her front porch in a glinting gift box with a scarlet bow. He drove around the outskirts of town with his window down, the afternoon sun on his arms, getting a look at all the places that were important to him as a kid. He drove by the high school, the old swimming hole, the fields where all the youth sporting events were still held.

It wasn't until the next day, after a morning working on his mother's yard and an afternoon nap that left him groggy rather than refreshed, that gloom began creeping back over Garner. He lay motionless in his little bedroom, absently listening to people argue on a sports radio show, his hair matted with sweat. Reality was upon him again. He'd settled one small card but there were several big ones still bearing down on him. He had his storage unit to pay, full of the stuff from his loft that he'd been unable to sell but unwilling to throw out. And then there was the damn watch. It was too much too soon. He'd gotten carried away, had fallen back into the mode he'd lived by in Atlanta, where he'd learned everything about money except how to respect it. Ainsley would think he was showing off or something, which he supposed he had been.

He clicked off the radio, on which a caller had been mocking a baseball player who'd cried after losing his team a game. Garner stared up at the fan. It wasn't spinning fast enough to push any air.

Wednesday Lucas didn't have to tutor and didn't have band practice, so Garner got him out to a rickety pier on the marsh flats where they'd gone fishing countless times as kids. The pier looked like it was about to collapse, but it had looked that way for decades. It was on a minor canal and in the first hour of fishing Garner and Lucas didn't see another soul. The sun was out, pale and strained, like a headlight that had been left on too long. That tropical storm had never shown up; it had dragged its skirts over Bermuda and petered out in the North Atlantic. Garner felt disoriented. This guy he was sitting with on this rotten pier had once been his best buddy. The years had changed him, but not by much. His voice was the same. He had the same cowlick in his hair, the same scar on his calf from when he'd wrecked his bike when he was nine years old. Garner had the sense of watching himself from afar. He'd talked himself into the first bet and now he'd talked himself into a second, had talked himself into what he was about to do. He was watching himself prepare to close a deal.

He'd brought out gin and tonic fixings and today, for the first time in a while, was drinking right along with his company. They'd brought out some lunch, too, but as midday approached Lucas seemed less and less interested in eating. They hadn't caught a thing but their bait kept getting stolen, which didn't seem to bother Lucas. He was an easy-moving, even-handed guy. As Garner had built an identity for himself out of success, Lucas had built one of composure, of fruitless but dignified perseverance. It was wearing thin, Garner could see. Lucas was gray around the eyes and his shoulders were slumped.

Garner poured another round of drinks, the ice mostly melted by that point, and got Lucas to talking. Garner complained about the town, the same complaints from the old days.

"They're a satisfied bunch," Lucas said. "I'll say that for them. Doesn't take a whole lot to keep smiles on their faces."

"I know what you mean," said Garner.

"They're proud of this place. I mean, look around. It's pride for the sake of pride, I guess."

"They think it's a virtue."

"Easy mistake," said Lucas. "Clerical error. They put pride in the wrong column."

"The main thing they're proud of is that nothing changes. Town doesn't change. People don't change. The achievement is lack of achievement."

"It's like my mom," Lucas said. "Bragging about me all the time. Always telling everyone about me. What the fuck have I done? Nothing. But at least I realize it."

"You're attempting to accomplish something worthwhile," Garner told him. "Worthwhile endeavors are risky and they take time."

"Maybe that's the problem around here. There's no risk and no reward. And nothing *but* time."

Lucas's eyes were animated, not so gray. The water was lapping under the dock to its own incoherent rhythm. Lucas told Garner he was only continuing to tutor and bus tables because he needed a dependable van. With a van, his band could play out-of-town gigs. Once they were playing steady, they could think about moving to Charleston. They could make a name for themselves in the Carolina college towns. There was a label called Bottle Tree that would sign them, once they had more of a fan base. Lucas wanted to account for himself, it seemed like—to declare his plans. He told Garner he played the upright bass and sang baritone. He hadn't allowed the band to be named yet. They went by Music Project. Lucas wasn't going to name them for real until they deserved it, until someone cared what their name was.

Garner was tired of baiting his hook and had quit reeling it back in. He took his Russian cigarettes out and there were two left. He offered one to Lucas.

"Trying to quit," said Lucas.

"Me too." Garner kept holding the clay-colored cigarette out until Lucas took it from him. They lit up and Garner tossed the pack away.

"What exactly is it that you do?" Lucas asked him.

"I'm in export futures," answered Garner. "That's what I'd call it."

"Exporting what?"

"Anything that's touchy to export."

"I've always imagined you going a lot of places, meeting a lot of people. Hanging out in weird foreign airports."

"It used to be fun," Garner said. "I won't deny it."

"Everything used to be fun." Lucas baited again, setting his cigarette on a damp plank and then picking it back up. "We're not catching them," he said. "We're feeding them."

"So do you have the name picked out, though? For the band?"

Lucas shrugged.

"I can keep a secret," Garner said. "That's another part of my job."

Lucas thought a minute then spat. "It's narrowed down to two. Proven Pelvis, or Lucas Graines and the Tufts."

Garner nodded.

"I don't know if I like either of them anymore. It's kind of stupid, anyway—not naming the band. Makes it a little hard to get name recognition, right?"

"Your mom said you were getting ready to make a demo."

"We're always getting ready to make a demo."

Lucas flicked his line around like it was caught on something. He took a drag from his cigarette and let the smoke leak out his nostrils.

"So which all players do you tutor?" Garner asked him.

"The dumb ones," said Lucas.

"Any of the good players?"

"To tell you the truth, I haven't really been following the team."

"How about Nigel Forde? That receiver. You tutor him?"

"He comes in sometimes. They all have to come every once in a while."

Just then Lucas's rod bent. He got a grip on it and dropped what was left of his cigarette in the water. The fish was stubborn but it wasn't running anywhere. Lucas didn't seem pleased to have hooked something. He was peering at the water and cranking. The sun was high above, and the tall reeds were leaning with a tepid breeze.

"Lucas," Garner said, sounding as sober as he could. "Lucas, you can't tell anyone I told you this but I'm having money problems."

Lucas's cranking slowed, but now the fish was visible beneath the surface of the water. It was chasing itself around.

"You're the only one who knows," Garner said. "I'm broker than you are. I'm scraping the barrel."

Lucas raised the dripping fish up into the light and stoically got a hold on it. The fish didn't flail. It had done all its fighting. It wasn't an eating fish and wasn't big enough anyway, so Lucas freed it from the hook, lowered it off the side of the pier, and released it. He and Garner watched it swim off casually into the dark water as if nothing had happened.

"Broker than me?" Lucas said finally. "That's a pretty brazen claim for someone like you to make. That's big talk."

"I need you," Garner told him. "I need you and you don't necessarily need me. I'm in a tight spot, but maybe you're not. Maybe you want to stay in this same life you've always been in. You have that luxury. You can put a plot on layaway over at the memorial gardens and sit next to it in a lawn chair until they lower you in. You can do that, if it strikes your fancy."

Lucas gnawed on a fingernail and spit it in the water, waiting.

"The other option, besides waiting at the cemetery, is getting a van and some gas to put in it and some better instruments and some real studio time and whatever else would help. That's another way to go. All in."

"Two choices," said Lucas. "That's more than I'm used to."

"It's more than most people get."

Lucas pressed his lips together and then he sat up straight. "I'm curious to know what you got cooked up," he said. "No denying that. I'm curious to see how your mind works."

"Nothing fancy. We're going to redistribute a little wealth is all." Garner looked flatly into Lucas's eyes. "We're going to make a wager and we're going to win it."

"Redistribute, huh?" said Lucas.

"An intelligent foray into gaming."

Garner told Lucas about his first bet, when the fullback had been out. He explained that with the fullback returning the Coastal offense was expected to recover its swagger, but if they didn't have Forde, the only deep threat, the opposing defense would put nine men in the box and stuff all of Coastal's pet running plays. He informed Lucas that they were going to accuse Nigel Forde of academic dishonesty. That was the easiest plan. They were going to make an accusation and that accusation would have to be looked into.

Lucas still hadn't cast his line back out. He rinsed his hands in the water and shook them dry. He was a patient guy, even now. "I was wondering why you wanted to go fishing with me," he said.

"Now you know."

Lucas looked vaguely in the direction where the boundless ocean was. He let out a laugh, not because anything was funny. "This is what we've come to," he said. "Ten years ago we were sitting out on this dock, ecstatic to have a couple beers in our possession. Remember?"

Garner nodded at him.

"I guess you always find a solution, don't you? You're the solution guy."

"It would appear that way," said Garner.

Lucas rested his forehead in his palm. He picked at one of the soft wooden planks of the pier with his fingernail. "I didn't like tutoring from the first day I did it," he said. "Helping those imbeciles write papers so they can keep bashing each other's heads in."

"If anyone catches onto this, there might be consequences more dire than losing your tutoring career."

"I'm aware of that."

"And this is still gambling, you know?" Garner said. "There's still a chance we could lose the bet. It's slim, but it's there."

"I'm losing now," said Lucas. "I'm getting whipped."

"Well, you and me both."

Lucas hung his hook on an eyelet of his rod and reeled the line taut. He rested the whole rig on the pier. He looked down at nothing for a time, his head bowed like an exhausted traveler, then he spat deliberately into the water. "So," he said. "I'm not agreeing to this, but how would we do it?"

Garner talked it over with him, encouraged that Lucas didn't seem drunk, and they decided the simplest method would be for Lucas to drop an anonymous tip into the Dean of Students' box. Just wait until the hallway was empty and stroll by and slip it in. There was a geology class all the athletes took, a class that was exactly the same every semester. Lucas could drop a typed note asserting that Forde had copies of all the tests. They only needed him to be held out of this one game while the dean's office investigated the claim. Forde would be cleared eventually, no harm done. Just a mistaken tip, an empty rumor, and no one to attach it to.

"I guess no one's going to look after my future but me," Lucas said.

"Can you do this?" Garner asked him.

"I can do more than you probably think I can."

Neither of them wanted another drink. Garner offered Lucas one of the sandwiches still sitting there in the cooler, but he didn't want it. The day was getting hot finally, the silvery sun getting a bead on the marshland, that sweet rotten smell rising up from the reeds.

*   *   *

On Friday, Garner parked down the block from Cuss Seafood, under a stunted myrtle that offered little shade. Lucas had not backed out, as Garner had thought he might. Lucas had, just minutes before, called Garner's cell phone and hung up when Garner answered, meaning the tip was planted. Early that morning Lucas had dropped off his $6,100 at Garner's mom's house, all the money he had.

Garner emerged from his mother's Honda and took a sharp breath. His date with Ainsley the night before had not gone well. They hadn't made it past the hors d'oeuvres course, the samosas Ainsley had spent half the day making. He'd arrived three or four gimlets in, and had immediately started working on an oversize Indian beer. He'd been too drunk and could now feel the proof of that in his temples. This was why Garner didn't usually drink. He couldn't handle it. He'd gone to the bar yesterday afternoon because he was anxious about dragging Lucas into this. Garner had felt impatient since the minute he'd arrived back on the coast, and it had all caught up with him last night. He'd kept trying to rush things to the bedroom, and Ainsley had kept slowing him down as politely as she could. He'd asked her why the hell she'd invited him over, and then watched injury bloom in her face. She'd stood up from the couch stiff and composed. He was different from his old self, Ainsley had told him. There wasn't any sweetness in him anymore. Not a trace. Whatever he'd been pretending to be in Atlanta, he really was now. She'd handed him the wristwatch and given him a long look that expressed mostly disappointment.

Maybe he could patch that up in a few days, but he couldn't let it distract him right now. It was a bad date with an old flame; that's all it was. It was time for business, time to look Cuss in his good eye. The reason schemes didn't occur to most people, he knew, was they couldn't pull them off. Garner could. This is what he did. He found the soft spots, and there were plenty of them. He swung the door of the Honda shut and stepped over a row of lilies and up onto the sidewalk, the day open and bright in every visible direction, feeling the fist of rolled cash in his pants pocket with each stride.

THE PICNICKERS

At the close of the spring semester, Kim drove from Galesburg to Chicago to visit her old friend Rita. She normally stayed a week, but after three days in the suburbs it began to feel like she'd been there long enough. Rita's neighborhood friends were always dropping by—Tuesday for health shakes, Wednesday for scrapbooking. This morning, roused by their noise, Kim had made her way down to the kitchen to find a group of them trying to convince Rita to go to the outlets. These women had plenty of money but nonetheless got a thrill out of finding a bargain. Rita was hesitant about the plan. She knew that Kim wasn't a shopper.

"Maybe it's time I learned," Kim said. "Maybe it's time I broadened my horizons. This is stuff other people didn't want, right—at the outlets? That might suit me. I usually like stuff other people don't want." She got a bottle of diet soda from the fridge and sat down at the table with it. She felt bad for Rita, having to juggle Kim and her other friends all at once. Kim so plainly didn't fit in that she'd begun to feel emboldened.

"It'll be all day," Rita said. "We grab lunch up there and everything."

"I have two hundred and twenty dollars and some change. Is that good enough for all day?"

Rita's friends had grown used to Kim and didn't often respond to her. They were regarding one another with tight faces and blowing into their coffee cups.

"I just don't want you to be bored," said Rita. "You have to promise you won't be bored."

"You don't need to worry about me being entertained," Kim said. "How long have we known each other?" She was smiling—a little crazily, it felt like.

It was very bright outside, but Kim could see a lot of clouds through the window too. The leaves on the trees were tender-looking and motionless. The kitchen smelled of whole things, grains and healthy shampoo.

One of the women, the youngest of them, wasn't drinking coffee. She made this conspicuous by fondling her cup, turning it upside-down. When the others finally questioned her, she played coy for a moment before announcing she was pregnant. *Might* be pregnant. She was almost sure. Squealing and flouncing ensued, the women all hugging each other and even deigning to hug Kim, though she remained seated. The other women jokily consoled the pregnant one about not being able to drink wine. Apparently she really liked wine. They all hoped she'd have a girl this time. Preliminary plans for a shower were put in place, duties assigned. Rita didn't want catering again. She wanted anything but catering.

"The Carter's outlet," one woman said. "I saw the sweetest animal blankets in there. Neutral colors too. They have a pale green and a mustard. And some adorable bibs. You can't have enough of those."

"I have a stack of ten-percent coupons," Rita put in. "They work anywhere in the whole mall."

"I have some for the kitchen place," said someone else. "Not Williams-Sonoma but the other one."

Now Kim stood with her soda. She didn't really want it anymore, but she opened it and took it over near the sink. There were more clouds in the sky than a minute ago but also more sunlight. Going to the outlets, she knew, was not a good idea. These women didn't want Kim around. Things would not turn out well. There was a time when Kim could go with the flow, could see the good in people, but that time had passed. She was grumpy now; she worried all the time, and about the wrong things. She worried that she was tired of all the music she owned, instead of that her bathroom was filthy. Her car's engine was about to give out, but she complained that the windows stuck. She had some money in the bank but no confidence she knew how to spend it. Right now she should've been worrying about the fact that she'd fallen out of friendship with Rita, but there didn't seem to be anything either of them could do about it. Their lives had diverged radically; the alliance of soul they'd shared when they were younger was dead on the vine.

Franklin, Rita's son, came down the stairs, his footfalls weighted and clumsy. Without acknowledging the kitchen full of women, he stuck his head in the fridge. He wore a wrinkled dress shirt and pants with numerous pockets. He was lanky, with sharp, slight shoulders. Franklin had a driver's license these days and didn't seem to eat meals. He didn't need anything from Rita anymore.

After banging around for a minute, Franklin emerged from the fridge with a bag of lemons. He dumped them on a cutting board and began halving them with a cleaver.

"Franklin," Rita said. "Dare I ask?"

"They're going rotten. The United States and Australia waste more food than the rest of the world combined. That's something I learned just this morning, doing random Internet research. It may or may not be true. I don't know what you bought these for, but they're on their last legs."

"I'm aware they're on their last legs," Rita said. "That's why I put them in the fridge. I was going to make pear butter, but I didn't get around to it. For the walk-run."

"Well, what I'm going to do is take the lemons life gave us and make lemonade."

Rita picked up a heavy peppermill and cleaned a spot on it with her thumb. "I don't think lemonade is a breakfast. Why don't I make you some eggs? I'll make over-easy eggs and rye toast like you like."

"Breakfast isn't really my strong suit anymore," said Franklin. He set the knife aside and squeezed a few of the lemon halves over a bowl. He paused and plopped in ice cubes, then found a spoon and fished out some seeds. "This day is starting off fun," he said.

Kim could remember Franklin as a small child. Rita and her husband had been worried about him, thinking he had Asperger's or something. It had visibly pained him to look anyone in the eye, and for some reason he'd refused to ever say hello or goodbye. He still didn't say hello, now that Kim thought about it. His verbal skills were always off the chart and he'd been a happy kid, but he didn't want to talk to anyone. He'd shown no interest in the cartoons the other kids adored, no interest in playing hide-and-seek or tag, but then he'd take a puzzle over to a corner of the room and keep putting it together and taking it apart for hours, until someone stopped him.

Somewhere along the line, he'd outgrown it. He'd learned to read people well enough. In grade school, they'd put him in a gifted class, and now he was in an expensive untraditional high school. The last time Kim visited, almost two years ago, he had been neck-deep in the collected letters of Vincent van Gogh. He'd found an enormous three-volume set at an estate sale, and was staying up nights with it. He'd sought Kim out one afternoon in the den, knowing she'd majored in Art History in college, and conducted a one-sided conversation with her in front of the cold, clean-scraped fireplace. He'd asked her unanswerable questions about the bond between siblings, made familiar accusations about the tastes of the public. Kim had asked him how he'd gotten interested in van Gogh's letters and he'd said he didn't think he was interested in them as much as hypnotized by their redundancy.

"We're going to the outlets," Rita was telling him. "Are you going to wear that shirt to school? It looks like you slept in it."

"I didn't sleep in it," he said. "Not *last* night."

"You know where the iron is," she said.

Kim hoped Franklin didn't lump her in with these other women. She didn't know why she would care, but she did. She was running her eyes over the sprawled sections of newspaper on the kitchen counter. They were full of the same stories that were always in newspapers. Unemployment was down, but not enough. A species of warbler had gone extinct. The smell of the women and the coffee and the lemons on an empty stomach was making her a little sick.

"I wonder, Mom, if you could spare one of your gang." Franklin's hair was messy by design and there was a scuff of acne along the curve of his jaw. "There's an extra-credit thing I need to do. It's on the Gauguin exhibit at the Art Institute. It's a two-man deal, though."

"At the Art Institute?" Rita said.

"I'm supposed to go with someone and then interview them about the exhibits. Anybody except a classmate. There's a whole list of questions, then I'm supposed to think of my own follow-up questions based on the answers to the first questions. It can't be a classmate, though. It has to be, like, a member of the public."

Rita's face was resigned, faintly amused. "Let me guess. Today is the last day you can do it." She looked around at the other women as if for sympathy. "I can always tell the last day something can be done, because that's the day he'll mention he needs to do it. I thought we talked about you having a schedule," she told Franklin. "Writing it all down."

He nodded, but he was in the middle of slurping more of his lemonade. When he came up for air, he shuddered, as if he'd done a shot of whiskey.

"And what about school?" Rita asked Franklin.

"This is the morning the class meets. You can miss a class meeting if you're doing the extra credit."

"What class is it for?"

"The Politics of the Image. I've got an atrocious grade in there, so I could use the points. I mean it's really alarming, how low my average is. The teacher says it's sad, because my insights are of uncommon quality."

"The Politics of the Image?" said Rita. "When I was your age, they called it Art Class."

"You're the one who put me in this school. None of the names make sense. We talk about Freud in Civics."

It seemed it was Rita's turn to talk again, but she only shook her head. The air conditioner kicked on. The woman named Teresa or maybe Tessa slipped a thin sweater off the back of her chair and hung it on her shoulders.

"Education first," said Franklin. "That's what I've always heard."

Rita was looking at Franklin with a face Kim guessed was tough love. "You should have planned this out ahead of time," she said. "You always do this. You always want people to change plans around you. You always want to get bailed out."

"I planned to plan ahead, but that plan fell through. Kind of like with your pear butter." Franklin shifted around inside his shirt. "I just need someone to respond to art. It's not a terrible thing to ask. It's not breaking rocks in the sun."

Everyone was quiet. Kim could tell Rita's friends wouldn't get involved. The etiquette was to mind your own business when someone else's kid was being difficult, to not say a word. An airplane could be heard passing over the house. The coffeemaker made a gentle gurgling noise.

"We should all get going," Rita said. "Us to the mall and you to school. Manage your schedule better next time."

Franklin exhaled dramatically. He was standing still, his eyes wide, and Kim thought he was trying to look toward her. He was looking at the area of her knees, his face stiff and apprehensive. He let his eyes flash up to her face for only a second. "If no one wants to go, no one wants to go," he said. "I can't force anyone." He waited a beat. When no one spoke up his shoulders went slack and his head slumped forward onto his chest. He started fishing around in his pants pocket for something. Rita had opened a drawer and pulled out a little accordion folder where she kept her coupons organized, and was flipping through it with a fingernail.

"I'll do it," Kim said. She pushed the newspaper into a pile and pushed it away from her. "I'll be the subject."

The kitchen went silent again. Kim could feel the skewering looks of the women in the room. At this point she was enjoying them. She'd broken the noninterference code, compromised the unified front.

The look Rita rested on Kim was one of tart curiosity. Kim didn't look away from it. Rita still had her fingers in her coupon book. She cleared her throat, and quickly enough she was smiling again. There was something brave in her smile nowadays.

"All right then," she said. "I guess that's settled." She pulled what she needed out of the coupon book and placed it back in the drawer, which she closed very softly. Then she reached for her purse and gave the contents a shake. "Franklin, it looks like you're going to slide by again." She removed her wallet from her purse and found some cash. "Take this," she said to him. "If Kim's giving up her day for you, you can at least buy her lunch."

"That's not necessary," Kim said, but Franklin was already accepting the bills and stuffing them into one of his pockets.

The rest of the women were gathering up their phones and sunglasses. "We could try Barbette for lunch," one of them offered uncertainly. "They're supposed to have really good soups." Franklin smirked at Kim and returned to his lemonade, sniffing it and adding more sugar.

"Isn't Gauguin the one that molested all those island girls?" Rita asked.

"That's what they say," said Kim.

"In Tahiti or whatever. That's him, right? He was always having his way with the natives."

"There was so much molesting going on in those days," said Kim. "Hardly seems fair to keep bringing it up."

She excused herself and went upstairs, her blood quickening with escape. She couldn't be around Rita's new friends another minute. She reached the landing without a backward glance and strode down the hallway. The second floor of the house was a whole different kingdom. It smelled different up here, like brand-new furniture, like bamboo.

In the shower she rubbed herself up with gel, breathing the steam. She soaped her thighs, her shoulders, massaged the back of her neck. Kim still liked her body. Her lips were plump and her legs were firm and shapely. Her skin was soft enough. A stranger would never have guessed that she'd used up more than half of her thirties.

She stayed in the shower long after she'd rinsed off, enjoying the warmth, and then she stepped out onto a plush teal rug, water streaming off her. The mirror and fixtures were fogged. She wrapped a towel around herself and wandered into the closet connected to the guest bathroom, dripping on the carpet among a hundred dresses, many with their tags still on. This was Rita's runoff area, for the clothes that wouldn't fit in her primary closet. Kim thought of her own cramped bedroom closet back in Galesburg, her bulky coats and worn sundresses. She couldn't have fit another hanger in there, yet she didn't own one article of clothing she still liked.

Staying in Galesburg had never been the plan, of course, and she thought about this often now—just how she'd wound up where she was. When she'd graduated, the part-time position she'd taken as a senior in college had been offered to her full time. She could still remember how grateful she'd been. She'd wanted money, not more loans. She'd wanted aimless weekends and a little cash to spend, not more Sundays of homework. Her job as an assistant became a job as an adviser. She went as far, those first couple years, as sending off for the grad school applications. Places like Arizona, Oregon. She felt herself envying the professors on campus, with their consuming research, with their peculiar, prized minds. But then she was moved laterally and promoted; she decided to buy a new car, and take a trip to Italy. She was administrating the honors program now, a position of accomplishment. The higher-ups loved her. She had great insurance and a retirement account and summers off. For the last sixteen semesters she'd been making sure all the hottest shots at the school—so many twenty-year-olds with cutesy snow hats and ear buds hanging down their shoulders and knobby knees and cheery jewelry—had the ducks of their futures in a row. The years were coming and going, the seasons slipping past.

She tightened the towel around herself and sat down in a rustic ladder-back chair that Rita had, for some reason, put in the bathroom. When Kim had first started visiting her, in her new neighborhood, they had laughed at the fact that Rita had started playing bridge and had joined a book club. They'd laughed at the invitations Rita received to attend Tupperware parties and lingerie parties and other types of parties that weren't really parties. Now Rita didn't make excuses. Now these women were simply her friends. These women were fast becoming her *old* friends. Rita had had Franklin young, a surprise, but becoming a mother hadn't changed her. It was being around these other mothers, all of them kept women, that had made her different.

Kim got dressed and brushed her teeth and went back down to the kitchen. She entered the walk-in pantry and surveyed a row of cereal boxes, each a version of granola. There was a case of pomegranate juice, unopened bottles of vinegar and marmalade and steak sauce and brown mustard. There was an entire shelf of whole bean coffee. Kim heard footsteps and turned to see Franklin leaning in the doorway of the pantry.

"You're already getting dirty," he said.

Kim looked at him neutrally. He'd changed his shirt to a yellow polo. His eyelashes were long and thick like a girl's.

"It's like they say how once you're born, each minute brings you closer to death. After you shower, every minute brings you closer to being filthy. It's exhausting to think about."

"Unless you like to shower," Kim said. "Unless that's a highlight of your day."

She brushed past Franklin, getting out of the pantry, and sat at the table. He followed her over. He picked up the soda Kim had left before and drank half of it down with a series of hard glugs. The clouds were clearing off and the sunshine was softening, a reasonable springtime sky prevailing.

"You had me worried there for a minute," Franklin said.

"How's that?"

"When I brought up the museum."

Kim's bare feet were cold on the tile. She pulled them up under her on the chair.

"I knew you didn't want to go to the mall," Franklin continued. "It's funny, I outgrew hanging out at the mall right around the same time my mom got back into it. We just missed each other. Of course, she prefers the outlet mall and I always went to the proper mall."

"So is there really a Gauguin assignment?" Kim said. "Or did you make that up?"

"Oh, the assignment exists. It's just a matter of getting ourselves to do it." Franklin's lemonade was still sitting out on the counter, and now he dumped it down the sink. He opened a drawer and found some kind of protein bar, which he ripped open and took a chewy bite of. Kim could smell him now, a combination of ordinary scents—clean laundry, lotion, unwashed hair.

"Do you ever miss your old house?" Kim asked him.

"All the time," said Franklin. He was chewing with effort.

"I can't get used to this one. I've been here twice now and it still feels like a bed-and-breakfast."

"You can get off by yourself in this house. That's the silver lining. You don't know anyone else is home."

Kim felt her stomach growl. She wasn't going to do anything about it.

"I feel sorry for men who have to live in houses like this," she said. "It's a big dollhouse. I feel sorry for you and your dad."

"Well, sometimes I go weeks without a Dad sighting. He lives at hotels. Not that I don't like the guy. Not that I'm complaining or anything. Somebody's got to bring home the bacon."

"It can't be good for a man's soul to have a cutesy mailbox."

Franklin craned his neck, as if to look out at the mailbox. It couldn't be seen from where they were sitting.

"Do *you* have a job?" Kim asked.

"Yeah, right. Me with a name tag, speaking to customers."

"So what do you do with your time? I'm sure they're big on extracurricular activities at that school of yours."

"My time?" Franklin took a moment. "I guess I lose track of it quite a bit."

"No volunteering with the poor? No socializing?"

"I steal mail sometimes. Speaking of cute mailboxes. That's something I used to do. That's pretty much the opposite of volunteering with the poor, huh?" Franklin gave up on his protein bar, or maybe he was only taking a break. He set it on a paper towel on the counter. "It's not like I *never* make friends. Girls seem to like me okay. A couple of them." He lowered his eyes, which were a wan green. Kim could hear the ticking of clocks from other rooms, all slightly off rhythm with each other.

"Full disclosure, I'm suspended right now. From school. My mom doesn't know. I had my dad talk to the Assistant Dean of Studies and sign the papers and he promised he wouldn't tell her. I'm suspended this whole week." Franklin produced a chuckle that didn't make it past his throat. "Dr. Crantz told me the suspension would be in my file forever and I told him it was important to me to have an interesting file. He didn't think that was humorous. I told him I wanted my file to be a fun read. I think I saw somebody say that in a movie once. It was pretty lucky I got to say it in real life."

Franklin insisted on driving. He had a used Audi sedan he was letting go to hell. He'd tried to peel the bumper stickers off it, but you could see where they'd been. The hubcaps were missing. As they walked down the driveway toward the car, which was parked half on the curb, a little boy wearing a loose jersey hopped over a bush from the yard next door and winged a football toward Franklin. Franklin didn't see it in time to catch it, but he managed to flinch so it wouldn't hit him in the head. The ball glanced off his forearms and bounced out into the road and came to a stop. Franklin's face was red. He looked at the boy in exasperation, before taking a breath and regaining his composure. "I'm the quarterback," the boy declared. He scuttled past them and retrieved the ball from the road, then ran back over to his own yard, leaving them standing there.

Franklin unlocked the driver door and opened it, still flustered, and hit a button on his armrest that unlocked Kim's door. Before he got in, he placed a hand on the roof of the Audi and poised himself to speak. "I fucking hate kids," he said. "Let me be clear on that. They should be kept somewhere until they're twelve. Like a bunker. Until they're at *least* twelve."

Franklin drove them to the entrance of the neighborhood, then turned in a direction opposite from the museum's. Kim knew which way the city was, and this wasn't it.

"So I decided we're not going to do the extra credit." Franklin was picking things out of the cup holders in the console—gum wrappers, paperclips, parking garage cards—and tossing them into the back of the car. "I hope you didn't get your heart set on seeing paintings. My grade is beyond help. It would be a waste of time in that respect. And really, you've seen one museum, you've seen them all."

There was a huge book on the floorboard by Kim's feet. She picked it up with two hands and twisted around so she could set it on the back seat. "Okay," she said. "So no museum."

"We can find a better use for a nice day like this, so here's what I'm thinking. We go to this farm I know where we can get fresh fruit, then we go to this... well, it's like a sculpture garden, and then we'll have a picnic where we can eat the fruit we got at the farm. It doesn't sound like much of an itinerary, but believe me, it'll be enough."

Kim couldn't help but laugh. Nothing was funny. She felt a little snuck up on. "I'm not the one with a GPA to think about," she told Franklin.

"Don't remind me. Do me a favor: I'm going to take a vacation from GPAs and permanent records today. Let's not mention any of that."

Kim ran her window down with the button, then changed her mind and rolled it back up. She had a feeling she should protest, that she shouldn't allow herself to be swept along on this new course, but the feeling was too remote. She didn't know what the grounds for the protest would be. She looked over at Franklin, and his face betrayed nothing at all, just concentration on the road, peaceful focus. There was something about him that seemed above dishonesty, like he wouldn't bother with it.

"Hope you don't mind if we abstain from the radio today," he said. "I'm taking an indefinite break from music. I think I listened to too much of it in too compressed a time frame. I'm really sick of songs."

They proceeded over a couple overpasses, then a low bridge that spanned a still river. They were taking a back way out of the suburbs. There were a bunch of quiet apartment complexes out here that were neither upscale nor crummy. A big hardware store that didn't seem open for business yet. Franklin had a firm grip on the top of the steering wheel, his wiry forearm muscles tensed. He had wispy sideburns, the kind you'd trim with scissors rather than shave. His lips were bright red, his skin healthy-looking against his shirt. Kim suddenly thought about how *she* looked, what she was wearing. Her toenails were freshly painted and her navy blue shorts were probably a little shorter than they should've been for an outing with a teenage boy, especially when she was sitting down. She rested her hands on her thighs and tugged at the material. She'd packed these shorts, she remembered, thinking she and Rita might go down to the lake, to get some sun and catch up. Turned out they hadn't gone anywhere alone, hadn't done a bit of catching up.

They passed an ice cream stand with a lone customer standing in front of it, then a big empty lot with a hill of reddish lawn mulch at its center. There was a part of Kim that was happy in a simple way, at being away from Galesburg and now away from Rita and her friends, getting driven around on a warming aimless weekday. The houses around them were growing austere, the yards turning into fields. Franklin slowed the car in front of an out-of-place Tudor-style strip mall, but he didn't pull into it. Just past the mall he made a left, and they rolled down a bumpy lane lined with homes of all styles and sizes. Some of the yards were overgrown and strewn with tools or toys, and some were neat as a pin. They passed under a series of huge shade trees, which gave Kim the feeling of driving through a tunnel, and when they came out into the sun again Franklin raised his hand and pointed excitedly.

"The red pickup means she's home," he said. "This *is* our day. Luck is playing nice with us."

He pulled onto the pale dirt drive and put the car in park. The house had a shingled roof and beige siding. There was a chimney on one side that seemed too big. Franklin squirmed in his seat, getting at one of his pants pockets, and yanked out the money Rita had given him.

"You don't mind if lunch is vegetarian, do you? I know some people like a more substantial midday meal."

"Whatever floats your boat," Kim said, sounding odd to herself. This wasn't an expression she ever used.

"I have a picnic spot in mind, but maybe when we're out there we'll see something better. A covered bridge or some such, or a broken-down tractor. Something in that ballpark." He unfolded the cash. "Thirty bucks. That ought to do it. Two people like us ought to be able to have a rewarding day for less than thirty dollars. There was a show on TV like that, where this lady tried to do a day in different cities for thirty dollars. I think it was thirty. She had to leave a crappy tip if she went to a restaurant."

Kim thought she remembered the show Franklin was talking about. For years she'd been trying to get herself to watch more TV, but none of it seemed intended for her. She wasn't a target audience, she supposed—there wasn't a spinster-in-training-of-above-average-intelligence demographic. She hardly even watched movies anymore.

Franklin led her around the back of the house, past a latticework apparatus covered in ivy. In the yard they found an old woman sitting in a lawn chair. The woman set her book aside, but didn't stand up. She told them everything was the same price and sold by the bin, and you could fill your bin as much as you could manage not to spill. The old woman wore her hair up in a soft bun, and her jewelry was all of a set, silver with large scarlet stones. Franklin went and grabbed a bin, and stepped over to a row of crates that contained different sorts of onions. He picked a few up and sniffed them with gusto.

Kim heard music from inside the old woman's house—dreamy electric guitar, Hawaiian-sounding. She let Franklin wander off by himself to choose the fruit, and stood by the lawn chair as the woman began talking as though continuing a conversation that had been interrupted an hour before. She told Kim she was taking a class at the junior college about the Mayans and the Aztecs. She was able to attend the class for free because she was old. The teacher was a handsome Spanish guy with an accent, who often told hunting stories. The woman said the seasons had been perfect lately. Fall and winter and spring, all perfect. Right on time, like the movements of a symphony. Franklin was at the far end of the crates now, holding in one hand a vegetable Kim didn't recognize. He was spindly, too tall, but she liked that there wasn't a bit of put-on in his mannerisms, no practiced reluctance, no breeziness, no mope. Perhaps he'd given up on being something other than himself.

"Your boy there's a spitting image of my first husband. When I first met him, I mean. In those days, you got married young. You didn't wait until you had a million dollars and all your towels matched. And of course people dressed different. He was always wearing a pressed white shirt and a vest and good shoes."

The old woman cautiously pulled a stick out of her bun and let the hair fall in sections down her back. She set the stick on the table beside her. It was a regular stick from outside; it looked like a twig from the oak tree that was shading this portion of the yard. Kim had no idea if the woman thought Franklin was her son or her brother or what.

"He died young, in his forties. There isn't anything I wouldn't give for one more day with that man. I knew the first time he held my hand there'd never be anything else like him, and I was right."

Franklin walked up close then, carrying the bin and eating a strawberry. He gave the woman a twenty and thanked her, and she tucked the money into the pages of her book.

As they were walking back around to the car, Kim noticed there were flowers in the bin. Daffodils, the same color as Franklin's shirt. As soon as Franklin found a place for the bin in the back seat, he emerged and presented the bouquet to Kim. He wore a daffy, bright-eyed expression, bowing slightly. Kim looked at him and at the flowers, and took them.

"I thought you might like these because you're a woman and women enjoy when men buy them flowers. That's one of those things you can depend on. It'll never change. It crosses cultures."

The stems of the daffodils were warm in Kim's hand, still alive and doing the work they'd been doing before they'd been cut. "What if the man's mother bought the flowers? Does the woman still enjoy it then?"

Franklin wanted to grin. "I don't think when a woman gets flowers, she's supposed to worry about exactly who financed them. Seems like a vulgar thing to worry about. It's just something simple that both parties can feel good about."

Kim could remember when Franklin was a toddler, could recall Rita forcing him to be normal, forcing him to eat what the other kids ate and play with balls and stare at cartoons. She couldn't believe that that little kid was the guy standing in front of her. She couldn't believe that so much time had passed. He was taking her out for the day, buying her lunch, giving her flowers. His expression was open and artless, without agenda, and maybe that's what was making Kim feel disarmed. Kim was the adult and should've been the one steering the direction of the day. She found herself thanking Franklin for the daffodils, putting her face near them to breathe them in. She found herself trying to remember the last time she'd received flowers. Valentine's Day a couple years ago—the obligatory roses, probably from the supermarket, picked up at the last minute.

Franklin was driving again. Kim felt dazed, adrift, and she wondered if that was willful. Of course, she'd barely eaten all day. She'd had a few strawberries in the car as they tacked along on nondescript roads that seemed to take them back toward town, but the berries had only made her hungrier.

When Franklin shut the car off, the world seemed inordinately peaceful. They were parked next to someone's patchy front lawn in a lower-class development. A dog was barking, but not nearby. It was baffling that all the years of her life had led to this spot. This is where she'd arrived. This sensation—of being the prisoner of a strange, serene afternoon— was something she remembered from childhood. It had been a pleasant feeling then. But now she was *too* free for someone her age. The people who lived in this subdued ward Franklin had driven her to were at work right now, or washing dishes or clipping coupons or reading the Bible. They were married, some of them divorced already. They had families, and the intrigues that came along with families. They had illnesses. They could barely make ends meet. Their kids were hanging out with the wrong crowd or putting on airs.

Franklin was gathering himself to rise from the car when his phone started ringing. It played a muffled snatch of some old Motown song Kim couldn't place. The phone was in his pants pocket, and Franklin looked down toward his hip with mild interest. Then he went ahead and stood up and closed his door behind him. Kim could still hear the music, repeating itself and then repeating once more. Franklin leaned against the closed window, his posture content, as if they'd pulled off on a scenic overlook in the mountains.

After another moment, as Kim half expected, her phone made its own buzzing signal. A text message. From Rita. She was asking how the museum was. Kim wished she could just not answer, like Franklin. Ignore whatever didn't suit her at any given moment. But no, she had to say something. She wrote, *super crowded—fun though*, and hit SEND. And in an instant her phone buzzed again. Rita asking where they were now. Kim looked over toward Franklin, the back of his shirt pressed against the window. His arms were folded on his chest, she could tell. He was gazing at something in the distance, or just staring into space. She typed in, *grabbing a bite. battery dying—sorry!* She sent the text and then held down the power button on the phone until it shut down. Guilt was present in her, but at this point it was something she understood more than she felt. And part of her resented it, to be honest. Resented Rita and maybe resented the whole idea that someone with as little as Kim had was supposed to feel guilty at all. She slid the phone into her purse and stuffed the purse under her seat. When she opened the car door, fresh air rushed in.

Just like at the old lady's farm, they walked around the outside of the house instead of knocking on the front door. The house was a pale blue split-level with peeling paint, and there was a low chain-link fence enclosing the backyard. Franklin pulled the gate open and stood aside, beckoning Kim to enter. He said the guy who lived here was on the road, but he didn't mind people stopping by to look. Kim went into the yard and Franklin followed, reclosing the gate.

This man's art, Kim saw, was a dozen or so enormous padlocks spread over his property. The bodies of the locks were tin sheds, and the steel loops on top were some kind of light, flexible pipe. Kim and Franklin strolled toward the center of the yard, but the effect was mostly lost once they were in the middle of the locks; you had to see them all at once. The sheds had no doors on them. Franklin said the next step was the guy putting big combination wheels on the front of each one. They walked all the way to the rear of the lot. Kim could still hear that same dog barking in the distance.

Franklin was facing away from the locks, out past the fence, where the land fell into a hollow and grew marshy. "It's not a museum, but it's better," he said. "We're seeing this before it's institutionalized."

Kim could feel the sun on her face, the mild warmth of spring. She closed her eyes for a moment. "It's pretty great," she admitted.

"You really think so?" Franklin said. He turned to face her, taking a step closer. "I thought you would like it. It's one of the coolest things I know of, so I thought you should see it." He was close enough to Kim that he seemed taller than before, almost towering over her, wielding his enthusiasm.

"You'll dream about these things," he said. "Once you get them in your mind, they never leave. I find myself drawing them in school, doodling them, like a compulsion."

The sun was focusing on them now, coming into its full strength, bringing a rich odor forth from the ground they were standing on.

"This is the reason to envy artists," Kim said. "Because they get to have these nutty consuming projects going, instead of being consumed with, you know... whatever."

"When I saw these the first time I thought how I'd like to be locked away for a while. Not like in prison, but *totally* alone. Not in trouble, just away from everything for a long time. I don't know how long, but it would be a long time. Have nothing to look at and nothing to listen to. I think that would be really good for me. I could figure out what my business is and mind it."

"You could probably do something like this," Kim said. Franklin had been gesturing a little wildly, and she was still looking at his hands, at his long tan fingers and the swirls of blond hairs on his wrists. "You could be an artist like this guy. I could see that."

"But I'm not mechanical. You have to be a craftsman to do this stuff."

"I don't think you have any idea if you're mechanical or not. Anyway, being mechanical isn't the rare talent. The rare talent is having a weird soul and also not being lazy and also being able to concentrate. That's the combination."

"It's not polite to call people weird. It's not polite to talk about people's souls like that."

"These days it's not polite to call people normal, either. They get just as offended."

Franklin looked at her appreciatively, ticking his head to the side like a dog. "I like you. I guess you already know that. I don't like many people and I like you a lot. Not that everyone's wishing I would like them or anything. And it's not just because you're pretty. I saw a study that said that good-looking people are 30 percent more liked by others, or 30 percent more people like them. But that's not why. That's not what made me want to plan this day."

He kept looking at her, pleased, like someone surprised not to be disappointed. The wind gathered steam, bringing a dull roar up from the trees in the hollow. Kim wanted to say she liked Franklin too, because it was true, but she stayed quiet. She felt the sun, soft but heavy, tightening the nape of her neck, but deep inside her there was another warmth, unwelcome: the sneaking perk of desire. She didn't want it, but there it was, tiny and unmistakable, shameless in its way, sure of itself. Kim's hands were clasped behind her back, her fingers all squeezing each other. She felt ridiculous. Franklin hadn't even been flirting with her—not really—he'd just made an honest declaration of affection. He hadn't made a move to touch her. This nonsense was all on her side. It was *her* problem. It really was ridiculous. Was she this unhappy? Was this all it took? He was a teenager. He was a gawky kid. She could hear the correct and responsible words in her head. They had to go back home now. That's what she needed to say. She wouldn't even have to give an explanation. She could just say they needed to start heading back and Franklin would have to do what she wanted. But she knew she wasn't going to say it.

He kept gazing at her, his arms crossed, his honey-colored stubble shimmering in the light, until he saw that she wasn't going to say anything. He gave one inscrutable nod and started walking back toward the dumpy split-level, weaving without hurry through the glinting sheds, reaching out as he passed each one to graze the baking tin with his fingertips.

* * *

This time they got onto a straight two-lane country road and worked up some speed, the townships petering into homely grain country, pockets of darkly shaded woods here and there. Kim watched Franklin guide the car, navigating through the minutes of his life. His existence was luxurious and vexing, and he was probably doing fine with it. The clock on the radio of the Audi was broken, reading *9:13*. More clouds had piled up, ragged and low like rocky hills, the sky like something you could march up into if you had the energy.

Franklin took his foot off the gas and let the car coast. There wasn't a park or even a kept glade in sight; the land had grown less tended. There were no cross streets, no signs. At a wide spot in the road, Franklin veered over and stopped the car. He seemed relieved.

"Thought I forgot where it was for a minute," he said. "My memory is terrible these days. My teachers say it's early-onset senioritis."

"I've always wished my memory could be spottier," Kim answered.

Franklin waited a moment, but Kim didn't elaborate. He opened his door and stepped out. Kim turned in her seat and watched him pull a blanket out of the trunk, the bin of fruit from the back seat. He stepped around and opened her door, proffering his hand.

She followed him down an overgrown trail that seemed to materialize in front of him as he went. The Audi disappeared behind them. There was only the dry leaning grass, hip-high to Kim, and the faded, half-cloudy sky. Franklin kept sweeping swaths of grass back out of the way with his free arm, holding them bent as Kim kept up with him in her flip-flops. They were heading toward a giant tree with very dark leaves, and when they reached its shade there was a break of clear ground. It was cool under the boughs. Franklin spread the blanket and set the bin down. He took off his shoes and socks and reclined flat on his back. Kim joined him, also on her back, on the other edge of the blanket but still in arm's reach. She kicked her flip-flops off and stretched her legs out, aware of the flattering arch of her torso.

Franklin was the first to speak. He asked Kim if she'd ever been engaged, his voice sounding a little grave. Kim brushed her hair out of her eyes. She told him she'd been engaged for a while, and that now she wasn't. She was looking straight up, but could sense Franklin nodding, contemplating what she'd said.

"I got proposed to last summer," he told her.

"Proposed to for marriage?" Kim said. She had no idea whether to take him seriously. It didn't seem like he was being cute, looking for a laugh.

"What happened was we went to a cornbread festival in Tennessee and we drove down in her Volkswagen Bug. At the festival, she entered a raffle and the prize was a scooter. She was the type that enters any raffle she comes across. And this time she wins. They call her name while we're standing there eating free samples of honey. We get back over to the raffle place and they're like, 'Here's your scooter, miss.' Just like that. She signed some paper and they're like, 'Y'all enjoy the parade.' One problem, though. We get out to the parking lot and the scooter wouldn't fit in the car, in the Volkswagen, so I offered to drive it back to Chicago. I said we could take the back roads. I'd just follow behind the car."

"That was a sweet offer to make," said Kim.

"She was of the same opinion. She thought that was a pretty touching gesture. Right on the spot she bought me a ring from a booth at the festival, with a big orange stone, and asked me to marry her. I couldn't believe it. We ran around the whole night kissing each other's hands, and then we managed to get some wine and we watched movies all night right in her car and slept in there. We were still holding hands while we were sleeping. We just drove down off the road by a little stream. Well, as you could probably guess, the next day we thought better of the whole thing. We were both embarrassed. It felt like a stunt or something. It made us feel like silly young people who wish they were older. It was her fault, really. She's the one who asked. We fizzled out after that trip. We saw each other maybe one more time."

Kim rested her hands on her stomach. She had an image of the orange engagement ring in her mind. "So you didn't end up driving the scooter back or you did?"

"No, I did. I meant the offer when I made it. It was fun, too. The weather was gorgeous, pretty much like today."

Franklin turned toward her, propping himself on his elbow. He pulled the bin of fruit in between them. Kim stayed on her back but she found the bin with her hand and ate one strawberry and then another. She tossed the stems behind her, into the weeds, and it was like throwing something overboard. The juice was staining her fingertips. She had a feeling like she didn't want to be let back into the fold. She didn't know where she wanted to be, but the fold had nothing to offer her. She could feel conviction in herself, or perhaps the complete lack of it.

Kim rose up on her hip and looked at Franklin, and he made a slow appraisal of the length of her. She could feel the blood moving in her feet. All the buttons of his polo shirt were undone now—she hadn't seen him do that—and she could glimpse the top portion of his lean, soft-lined chest as it rose and fell. Kim could smell Franklin's sweat and she could smell pollen and she could smell the air itself, the oxygen and ozone.

"What do you want?" she said. "Tell me right now."

Franklin cleared his throat, sitting up a little and unclasping his hands.

"With this day. What are you after?"

At long last, he seemed nervous. "I think I just wanted to be around you while I have the chance. I didn't want us to miss our window and never connect." He rubbed his eyes and looked off, as if into a vast and varied landscape. There was nothing around but Illinois. "My mom always used to say to be nice to you. Before you'd visit, she'd sit me down and say how important it was to be nice to you. Which of course I never paid much attention to. I don't know what she was talking about—I guess that you're not married or rich or whatever, and you live in Galesburg. I don't know. But now I *want* to be nice to you, for my own reasons. I just think it would've been a travesty if we never knew each other." He frowned then, in a tranquil way, contenting himself with his answer. His eyes were gazing out wisely from under those brushy lashes.

Kim could feel a wind in her mind, blowing things away that she didn't need. She closed in on Franklin and took hold of the scruff of his neck. She wasn't going to say another word and wasn't going to allow him to either. She'd talked herself into wanting so many things, and here was this pure, unbidden craving. The juice on her fingertips was leaving dark smudges on Franklin's collar. She was reaching for his hair now, limp-looking but coarse, and he was moving toward her, meeting her. She felt the sensation of falling, but she was down on the ground already.

THE MIDNIGHT GALES

There's a guy from New Mexico who arrived recently. He stays at a one-story motel over next to the power substation, and he makes no secret that he's obsessed with aliens and that's why he's here. One of his T-shirts proclaims as much: OBSESSED. He's got another shirt that says SITTING DUCK, and another that says MIDDLE SISTER. He spends a lot of time sitting next to the weed-cracked motel pool with his feet in the sun, a jug of iced tea underneath his chair. He wears colorful hats and a beard and his jug of tea has halved lemons floating in it. My father says that if this guy were any kind of respectable crazy he'd read library books all day, books that smelled like piss and hadn't been checked out in ages, not glossy magazines full of cologne samples.

We have no downtown, no police station or city hall of our own. There's a concentration of dwellings near the highway, but it's hard to say why. The highway is convenient to nothing. If you want to drive eight or nine miles down country roads, you have your pick of towns—franchise restaurants and car dealerships and jails. My parents rent a post office box in one of those towns, and hope not to get much mail. Occasionally my mom drives over for an out-of-the-way recipe ingredient or to see a movie in a theater.

My parents have a system for me. Every other year I go with the rest of the kids to a school in Larsboro—that's one of the nearby towns—and in the odd years I'm homeschooled. My mom says the state discourages this by making the paperwork daunting, but what they don't know, she says, is that she *likes* paperwork. She enjoys filling out forms and composing statements. She likes being put on hold. Resubmitting information she's already submitted blows her dress up, she says. Driving twenty minutes to get a document notarized makes her all tingly. And then if the notary's at lunch when my mom gets there, forget it.

She's got a sense of humor, unlike my father. They moved here to get away from red tape, among many other things, but for my education, she says, she can weather the red tape. She administers book learning on Mondays, Wednesdays, and Fridays, and on Tuesdays and Thursdays she encourages me to wander. She sets me loose with a pack of oatmeal bars. I'm supposed to observe and reflect and interact and get some exercise. Huck Finning, she calls it.

My father says no one believes in miracles anymore, or in the impossible. He says the Catholics want to wax their cars and burn incense and the Baptists want guns and frozen yogurt. The corporate churches, in their newsletters, say we're perpetrating a hoax. Newspapers from tourist-trap towns down on the coast have suggested we're running a scam, trying to drum up tourism in tough times. *What* tourism? Besides the guy at the motel, what tourism? At first, people came off the highway and slowed their cars as they passed the sites, but there's not much to see, really, unless you appreciate that unearthly violence leaves profane scars. We've come to suspect that time spent here is stolen time, and precious.

We are an area of unnamed, interchangeable churches. We decide things in church. Votes are taken and the losers are gracious. We decline to deem people ignorant. We don't mind not knowing, don't ask questions and then get angry at the answers. We don't gather around anything that moves and beat it with sticks until money falls out. Our services aren't an excuse to figure out who you hate and who you're supposed to vote for and what you're supposed to wear. We took all the fun out of religion, is what my mom says. She says it's better than razor wire for keeping out bad elements.

A kid who was in my class at school last year and his family were chosen. The kid was special at baseball. His arm was as skinny as anyone's, but he could throw runners out from deep in centerfield. He was a switch-hitter. Eleven years old, switch-hitting doubles off the fence. I wonder sometimes if, wherever he is now, they have baseball.

A family that ran a custom ball cap company was chosen. You still see people wearing the caps, each a one-of-a-kind.

A woman who lived alone.

A guy with a limp who ran a used-furniture shop.

An old-timer who was an assistant coach for FSU before Bobby Bowden came along and cleaned house.

The homes get tarped over right away by the church deacons. Since most everyone in the area has moved here from some other state, it takes the relations a couple days to arrive. They come and go without talking to anyone, carrying off the random remaining possessions. They are ashamed. They feel tricked. In the cold, crowded places these people come from, there is nothing more regrettable than being tricked.

The college-age kids leave, and the old people when their health fails and they need to be near hospitals. The parents and the children, we stay. This was decided in the churches, and the votes were not close. We will all stay until we all leave. Common sense has been propounded—all places have their dangers, their earthquakes or tornadoes or robberies at knifepoint or government-sanctioned poisonings or avalanches or wildfires or schizo-phrenics with machine guns. And then there are some who believe that when fate calls you, it won't matter where you are.

People do ask *why* the little baseball star and his dimpled sister and his strict but patient parents were chosen, *why* before them it was the old lady who kept sweet-temperedly to herself, who spent hours and hours tending the citrus trees in her backyard. You can hear the unspoken complaint: Why not me?

My parents are worn out, but also they've grown proficient at being worn out. They toughen as needed, like people throughout history. My father has always kept odd hours, but now my mom makes excuses to stay up at night too. She'll say she just put a pie in, or that she's going to finish a book. She'll stay up and knit scarves far too warm for this part of the world, and in the morning I'll find her kitchen chair over near the big floor-to-ceiling window in the living room. They'd gotten out of the cross-hairs, as my father used to say, had made their escape from teeming vulgar commerce and my mother's insufferable family and cold weather to boot. They'd found this sanctuary and made it home and had a child here. But now something else has found this place too.

The guy at the motel is in his customary lounge chair. His T-shirt says NEVER SAY ALWAYS. I'm Huck Finning—interacting, which is a lot easier than reflecting. I'm a couple chairs down from the guy. He's seen me plenty of times walking by, has eyed me through the chain link.

"What's it like in New Mexico?" I ask.

He takes his time, tries to rub something off his lounge chair with his thumb.

"I live in North Hollywood," he says. "In a penthouse."

Now I think of vast, hazy views and bartenders in bow ties. Trees growing indoors.

"The building calls the whole top floor the penthouse, but it's the exact same apartments as the rest of the building. In the elevator the buttons say *1*,

2, 3, and *P* and I get to push *P.*" The guy's smirk brightens. "I have a more commanding view of the industrial park than the folks on the third floor."

"Why do you say you're from New Mexico?"

The guy produces a glass and pours me some tea. He explains that he's a scout for a company that makes documentaries. They did one on the ivory trade, he says. They did one on these hundred-year-old Nazi officers that turn up now and then.

"What does a scout do?" I ask.

"Absorb and process the available narrative. Also make sure no one else is poking around. Make sure there's no one to buy out or partner with." After a moment he says, "We're a relatively small company."

I sip the tea and it's so sweet it makes me squint.

"This isn't far from where Errol Morris made that movie," the guy says. "The one with the turkey hunter."

"That movie celebrates rednecks," I tell him. "Not all turkey hunters are like that. My father's best friend is a turkey hunter."

The guy smirks again. The way his face is, he's always either smirking or failing to smirk. "There are religions way off in the Far East where shooting a turkey would be a sin," he says.

"I've heard of that."

"Sin isn't the correct term, but ending another life is an act you'd be judged for. You're not allowed to harm another creature."

"They're innocent," I put in. "Animals are innocent."

"Do you think that's possible, to live your life without causing suffering in any other creature?"

I know this is one of those questions that aren't meant to be answered, so I don't try to. I watch the guy extricate a pack of cigarettes from a pocket in his shorts. He wrangles a lighter out of there too. He pulls a cigarette out and rests it on the ground, and lays the lighter right next to it. I guess he's going to wait until I'm gone to smoke.

"My problem is getting caught up in earthly judgments," he says. "It's hard not to when you live in LA, and when you work in the entertainment industry."

"My mom says LA is no worse than anywhere else. I heard her say that one time."

"Well, that's mighty generous of her." He looks down at his cigarette and lighter. They seem to have a peaceful effect on him. "No matter what you do out there, they've got a prize for it. And if you don't get nominated for these prizes, it's the end of the world. The absolute end of the world. And if you get nominated and don't win, that's worth getting upset about too. That's called getting snubbed. Awards, awards, prizes, prizes." He looks upward a moment. There's just clouds up there, but he seems surprised to see them. "As you can probably surmise, we haven't won any."

"Prizes are demeaning," I tell him.

He stays with his thoughts a moment, still gazing upward, then he looks at me. "Who told you that? Is that your mom again?"

"No, my father. He says children are motivated by prizes. 'If you do real good, I'll give you a candy.' He says that's kids' stuff. He says I already should've outgrown it."

"Have you?"

"I think so," I say. "He says if you're an adult doing adult work, having someone pat you on the head in approval is patronizing."

The guy nods. He presses his thumb against his front teeth. "It's patronizing," he says, "but it's also how you secure patronage." Then he leans forward and kills an ant in an expert fashion, cutting it in half with his fingernail. He watches the two halves of the ant continue to move, limping around in antic little circles, until they finally stop.

"That ant was scouting your jug of tea," I say.

There are two women in our area who have both opened restaurants serving Northern Italian cuisine, and these are the only restaurants of note. The women are sisters who moved here after they got tired of Dallas. The competition between their restaurants is fierce. Most people don't take sides. Most people dine in both. Each time my parents and I eat at one, the prices are lower and the ingredients more exotic. The sisters are wealthy, the daughters of a pioneer in the cable TV industry. My father says he brings me down to the restaurants for one because the food is world-class, and for two to show me what kind of silliness can come of having siblings. He says a sibling is one more thing you're tied to against your will, more toxic clutter in your life, more stale drama.

Our churches are plain white buildings with piney, unpaved parking lots. Our men wear ties to church and our women wear whatever they want. Our preachers go on and on for hours, but never about right and wrong. They don't want to hear about our shortcomings.

A long-standing, moneyed Protestant church sent a guy down here to check things out. He's been around the block. He's not unfamiliar with the impossible. They sent him from Canada. He doesn't stay at the motel. He stays down on the coast and drives up every day. He eats at the Italian restaurants, sits in the back row during church services, listens to the joyful noises raised by the young during the songs at the beginning and the end.

My father designed memorials. His first one, when he was starting out, won him distinction. It's on the campus of FSU, dedicated to a scientist who spent his life improving tomatoes. It's a fountain inside a huge beaker. There are these transparent wires with copper tomatoes hanging from them, and the falling water is always nudging the tomatoes so they sway. A day of imagination and then a year of math. That's what my father says about his job. He always has a pair of glasses in his shirt pocket and when he hugs you he does it with one arm so he can protect the glasses.

There were others after that, in Florida and elsewhere. One was for a man who modernized the flower industry in Mexico. One was for a genius Mississippi bluesman. He hasn't done a memorial in years, but he still goes out to his studio for hours at a time and returns looking exhausted.

My father's only friend now is the turkey hunter, a mason who spends all his time in the woods. He and my father were partners, years ago. My father doesn't get on well with others these days, even at church. My mom is the one with all the friends, all the confidants. She told me once that she'd married my father because he didn't have a phony bone in his body. It was the greatest thing about him, she said, and his biggest problem.

Some people from the area instituted an all-night patrol a while back, attempting to be more vigilant than the heavens themselves, but it didn't last. Too few folks participated. The patrollers got exhausted and started falling asleep on people's porch swings and in cars that were left open.

Someone else, a retired high school physics teacher, calculated a radius beyond which no one would be chosen. But then someone was. It happened barely outside the range he'd defined, as if to teach him a lesson. It was the furniture shop owner that time—his cottage found roofless and purified, not even his walking stick left behind. Some people said the physics teacher was responsible, that whatever was happening to the furniture shop owner, good or bad, in some unfathomable dimension, was the physics teacher's doing. Maybe the furniture shop owner was being tortured. Then again maybe his limp was healed and he was drinking something cool in the shade. That's why the TV channels lost interest, my father says—because they couldn't prove anyone was suffering. He says when you get to the front of the traffic jam you want to be rewarded with stretchers and ambulances.

The furniture shop is still here, on the edge of our area, looking like a museum exhibit, the furniture inside growing antique.

The county police call it an ongoing situation, rather than a case. If not versed in the impossible, they're at least practiced in the unsolved. Even folks who hold cops in the lowest regard agree that they've been graceful. The first couple times they swooped out in a fleet of lit cruisers and dusted every surface and put samples in zipper bags and stood around with coffee all day, keeping the reporters behind an orange ribbon. But they've wised up.

Now they send a single deputy to do whatever paperwork is unavoidable. Sometimes the cops wait until the next night to sneak someone over—in part, I imagine, because they have comprehensible problems to battle, and in part because they don't want to be asked if they've made any progress.

I walk out of the corner store where they sell used books and homemade ice cream, and a man sitting on a bench speaks to me. I don't recognize him at first because he's wearing khaki clothes and a floppy hat. It's the investigator, the one sent by the rich Protestants. He asks me about fishing, about where to get gear and bait and a permit, and I tell him we don't believe in permits around here.

"Have you decided anything?" I ask him.

He removes his hat. Now he looks exactly like himself.

"In fact, I have. I've decided nothing noteworthy is afoot, nothing worthy of further investigation. I think I'll report insufficient findings. I'm going to recommend this area be left the hell alone. Close this baby up, as we say."

I don't know whether to be glad about his answer. There's a part of me that feels slighted. The investigator looks deeply unconcerned.

"So you're going back to Canada and you're going to lie," I venture.

His face doesn't change but I can tell he likes me. Old people always like me. "I'm going to fib all right, but I'm not going back up there. I'm staying. The natives are going to be even more outnumbered than they are now."

"You're going to live here, just like that?"

"Well, I'm retiring. When people retire, they head south."

"Yeah, but there are places more south than this," I say. "Places that don't have... what we have going on."

"Exactly," he says.

We're under a few massive old pecan trees, birds flitting branch to branch above us. It's the middle of the day but it's dim here in the shade.

"Isn't it against all religions to lie?" I say.

"First of all, there's a lot of gray area in my line of work, religion or no. Second of all, yes, it is."

"If you were Catholic, you could lie and then go to confession and admit it and it's like it never happened."

The investigator shifts on the bench. He's not going to stand anytime soon. He's probably not going fishing. He's going to be one of us.

"I'm a native," I tell him.

I watch him nod appreciatively. "I know it. And natives like you speak well of a place."

"I think confessing sounds fun," I admit. "You go in that wooden booth and nobody knows it's you."

"Somebody always knows it's you," says the investigator. "Someone's always totting your omissions."

That night my parents head over to one of the towns to see a movie, an old-fashioned date sort of thing. I practice juggling for about an hour in my room, a skill I've been trying to pick up. Then I listen to music in the parlor for a while, a subdued jazz record my father is partial to, but I can't get sleepy. I go to the kitchen for a glass of milk, but instead I find myself rummaging in the drawers for the spare key to my father's studio.

It's a flimsy key, not full size, like a key for a file cabinet or something. I find it in a junk drawer underneath a calculator and a tape measure, and then I slip out the back and walk across our shadowy little yard and fit the key into the doorknob. There's a palm tree growing right in front of the studio, leaning down over the entrance. When I open the door it shushes against the hanging fronds, and there's the shush again when I close it behind me.

I've been in my father's studio many times, but not lately. I know there's a pull cord for the light, and I grope around above me until I find it. With the place lit up, I can see that everything is the same as I remember. The walls are bare white. There's a case of mineral water under the drafting table, pencil shavings scattered around on the concrete floor. The air smells like things heated, things overused—hot glass and leather and stale coffee.

On the table is the book of all my father's sketches. There must be a thousand of them, in clear plastic sheets. On the page that's showing there's a three-dimensional drawing of a clock tower. One wall of the tower is filled in—with irregular, soft-looking bricks—but the others seem like they're transparent, so you can see that inside the tower, on the floor, is a pile of heavy chain. I look closer and there are cuffs attached to the chain, like to hold a person prisoner in a fairy tale. The clock has numerals but no hands. I turn to the next sketch and it's the same drawing. There are small alterations—the size of the clock face, the shape of the bricks. Next page, the same thing again, but now the tower is stouter and instead of a pile of chain there's only the cuffs, moored directly to the wall.

The studio is shaped like an L. I still my breathing and listen for a car out on the road. When I hear nothing, I go down around the corner, and what I see, arranged on a pallet of plywood, are a dozen identical metal eggs. They're about two feet tall. They're not eggs, though—they're shaped more like tears, or a moon that's begun to melt. They're fashioned of a dull-colored metal. I step closer and see that they all have little holes punched into them, companies of tiny sharp punctures gathered around the tops. The moons, or the tears or whatever, are hollow. I put my hand on one and it moves easily, so I pick it up to assess it in my palms.

There's a candle underneath. Now I see. There's a candle under each one. I put the one I'm holding back where it was and look around for matches, which I find handy on an otherwise empty shelf. Big camping matches.

I get the candles burning, one and then the next and then the next. I pull the cord for the light, and when I come back around the corner I see, there on a screen my father has tacked to the ceiling, a host of wide-open eyes staring down at me, incurious and knowing at once.

If you look under one of the tarps you'll see that the roof of the house is gone—not caved in or blown over or burned to ashes, just gone. The big appliances are left, and some compact heavy objects like cans of beans or a bowling ball in a leather bag. The buildings look at once frozen and scorched. The walls are blackened as if by heat, the floors cracked as if by cold.

It's dark still, and I'm in the mason's pickup. We're going hunting. It's a Huck Finn day, and this is a little field trip of sorts—my mom's idea. The radio plays music like I've never heard.

He has a place set up, he tells me, not far into the brush—a hideout. You're supposed to ramble around the live oaks lugging a pop-up blind, he says, but today we're going to let the gobblers come to us. "And if they don't," he says, "it's just not our day." He pulls halfway off the dirt road and stops. It doesn't seem like there's enough room for another car to pass. He grabs a shotgun off the rack and I carry the pack. The mason has unevenly cropped hair and he's wearing a tracksuit that does not look new.

We round a thicket at the base of a beech tree and there's the hideout. The mason pulls aside a flap and we crouch in and get settled. You can see a lot from the mason's hideout and nothing can see you. It's roofless, and roomier inside than it looked from the outside. "Thing about shooting a turkey is then you have to clean a turkey and cook a turkey," he says. He turns his head and coughs. "I don't have much energy for chores lately, or much appetite."

He handles the gun and shows me how it works, and I'm impressed. There's nothing extra to the gun. It's beautiful, a little monument to its own function. The mason says we probably won't have much luck with the turkeys, but he'll let me practice on some targets later with a different gun. He likes to shoot at textbooks with that one, he tells me. He takes out a little wooden device that reminds me of the pitch pipe I use when I sing at church and he makes turkey noises with it, just a soft clucking for a while, then a series of shrill yelps. I listen hard for a response, for a garbling out in the bracken and the briars, but the mason seems more interested in his instrument than in any quarry it might draw. In the pickup I'd been waiting for the sun, and now somehow I miss it rise. There it is off to the left, an overripe grapefruit pulling clear of the scrub.

The mason keeps sipping off his thermos but his eyes look sharp. Maybe he's not going to say anything about what's been going on—the chosen, the incidents—and he doesn't have to. It's in the air we're breathing. We're due, everyone knows. We're close to due.

The mason plunges his hand into the sack of shotgun shells and absently kneads them, like he's petting a dog. He's ready to talk, ready to lecture. He tells me the history of his pickup truck, which he bought off a man who used to collect debts up in Georgia. The pickup has been in shoot-outs. It has been rolled in a chase, and clipped on the back end by a train. He tells me about Georgia, how there are spots up there hotter and flatter than Florida. The mason is a native here, like I am. He says in the old days a sweet potato that grew right out of this yellow dirt tasted better than anything at those Italian restaurants. His mother was prettier than any of these women around here now.

"Your mom's the pick of the current litter," he tells me, "but she wouldn't have been fit to carry my mother's lipstick around for her."

There's a laugh in his throat, but he clears it. He does something rough but precise to the knuckles of his left hand, producing a roll of cracks, and his demeanor changes. He peers out sternly into the broad, mostly quiet woods. His voice goes even and he explains that recently a tree his great-grandfather planted died on his watch. Among the biggest sycamores he's ever seen. It just quit living. He'd had to chainsaw the thing down and limb it and cut it into pieces small enough to carry and burn it. Not a leaf on the thing. A couple days' work. He wants to know why a tree would up and die like that, but he knows he won't get an answer. He lost an infield of shade easy, but worse he lost something grand and noble that his fore-bears had given start to. He'd sat by his nightfire, sweating, feeling watched by black quiet eyes. He doesn't care about getting taken; something has to take you in time. What he doesn't like is feeling monitored. He doesn't deserve it. He looks at me, maybe wondering if I have anything to say about it, but I don't.

The mason brings out a sleeve of smoked nuts and shares them with me. There's no water, but I manage to get down a few handfuls. "So," he says.

"What we got right here, where we're sitting: this is a sanctuary inside the sanctuary. For natives only. Nobody can find you here. And I mean nobody. And you, little friend, can use this place whenever you want."

I thank him and he nods in an upbeat way. It's almost regular daytime now. I can see everything. I can see every stitch in the canvas of the hideout, and a black and pink bug bumbling around on a pinecone. A ray of sun is finding its way through the foliage and glinting off the barrel of the shotgun, the heat beginning to thrum in the treetops.

The sisters live together now, the ones who run the restaurants. They told my mom they don't want to be left behind if one of them is chosen.

Before they get the tarps up the houses look like hungry baby birds. Mouths agape to the sky, like despite everything being taken away they still expect something to be given. That's how they look to me.

PALATKA

auline awoke to Mal's voice outside her window. Mal was the seventeen-year-old girl who lived by herself in the next apartment. She was always talking on her outdated cordless phone, always helping some far-off person navigate a problem. Pauline went out to their shared back balcony in her bare feet and snuggled into a camping chair. Mal, standing with her weight all on one hip, grasping a big cup of iced tea, winked at her. She was as skinny as a rail; her fingernails were painted in stripes, and her elbows were raw. Pauline never saw her come home with groceries. The girl had a look in her eye sockets like she didn't get enough red meat, or enough green vegetables. Pauline felt a mothering urge toward Mal. She had never gone through a wild phase herself, and so Mal's carelessness fascinated her—her carelessness about things such as nutrition and education, but more so her general carelessness with herself. She didn't seem to realize that a cute young girl shouldn't treat her body and soul like they were rented.

Mal hung up the phone and chugged enough of her tea that she had to recover her breath afterward. She hoisted herself onto the banister. Pauline asked what the call was about and Mal said she had a friend who, when she met up in person with a guy from online, always felt too guilty to bail if she didn't like the looks of him.

"She feels bad about wasting the guy's time, after they got gussied up and used gas in their tank. And she's like, what if that happened to me? I said, nobody's going to be walking out on you because of the way you look. She's like, yeah, they walk out later for other reasons."

Pauline was only six years older than Mal, yet the dating world Mal inhabited seemed foreign to her, insane. There was no normal dating world anymore, she knew. A guy wasn't going to approach Pauline with his hat in his hands and ask if that seat was taken, then give her an elegant little compliment and ask if he could have her phone number for the purpose of asking her out on a date that weekend.

"I'm telling you, you gotta try it," Mal said. "It's a hoot. Why not put up a profile and see what happens?"

"It just seems dangerous," said Pauline. "I need to do something, but not that."

"Dangerous? I've stopped keeping track of what's dangerous. It's tiring."

"There's a bunch of perverts in their underwear leering at your picture, Mal. Thinking God-knows-what."

"I just want to go on a few dates. A girl used to be able to do that. Anyway, the picture I use is tasteful."

"I'm sure it is," Pauline said.

"It's fun browsing through the guys. You get a bunch of likes and dislikes and hobbies. Then sometimes they'll brag that they have a job." She smiled. "Rick couldn't brag about that. He bragged about his dad's boat."

Rick had been Mal's most recent semi-steady guy, a man easily older than Pauline, way too old for Mal, with a tattoo on his neck and a hairline that had begun to recede. Pauline hadn't seen him in a week or so. "What ever happened with Rick?"

"Yeah, that." Mal ran a palm down her cup, wiping it dry. "His friend called and asked me out and I said no way, then I told Rick about it and he says, 'I know, I told him to. It was a test.' I was like, these fuckers are weird."

"Did you have to lie about your age, for the site?"

Mal spit ice into her cup. "Been doing that all my life. Sometimes I forget how old I actually am."

Mal pulled her hair back and bound it with a rubber band. It was a light shade of brown and always looked a little greasy. Though Pauline talked to Mal most every day, she still knew almost nothing about the girl's childhood. She'd been raised a couple counties away, Pauline knew, in a place she'd said was even more raggedy than Palatka, by an old woman she called Granny who wasn't really her grandmother. The old woman had passed away a couple years back. Pauline didn't pry; Mal was the type who would tell you everything she wanted you to know.

"What have you eaten today?" Pauline asked her.

"Eaten?" said Mal. She tipped off the banister stiffly toward Pauline, as if falling, then shot her feet down and landed like a gymnast. "I don't know. I eat biscuits every morning, then I don't get hungry again." Mal gave the ice in her cup one sharp shake, then swished inside, the screen door swatting behind her.

Pauline rose and climbed into Mal's spot on the banister. She pressed her back against the beam and gripped the railing under her legs. The balcony felt solid enough, though its planks were discolored and warped. After several minutes Pauline grew comfortable with her balance, though she knew she didn't look at ease, like Mal had. She didn't look like a wise stray kitten.

Pauline hadn't had sex for over a year now. She was too picky, was the problem. There was a certain type of guy she was comfortable with, and that often liked her in return—guys who were nowhere near handsome but were cocky anyway due to some offbeat talent they possessed, who were gentlemanly without overdoing it—and that type of guy existed in college towns, not in regular Florida. Those were the guys who hadn't minded entertaining and winning Pauline, guys who spoke useless languages and played outdated musical instruments. Pauline remembered what it was like to be with one of them, how each hour had seemed unique. They'd been so sweet and honest. They'd been boys, she supposed, not men.

The last night Mal had brought Rick home, Pauline had turned her seldom-used TV up as loud as it would go, blaring a news story about a museum burning to the ground. The noises Mal made were like giggling. His were like someone getting burned by a cigarette.

Mal burst back onto the balcony. "Believe it? I'm officially one hundred percent out of tea. How do I let these things happen?"

Pauline lowered herself from the banister and curled back up in her chair. The heat of the day was taking hold. She could feel sweat trickling down her neck. "Mal, how many friends do you have?" she asked.

Mal's face went blank a moment. "No close ones, I don't guess. None like when you're a kid and you're friends with someone. Friends like me and you, maybe seven or eight. If I have a friend long enough, I get in a fight with her."

"Why? What do you get in a fight over?"

"Different things. Usually their boyfriends come on to me. This one dude, I threw a candle in his face, then my friend took his side. Says I could have blinded him."

"A lit candle?"

"Hell yeah, a lit candle. She said I was jealous of her because she had this great guy, so I was trying to ruin it for her. Meanwhile he's got a crossed eye. He was part-owner of a roller rink." Mal crossed her arms. She was wearing a tank top that revealed the flat bones of her chest. "She said I was always flirting, even if I wasn't trying to. The way I bop around and, you know, look at people. Maybe she's right." She bit the inside of her cheek. "Do you think she's right?"

"I don't know," Pauline said. "Look straight at me."

Mal arranged her face over-seriously and rested her eyes on Pauline. It certainly wasn't flirty. Mal wasn't blinking; she was waiting for some sort of verdict. And as Pauline looked back at her, thinking of what to say, she began to suspect that the face Mal was making was Pauline's face, that she was unconsciously mirroring Pauline.

* * *

Pauline had been so happy, a year ago when she'd finished college, to find a pocket of the Florida peninsula that had not yet been subdivided and sodded, a swampy area with no easy access to a beach or to Disney World. She'd wanted a bold move, a move she wouldn't have expected of herself. She'd wanted an escape from the familiar, a place where she could find something out about herself. Her friends from school had gone back to their hometowns and were predictably stepping into the molds of their young-adult lives, and Pauline was here, in Palatka, with no one to catch her if she faltered. She was proud of this original little life she'd forged, proud to have a consistent freelance job that paid the bills and then some, but whatever test she'd been hoping for hadn't arrived. She felt more capable than when she'd moved here, but nothing important about her had changed. She was the person she'd always been—cautious, a judger of character and debunker of myths.

And what of Palatka? It was less a town, more a tangle of numbered roads lined with lethargic trailer parks and dusty farmhouses. The daytime was uneventful, and most people stayed in at night because there was nothing lurking out there but trouble. Pauline's apartment was one of eight in her building, only two of which were rented—hers and Mal's. The whole row was on stilts. The apartment, if she looked too closely, was shabby, but it was a big space for one person, and out the windows she could see the sun rising and setting. Out the windows there were mucky cypress bogs, and in the near distance a strip mall that contained a tidy thrift store and a low-rent lawyer's office. A little farther off was a field of soybeans in perfect rows. And beyond all that was an unlabeled water tower, painted a pale yellow, peeking up over the treetops.

Pauline finished the work her company had sent her around midday, and then began feeling generally anxious for reasons that were hard to narrow down. She put in a hairclip, slipped her flip-flops on, and drove over to the outlet mall. This was another thing that hadn't changed about her—when she felt anxious, shopping helped. She waded inside with the old women, who all wore sweaters against the pumping chilled air. She passed a shop for kitchen gadgets and a discount store for bras, then wound up walking into a depot for outdoor gear and drifting to a huge bin marked LIQUIDATION. She picked through all variety of backpack, fishing vest, and cozy hat, then turned the price tag on a pair of men's boots: WAS $230.00 / IS $19.99. The boots were bulky and sleek at once, seasoned-looking yet pristine, rugged yet soft as a cloud. They were from Italy. She could smell the boots' neutral scent—the odor of a very clean and organized workshop. She hung them over her arm by the laces and started looking around for the registers.

From the mall she followed a two-lane highway in the approximate direction of St. Augustine. Through many forks and hard turns, the road remained the same number. After about fifteen minutes she crossed a short bridge and pulled into the lot of a restaurant with stuffed macaws in the windows and glazed tile on every interior surface. There was a bar in the middle of the room, and Pauline chose a stool and nursed a beer. A television hung from the ceiling on a complicated stand. The sound was off and the man on the screen was reviewing something—horror movies, it seemed—and making a show of being despondent. The bartender, a middle-aged woman wearing big pastel bracelets, had her mixing tools out and was polishing them with vinegar. Pauline had been served by this woman before, had made small talk with her before.

"Would you mind turning that TV off?" Pauline asked.

"They won't let me. I can turn it around for you, so it'll face the other way." The bartender stood on her toes and nudged the TV over and over until Pauline was looking at the back of it, with all its plugs and bolts. "You don't like that guy who's on?"

"I'm not used to TV anymore," Pauline said. "It seems aggressive."

"Where you been that there's no TV?"

"Just my apartment, I guess."

The bartender tilted her head, appraising Pauline. "I'll tell you a secret, honey. You're never going to fit in around here. You're not white trash. That's the main reason your experiment's going to fail."

"I'm not running an experiment," Pauline scoffed. "And who said I didn't fit in?"

"The world needs white trash. I'm not getting down on them." The bartender held a shaker up to the light. "This country wouldn't be what it is without white trash."

"Okay, since I'm not white trash, what am I?" Pauline asked.

"Best I can tell, you're a levelheaded gal who likes to sip on a beer in the middle of the day because it makes you feel not so levelheaded. I wouldn't say you're happy, but you've managed to not have anything bad happen to you yet."

Pauline was quiet. Then she said, "Damn."

"Don't worry, I can do that to anyone. Trick of the trade." The bartender ate one of Pauline's chips. "Stale," she said. She gave the basket a shake, rattling her bracelets, and walked off toward the kitchen with it.

Pauline went out to the balcony and found Mal hanging things. Some shop had gone under and Mal had plundered a birdfeeder and a set of wind chimes. She had neglected to pick up birdseed, so Pauline emptied a can of mixed nuts into the feeder. The two of them sat as still as they could, occasionally making a kissy bird noise. Mal was in her accustomed spot on the banister, a chime dangling inches above her head. From what sounded like a couple miles away, Sunday church bells were tolling.

"I used to go to church," Pauline said. "I was Catholic for part of college."

"Because of a guy?" Mal asked.

"Initially."

"I was raised Church of Christ, until I wore out on it."

Pauline took a handful of nuts from the birdfeeder. She sat in her camping chair and sifted for cashews and almonds.

"The preacher's son used to touch my knees under the table," said Mal. "I wore a skirt usually but he never went higher than right here." She dragged a fingertip high across her thigh, and then something over toward the swamp caught her attention.

Pauline stretched up from her chair and saw a gawky bird striding toward them. The way his head lolled back and then stabbed ahead was vaguely threatening.

"You won't fit on this porch, buddy," Mal said. "You gotta get your own lunch."

The bird stood still then, like it was waiting for Mal to say more. A breeze kicked up, thick with the scent of reptiles and blossoms. Mal's stomach growled and the bird laboriously took flight, beating the air, scraping the weeds with its belly.

"You and I need a cookout," Pauline said. "I'm getting a grill. I think I might go get it right now."

"Can't. I'm seeing this guy Tug later today. He's named after a pitcher and that pitcher's son is Tim McGraw, the country singer. He wears a bow tie."

"Tim McGraw?"

"No, this guy Tug wears a bow tie. He came in the store while I was working and gave me a pin, only he called it something else."

"A brooch?"

"Bingo." Mal straightened her arm and admired her nails, each of which bore a green dot. "A beetle brooch."

"That's what I want," Pauline said. "A guy in a bow tie who gives me a charming gift. Maybe that was my guy and you intercepted him."

"You don't have a workplace," Mal said. "You don't have a place where you're stuck, where you're out on display."

"I guess that's true. I guess there's not much chance they're going to randomly stop by my apartment."

Mal yawned, stretching her legs along the banister and reaching her arms up alongside the wind chimes.

"Where are you guys going on the date?" Pauline asked.

"No idea. That's up to him. I ain't paying for anything and I ain't driving."

Pauline's reflex was to tell Mal to be careful, to remind her that she didn't know this guy at all, to advise her not to let him take her anywhere too secluded, but she kept her peace. Mal had made it this far. She wasn't helpless. The girl knew how to do a lot of things Pauline didn't know how to do, like change oil and sew up clothes when they got a rip. Maybe using men for pure fun was another thing she was skilled at. She didn't need an amateur like Pauline nagging her.

"Hope he takes you somewhere nice," Pauline said. She had nothing but peanuts left in her hand, and she stood and returned them to the feeder.

Pauline woke up late and worked most of the next day. She played Cyndi Lauper, covered her kitchen table with file folders and pens and her computer and her tea gear. She opened all her blinds and the sun-washed day cleared her head. She switched to some old Tom Petty, then a Motown mix. She ate a banana that was about to go bad. The time flew.

Pauline hard-boiled an egg and painted her fingernails. She took down a bag of trash and cleared the credit card offers and coupon books out of her mailbox. She walked past her car in the lot, and saw that Mal's car was there too. Mal hadn't been home all day. Maybe she was still on her date.

Back upstairs, Pauline dropped her blinds and turned on the overhead light. It was past three o'clock all of a sudden. She stretched out on the couch and started reading a book about the role of colonization in world cuisines. She read a chapter, then realized she hadn't been paying attention to what she was reading. There was a big brown spider on the ceiling, but she was too lazy to get up and kill it. She watched it for a while, hoping it wasn't on the move.

The next thing she knew, it was morning. She was still on the couch. She'd slept through the evening and through the whole night. The spider was nowhere to be seen. She got up, her hips stiff, and brewed some coffee; then she put the coffee in a thermos cup and drove down to the mechanic. Her car had been making a noise for weeks, laboring in the low gears, and she was finally going to take it in.

She had hoped to be first in line when the place opened, but when she got there the lot was already a hive of activity. She waited awhile until her car could be looked at, then waited while the guy at the desk, in over-explanatory terms, told her she needed a tune-up and a belt and some kind of gasket and also her front brakes could stand some attention. Pauline settled into the waiting room and flipped through magazine after magazine at a steady but unhurried pace, registering each advertisement and headline. Across the way there was another shop, one for gleaming, tricked-out hot rods, and Pauline watched the men over there gathering around the front ends of the cars to lean in and admire the engines, childlike satisfaction on their faces. She wondered if she ought to go stand outside where she could be seen. Maybe one of them would come over and speak to her—maybe the slow-moving, tall one with the parted hair. Maybe he'd look at her like she was one of those shiny engines. Of course she wouldn't do it. She wouldn't go out there in the sun and pose. She'd stay stuck on her ratty vinyl chair.

The morning after that, Pauline spent an hour clearing old junk off her computer's hard drive. She wanted someone to go to a late breakfast with, but Mal still wasn't back. She hadn't heard a peep from the girl. Pauline sat on the balcony, watching a gauzy cloud slowly disassemble and listening to the different calls the birds made. She wiped off her windowsills and shined the air conditioning vents and folded some laundry she'd let pile up, and then after that she had nothing else to do. Her apartment was spotless and organized. She made a bowl of cereal and ate most of it, then fetched a trash bag and took it to her closet, where she began scrutinizing each shirt or skirt or pair of pants one by one. She needed to do a Goodwill haul and thin out her wardrobe, she decided. The rule was supposed to be that if you hadn't worn something in a year, it could go, but Pauline hadn't worn most of her clothes in the past year. There was no reason to wear anything nice in Palatka. She was staring indecisively at a sleeveless chiffon blouse when it hit her that she was worried about Mal.

It had only been three days, but Pauline had a bad feeling in her stomach. Mal had never been gone three days. She didn't like sleeping over at other people's places—she always said that. She was fine, probably, off somewhere having fun, but the bad feeling wasn't something Pauline could get rid of by will. It annoyed her that the girl couldn't find the consideration to make a simple phone call. Mal was under no obligation to report to her or anything, but was a quick phone call too much to ask? She'd taken off somewhere with that guy Tug, and while she was having fun Pauline had to sit here and worry. What else was new?

Pauline went and got her phone off the arm of the couch and tried Mal's cell. It went straight to voicemail. About ten minutes later she tried again, with the same result.

The next day, Pauline chewed up several hours going in and out of antique shops and thrift stores looking for pieces for her apartment, end tables and lamps. After all this time, she still didn't have near enough furniture. A framed picture. Maybe a hat rack. She chatted with all the owners, but wound up buying nothing but candles and teacups and the like. She stopped at a liquor store on the way home for a bottle of wine, and as soon as she got into her apartment she opened it and drank down a big glass. She poured another glass right away but only stared at it, feeling very alone. She had felt alone when she'd first moved here, but that loneliness had felt natural and she'd waited it out proudly. She'd known it was part of coming to this place. What she felt now was close to defeat. She went out to the back balcony and went over to Mal's side and peered in the window. There was a light on back where she couldn't see, back in the bathroom or something. The place wasn't a mess, nor was it particularly neat. Pauline scanned the interior of Mal's apartment and couldn't find anything noteworthy, not that she knew what she was looking for. There was a big plastic pitcher sticking up out of the sink. There were a couple remote controls on the waist-high wall that divided the kitchen and the living room. A hairdryer on the kitchen table. An empty vase. The ceiling fan was spinning.

Pauline slept restlessly that night, using her blanket as a pillow, and as soon as it was morning she went down and looked into Mal's car. She saw nothing in there but a pair of purple sunglasses and a thing of hard candy sticking up from the console. Probably the candies had melted into a single block at the bottom of the box.

Pauline went up and knocked hard on Mal's door, knowing it was a silly thing to do. She pressed her ear against the wood and heard nothing. She dialed Mal's cell phone number again, listened as it went right to voicemail. She had the number to Mal's landline on a scrap of paper in a kitchen cabinet, and once she'd found it in there she dialed that number, too, knowing it was useless but not knowing what else to do. She listened to the ringing through the wall. Mal didn't have an answering machine for the landline. She'd gotten the line and the cordless phone free with her cable and Internet, she'd told Pauline. The ringing from next door was measured, aloof. It was hard for Pauline to bring herself to hang up and stop it. She had been reasonable for several days now, and had ignored the sinking feeling in her stomach, but maybe the feeling was right. The girl was so young and so tiny. It was hard to imagine her safe. She had made it this far, tempting fate all the while, only due to dumb luck. She'd enjoyed more than her share of benevolent fortune and now it had run out.

The next afternoon, Pauline sat outside a taco joint staring at a plate of stuffed peppers. She would feel better, she knew, only if she decided on a course of action. She'd give it one more night. She'd watch TV like a normal person, would try to distract herself with political news or cooking programs. And in the morning, if she still hadn't heard from Mal, she'd call someone. Maybe not the police, but someone. That was a semblance of a plan.

The landlord, a man who wore a thin leather jacket in the Florida heat, owned a bunch of minor rental buildings and seemed to live in constant acute fear that his tenants would abscond in the night. When Pauline met him on the stairs, he had a vindicated air about him. He wanted to know what kind of mess Mal had left in the place, what kind of drugs he'd find in there. He pushed the door open and Pauline rushed ahead of him to check the bedroom and bathroom, her eyes working clumsily, finding nothing out of the ordinary. The bedroom seemed very still, like places did when you weren't supposed to be in them. Sitting on the dresser was a tall cup of tea Mal had abandoned, the ice long ago melted. Pauline left it where it was. The bed was made sloppily, the way Mal would make a bed. The bathroom offered nothing. The hall light was on, and Pauline turned it off.

"Never heard of dusting, I guess," the landlord called. "If you don't own it, why take care of it, right?"

"She could be in trouble," Pauline said, coming out into the main area. She saw Mal's biscuit pans on the kitchen counter. There were a couple empty shoeboxes on the floor. The cordless phone was in its cradle.

The landlord nodded absently, his attention now on a bowl that held a nutcracker and a corkscrew. Pauline's urgency was not rubbing off on him.

"Anything could have happened to her," she forced herself to say. "*Anything.*"

"She won't be back," said the landlord. "That much I can tell you."

The landlord's casualness was making Pauline crazy, and she heard herself tell him that Mal could be dead for all they knew. It was true, but it was strange to hear herself say it.

The landlord looked almost amused for a moment, then he let out a long, beleaguered breath. "They're never dead, okay? If it helps you any, they're never dead." He did something to the buttons on the cuff of his jacket. "Dead*beats* maybe," he said under his breath. "Anyway, she's not dead in this apartment. We agree on that, right? I came over and we looked and she's not here and the place looks about how one would expect."

"I don't know what you mean by that," Pauline said. "'How one would expect.'"

She went over and looked in the refrigerator. Nothing in it was opened. A jar of pickles, a package of butter, some ready-to-bake cookies—all with the seals unbroken.

When she closed the refrigerator door, she saw it. Up on top of the fridge was Mal's purse, the yellow one, the one she always carried, sitting up there sadly like a child's forgotten baseball mitt. Pauline pulled it down and unsnapped it, turning toward the light coming in from the back window. The purse didn't have much weight to it and there wasn't much inside. About a dozen cheap lipsticks and, beneath them, Mal's fake ID. No wallet, no cash. There were a bunch of inside pockets that held nothing but nickels and old concert stubs.

The landlord had walked up next to her. "Let me guess," he said. "She took all the important shit with her."

Pauline stepped away, closing the purse defensively. "Why would she not just take the purse? Why would she take her wallet out and carry it?"

"Now I'm supposed to read her mind? I don't know, maybe she has more than one purse. I can't read my own mind sometimes. I know I can't read hers."

There were two chairs at Mal's kitchen table, and Pauline pulled one of them out and sat on it. She dropped the spare change and ticket stubs and whatnot back into the purse. She rested it on the table but didn't take her hand off it. Mal wouldn't have purposely left her purse. That just didn't make sense. And why would she set it on top of the refrigerator?

"I was hoping you'd know what to do," she told the landlord. "I don't know how to deal with something like this."

"I'm generally not a wise choice," he admitted, "for pinning your hopes on." He picked up a magazine and looked at the model on the cover, then returned it to its stack. He said he had to go to the bathroom before he hit the road.

The moment he was out of sight, Pauline found herself up out of her chair and stepping over to the door that led to the balcony. She didn't know why, didn't know what it would accomplish, except that she wanted to be able to get back in here if she needed to. She didn't want to have to call the landlord again. She turned the deadbolt sideways, opened the door an inch and then reclosed it. She looked out the window—the exact same view she had, of course, but somehow it seemed broader, less pinched. The sunlight looked thinner than she'd ever seen it, the air without its usual weight. When she heard the toilet flush, she hurried back to the table.

The landlord emerged and went to the front door. He stood there making a face that meant it was time to go, and then issued a grand sigh. "How you deal with something like this, I'd say, is wait," he told Pauline. "People take off and then a couple months later, by hook or by crook, some news of them will filter back. You find out they went out west or something. Giving the landlords out there some fun." He dug something out of his eye, then blinked deliberately. "One of these days I'm going to get rid of this business and dig ditches instead. Deep ones."

The cops opened a file on Mal, but only because the fact that she was under eighteen forced them to. Pauline admitted there were no signs of struggle at the apartment. The police already had a backlog of violent crimes to work on, violent crimes that had definitely occurred, they told her, with blood and weapons and such. Mal wasn't a native, so they figured she'd wised up and headed home. Putting her on file was all they would do right now.

Pauline didn't have any pictures of Mal, so they used the one from her Florida driver's license, promising to circulate it within the system. They weren't going to come poke around the apartment building, didn't care about the car as of yet. They weren't compelled by Pauline's second-hand description of Tug. Pauline felt surreal at the police station, like she'd entered an old TV show or something, like what everyone was saying had been decided ahead of time. She turned Mal's deflated-looking yellow purse over and the cops accepted it indifferently and found a cardboard box to rest it in. They smiled at her humanely, waiting for her to leave.

There was no extended family Pauline knew of, no one beyond Granny who had passed away. She didn't know the names of the people Mal always talked to on the phone. Pauline called the appliance store where Mal worked, but they didn't have anything to offer, either. The woman who owned the place said they'd been wondering if she was going to show up again or if she'd had enough of retail. The woman seemed amused, like Mal was pulling a stunt. She said Mal reminded her of herself as a kid. She said Mal would always have a place at her store, if she wanted it.

Pauline herself still half expected Mal to clomp up the stairs outside in a new dress and with another offbeat manicure, a knowing smirk lipsticked across her face. The police had told Pauline to let them know if anything changed, if anyone came for the car or anything. That was their line—let them know if anything changed. They told Pauline to continue with her life. They told her that fretting wouldn't help anything.

For the next few days, Pauline ate nothing but the occasional slice of bread. She kept her teapot continually heating and drank cup after cup of peppermint tea. She scoured the balcony floor and the banister, scraping off some mold that was thriving and a battalion of tiny off-white snails. She stole a glance now and again at Mal's unlocked door, knowing it would do no good to venture past it. She almost wanted to lock it again.

Pauline was justified for believing Mal needed guidance, for always wanting to warn the girl about the way she conducted her life, but that validation was only making her feel small and cynical. That's what a realist was: a cynic. They were one and the same. And what was the prize for it, for all the accurate cynicism? Here she was cleaning, killing snails. The world was a perilous place where fun had a price, and what would understanding that get Pauline? Her landlord and the cops and the lady at the furniture store thought nothing bad had happened to Mal, and they were going on with their lives; they were believing what was convenient for them. Pauline had been right, and now she was left to feel hollow and stymied in her prudence.

She went out to the balcony less and less. Being out there only made her miss Mal worse, and she didn't like being next to that damned door. There was nothing behind it but fresh sadness and uncertainty; she wasn't going to find a clue. She didn't want back in that apartment.

Instead she would look out at the balcony from her kitchen and see birds perched on the railing. They didn't want anything to do with the feeder. They would just perch on the rail and look around. Pauline saw more of the big white water birds, strutting aimlessly down below, jabbing around dumbly in the swamps of Central Florida, which they would be allowed to do until they wandered into some redneck's yard and got shot to pieces for fun.

During the day she felt trapped in her own mind, a feeling she wasn't unfamiliar with, but at night she could hear everything, near and far—dogs answering one another across county lines, insistent whippoorwills, the screeching of tires, breezes in leaves and squirrels in branches and frogs in the muck out behind her building. She heard a girl scream, surprised and giddy. She heard fireworks.

*   *   *

Pauline tried to turn back to her work, something necessary, a duty, but day after day she couldn't concentrate. She would work a half-hour and then lose focus. She'd never had trouble working before. It was something she'd depended on. She'd been an A student and then a model employee. Now she found herself way behind on two separate projects, too far behind to hope to meet her deadlines. She wanted to email the company and tell them what had happened, that a friend of hers had gone missing, but she couldn't bring herself to use Mal as an excuse.

On the morning the first project was due, Pauline took a walk. She left her corner of town and wandered down a two-lane county road she'd never driven. She walked past empty fields dotted with dying trees, a few muddy stockponds. And then she came into a development of some kind, with plain little ranch houses and dogs behind fences. There was a market and a one-room post office. Pauline said good morning to some polite high school kids who were all wearing ball caps and drinking coffee. She went into the store of a gas station and bought a bottle of water, then stepped back out onto the pavement. The sun was shining persistently though the cloud cover; people were cleaning their windshields. A mother yelled at her son because he didn't have shoes on. Music was playing over the gas station speakers, a country song about having fun because you'd worked hard all week. People were making inconsequential decisions, choosing regular or high-octane gasoline, choosing coffee or soda, the *Gainesville Sun* or the *St. Augustine Record*. None of these people knew a thing about Mal, and there were hundreds of missing girls whom Pauline knew nothing about.

Before she went to bed that night, dusk still clinging to the sky, she stood inside her front door and unlocked the deadbolt. She leaned against the wood, her cheek pressed flat. On the other side of this two-inch-thick plank were countless unknown threats, all gaining agency. She slid the bolt in and out of its little nook, listening to the sure sound it made when it dropped into its spot. She turned the lever all the way over, leaving the door unlocked, and backed away. This was the door she should've unlocked all along, she thought. She went to her bedroom and put on a cotton night-gown, then curled up in her bed and lay there wide awake, sweating under the ceiling fan, listening to the noises outside her window.

The next night she left the door unlocked again. She took a shower with it unlocked, then lay down on her bed in a towel. Mal would have laughed at this, laughed at Pauline thinking she was daring for leaving her door unlocked. Mal would never need to scare herself in such a small, stupid way. When she opened herself up to danger, it was in the name of chasing joy. Her version of it, anyway.

Pauline removed her towel, shimmying it out from underneath her back, and tossed it aside. She felt the air from the fan tickling her skin. She had always acted like Mal's mother, but in truth she'd been envious of the girl. And there was a part of Pauline that was envious even now of the fact that Mal could inspire someone to steal her away, whether against her will or not. Mal had aroused such passion that she was either in a shallow grave or nearly two weeks in on some wild romantic romp. Either way, she'd put a man out of his mind. Either way, a man had irresistibly needed her. Her skinny, pale limbs were flopped haphazardly about her in the ditch she'd been dumped in, or else her limbs were stretched leisurely on the deck of a boat, her body warmer and more alive than ever. She was in the middle of the ocean, cut off from civilization, being adored. Tug would be growing a beard by now. He'd be bringing Mal fruit and running ice cubes down her spine. He would lose his job to stay with her longer. He would lose his family, if he had one. He'd spend his last penny on her, dizzy with desire, wanting her over and over.

Pauline put on some too-short denim shorts she hadn't worn in ages and a snug white tank top, and walked outside into the evening. The air was sticky, the mosquitoes lackadaisical. There were no stars in the sky and the night smelled of moss and car exhaust. Beyond the parking lot there was a sidewalk for a time, running alongside the white-lined thor-oughfare she lived on, but instead of continuing that way she crossed the street and cut behind a high-fenced middle school, a couple cars in the lot seeming forgotten or broken down, an athletic field patchy with weeds.

At the far end of the school she walked past a knoll blanketed with cigarette butts, thousands of them. This end of the grounds was unfenced. The land in front of Pauline was haggard and she could see in the failing light that it lowered by degrees down to a retention pond. Beyond the pond was the territory where normal people didn't venture, where the rednecks and recluses still lived by their own rules. She stopped there on the humble vista, hugging herself in the heat, a sheen of sweat glistening on her arms and legs. She looked back in the direction of her apartment building and couldn't make it out. There was a blank spot in the tree line that must've been the strip mall. She wasn't going to be satisfied by walking over to a middle school and walking back home. She didn't want to view the edge of the grid; she wanted to get off it. She started down the mild decline, not feeling bold but not acknowledging fear either, advancing at a mechanical stroll. She skirted the pond on the side with less overgrowth, cautious with her steps. A mosquito buzzed close in her ear and she flapped at it. She could hear a deep croaking that was either a bullfrog or an alligator. One step at a time and she was clear of the pond. She kept going straight and entered a swath of woods that ran alongside a string of slovenly family compounds. She felt hidden. If someone saw her it would seem like she'd been spying. She would seem guilty of something. Her eyes felt darty in the dark. The woods here were strangely dry, palmettos and pine trees, the earth underneath her practically beach sand. She steered herself between the skinny trunks of the pines. The tense voices she heard came from behind screens, from porches and bedrooms. The houses and outbuildings were all bare cinderblock, and there were lesser sheds locked up with heavy chains, disassembled dirt bikes everywhere, no music at all. Pauline tried to find the sand with her footsteps, testing for fallen branches or dry leaves. She could see quick glints of light above her, so she stopped a moment and concentrated, letting her eyes work. She was under a big hardwood tree, an oak probably, and the boughs were hung with metal objects, revolving lazily with the breeze or with gravity. Hubcaps and saw blades. Squares of cut sheet metal. The unexpected beauty ran a shiver through Pauline. She looked all around her, making sure no one was near. In her mind,

Pauline saw the back pages of a newspaper. It would be dated about a month from now, a concise write-up about Pauline and Mal, two more girls gone—neighbors. That detail would make them suspicious. But no: there wouldn't even be a cursory article. There would be an ad in the classifieds for their apartments. That's what would mark their vanishing. She kept herself moving, clearing the last shed, and emerged on an unpaved lane, trying to keep track of where she was so she could find her way home. The weeds on the roadside were thick and high, so she had to walk right down the packed, pale limestone. The houses were hidden back off the road, no mailboxes or street number markers or signs of welcome. The road was empty of traffic for a few minutes, but then a pack of big pickups came along and rumbled past her one by one, harassing her with their growling engines, slowing almost to a stop as they passed, the men in the cabs astonished at her and the pasty, unkempt women looking alarmed and annoyed. Her legs felt so naked now. She tugged on the bottom of her shorts without much effect. She felt even taller than normal, conscious of the way she was forming her steps. Tiny cars with worn shocks trundled by, whole filthy families inside, the children staring wide-eyed at Pauline like she was an apparition. The moon found a spot low in the sky and Pauline could see the yellowish path in front of her feet, winding ahead, winding ahead. She could hear her inner voice telling her it was time to turn back, that she'd done whatever it was she'd wanted to do, but her body had its own momentum. She could hear what sounded like chickens. The air smelled fishy. She went around a sharp bend and came upon three guys working on a dune buggy by lantern, the buggy upside-down, propped on big black bricks. She quickened her pace, a sane reflex that felt all wrong. It felt wrong to show fear, but that's what she was full of. The tall one saw her first and tapped the other two on the chest. They were wearing unlaced boots. One had long thin hair and the other two had bristly crew cuts. One held a wrench, another a pack of cigarettes. They weren't the least bit amused. They were slack-jawed, but with steely eyes. They were wondering, probably, what they were supposed to do about Pauline—*something* had to be done—wondering what the opportune move was for them in this unforeseen scenario. She kept walking, even faster, trying to keep her arms causal while her legs hurried, passing them by and not looking back, hoping they wouldn't call out to her, hoping she'd be out of sight before their shock wore off.

A telemarketer named Justin called. He was calling from Macon, Georgia. He spoke for several minutes about the pitfalls of the stock market, avoiding any mention of what he was selling. His heart wasn't in it, Pauline could tell. He threw in friendly asides, for example that he liked the name Pauline. He told her that even for young people it was paramount to begin making sound financial plans.

"How old do you think I am?" Pauline asked.

"By your voice, I'd say you're around my age. You're thirty years old, give or take." Then he added, "We're in our primes, you and me."

"I'm not in my prime yet. And I don't have a lot of money, so I wouldn't be a very good customer for you."

Justin laughed. He said he wasn't laughing at her, that he was watching a movie on his phone. His personal phone. He could do a lot of things at once. The movie was a parody where a guy keeps killing people with poisoned apple turnovers and the cops hire a master baker to catch him.

"You're allowed to watch movies while you work?"

"No," he said. "The rules are getting kind of lax around here. The company's about to go under. I'm just riding it out for a little extra cash." Justin told Pauline he had his own ventures he was working on, his own start-ups. They mostly centered on golf.

"Can't you get in trouble for saying that to me?"

"They're not listening. I can tell when they tap in, there's a little click. It's just you and me on this call."

There was a pause then. Pauline didn't want to get off the phone. She'd never spoken to a telemarketer for this long. She went and sat down on the couch, blowing into her steaming cup of tea. There was a belt and a headband on the other cushion, and a sock, and she collected them up and tossed them into a decorative basket she kept against the wall. Someone had to say something, and Pauline knew what she wanted to say.

"What do you look like?" she asked Justin.

"Look like?"

"Yeah, look like. Describe yourself."

"Oh, wow," said Justin. "Okay." His voice was quieter. Pauline could picture him sitting up straight in his office chair, checking over his shoulder. "Is this happening? My friend who got me this job said this might happen."

"It's happening," Pauline assured him.

"Well, okay, so I have long sideburns, but not too long. No mustache or goatee or anything. And my hair's kind of wavy but I keep it short. And I have broad shoulders. Like a swimmer's shoulders."

"Uh-huh." Pauline raised the dripping teabag out of her cup and sucked on it.

"I have piercing eyes. People have told me that. Man, this isn't easy. Let's see. My hands are big, and they're tan from playing golf. Is that a thing girls like? Tan hands? I wear a sport coat a lot, but I'm not wearing one now. Um…"

Pauline couldn't think of anything better, so she asked if he was wearing boxers or briefs. She rested her tea on the floor and stretched out on the couch.

"Boxer briefs, actually. They're tight like briefs, but they go down your legs a little."

"What color are they?"

"Just gray. Like sweatshirt gray." Justin cleared his throat. When he started talking again, it was in a whisper. He told Pauline he did a hundred pushups every morning, that he was kind of obsessive about it, so his chest was pretty good, and his triceps. He said he was six feet tall, or just a shade under. Pauline could feel it all happening inside her. She wasn't trying to picture Justin; she was just listening to his hushed voice, relishing this wayward mischief. He said when he was a kid he used to hide in the hedge and spy on the neighbor lady getting dressed. He said one time he'd gotten a handjob in the back pew during church.

Justin asked Pauline to talk for a while, asserting that it was her turn, and she told him she had thick chestnut hair and nerdy glasses. She ran her hands down her legs, bragging on them, telling Justin they were shapely and smooth and supple. She said her toenails were painted red, which wasn't true.

Justin said he was going to put his hand under his desk now, but he couldn't unzip his pants because there were too many people around.

"When I saw Palatka next to the number, I thought this would be a dud. I drove through there one time. Most calls are duds, but when I saw Palatka I thought either I'll get hung up on right away or else some old lady will try to talk to me for an hour about her nephew."

Pauline said her tummy was flat and her lips were plump. "What all's on your screen there?" she asked. "Do you have my address?"

"No, we don't have that. But you could give it to me. Actually, you don't need to. I know sort of what you look like and I know you're about thirty. I could just come down and look around for you."

Pauline was thinking of asking him what he would do if he drove down to Florida and found her, but then she heard him curse, sounding defeated.

"My manager's telling me he wants to talk to me. He doesn't look super pleased. He's doing that thing with his finger like get over here. Maybe they were listening in after all. Maybe I didn't hear the click."

Pauline waited.

"I really have to go. Shit, he's coming over here."

Justin hung up, and Pauline looked at her phone a moment and then set it down on the floor next to her tea. She gazed up at the ceiling of her apartment, marked up here and there where previous tenants had hung plants or killed insects. She moved her hand to her hip, dug her fingers in and kneaded her flesh, but the excitement was already dissipating. Her heart was slowing back down. Her breath was evening out again.

She'd been given an extension on her work projects, but could still find no motivation. She got everything out and tried to concentrate, but after twenty minutes she closed her computer and pushed the files aside and drove over to the Mexican restaurant.

At the restaurant she ate a couple bites of an enchilada and then went to the bar and started on a beer, feeling the first sips trickle down inside her. It was afternoon, still early afternoon, but the place was busy. A guy with buzzed hair and glasses sat on the stool next to Pauline and told the bartender to pick a beer out for him, something seasonal and with some bite. It wasn't the lady bartender Pauline had talked to a few times, just a nondescript Mexican kid. The TV that had been hanging in the bar was gone, along with its hanging stand. There was a vacant spot where it had been. When he was ready, the guy with the buzzed hair looked squarely at Pauline and introduced himself as Herbie. He was already sitting where he was sitting and had already ordered something, but he went ahead and asked if the seat was taken. Pauline told him she couldn't care less where he sat, and he looked at her with amusement. He told her he was writing a feature for a magazine based in Mississippi, and made a surprised face when she hadn't heard of it. He had a pronounced Southern accent but he didn't speak slowly. Pauline watched him take down half his beer in one greedy pull.

"You mind if I talk to you for a spell?" Herbie said. "So I can see if you'd be a good character for me to use."

"I wouldn't be," Pauline said. "I'm the boring friend."

He grinned, then he knocked on the bar like it was a door. "Nobody who calls herself boring is boring. And in my experience boring folks don't go out drinking alone. That ain't foolproof, but it's a general rule." Herbie held his beer at an angle in front of him, like he was examining the color. "I won't grill you with questions. We'll just shoot the breeze and see where it goes."

Pauline wondered how she looked. Her hair was pulled straight back and she didn't have any makeup on except some eye shadow. She was wearing cute shoes, at least. She had no idea why she'd worn cute shoes, but she had. No one had hit on her in the year she'd been in Palatka. She asked Herbie what his story was about, exactly.

"It's a series of stories, interrelated I'm hoping. I start them out sounding like corny Southern tales, and then I stick in profiles of real people. Then what I do is imagine meetings between the real people, if that makes sense. Fiction and nonfiction have a lot of gray area now. As does the South."

"I don't want to be in a gray area. I feel like I've been in a gray area for too long."

"Whoa, see, that's a line. I could use that. That's sharp dialogue."

Pauline took a hard gulp of her beer. It was still ice cold. She didn't look over at Herbie but instead kept her gaze vaguely ahead—on the bottles, on the string of plastic peppers hanging from the shelves, on the blue and gold macaw perched up among the tequilas.

"Why do you get to judge who's boring or interesting?" she said. "I think you're kind of boring. I think writing magazine articles is boring. I wish you'd just come out and ask for what you want. I've already decided the answer, so you might as well ask."

Herbie laughed through his nose, his straight white teeth lined up in a showy smile, but Pauline had cracked his cool veneer. He tried to think of what to say, fooling with a stack of coasters on the bar. "Hey, take it easy with the insults," he told her. "Maybe I'm just in need of a pal. I been on the road a long time. It gets lonesome. I need characters, but I need a pal too."

The lights in the restaurant dimmed a little and Herbie traded out his glasses for a pair he pulled from a pocket in his shorts. The new ones had less tint in the lenses. Pauline's heart was beating fast and she could feel that she was holding her shoulders tense.

"We don't even got to talk if you don't want," Herbie said. "I can learn plenty about a person without talking to her. Just by observing with the five senses."

Pauline kept looking ahead into the bottles, thankful there wasn't a mirror behind them. She liked being able to look away from Herbie and know he was looking at her. Men were certainly cunning. He had smelled the recklessness on Pauline. They did have their senses, men, and not just the five. Now he was doing something with his hands, sign language or something. He kept tapping the side of his head, then tracing his jawline with his finger. Pauline didn't believe he was really a writer. She didn't believe a word he said. She felt disoriented by him—his accent seemed to thicken and thin, and his grin had something sinister in it.

"What's the first line of the story you're writing? What's the first sentence?"

"I've done South Carolina and Georgia. Now I'm on Florida, obviously. The Georgia part's about this guy from Australia who opened a Civil War restaurant. It's called The Hardtack. They serve legal moonshine. Let's see, the first line. It's something about how in the South fun and trouble have something in common: you can't plan when you're going to have either. I can't remember exactly how I put it."

Pauline adjusted her sleeve and her bra strap. "So basically you're getting paid to mess around in bars for weeks on end? They pay people to do that? In this economy?"

"They do if your grandfather founded the magazine. He passed last year and I inherited his big old Cadillac. I was his favorite. Everybody wanted somebody from the Crontcow family to be associated with the magazine, so I quit science and became a writer."

"Science?"

"Herpetology, to be precise. I studied enzymes in snake venom. I always had a thing for snakes. That's a misunderstood, maligned creature right there. You work up compassion for snakes, you really did something. That compassion's hard-earned."

They were looking at each other and Herbie reached over very calmly and touched Pauline's wrist. His fingers were callused, but his touch was gentle. She waited a moment before she took his hand and moved it back to his beer.

"Your name isn't Herbie Crontcow. There's just no way that's somebody's name."

"What difference is it what my name is? A lot of people have a few separate names. In Georgia I was Sonny Martin. If anybody goes looking for me they'll be looking for Sonny Martin. I have a pen name too."

The bartender had brought Herbie another beer without his asking for it, and he was already more than half done with it. He raised it to Pauline, like he was happy she was coming around to his viewpoints, whatever those viewpoints were.

"What's the worst thing you've ever done?" Pauline asked him. "What's the worst single act in your history?"

He looked at her deliberately, not ready for the question, filling his chest with a breath. He finished the rest of his beer with an easy swallow and then held his hand up to stop the bartender, who was getting ready to get him another. He rested his hands on the black wood of the bar. There was a ring on his left hand featuring a silver scorpion. His arms were wiry. The sleeves of his T-shirt were short enough that Pauline could see his hard, oval-shaped biceps.

Looking at Pauline with an overly mild expression, he said, "Oh, I've always been pretty sweet." His eyes behind his glasses were meek. "I wouldn't have much to report in the way of evil acts. I never been too wieldy in a fight. And I don't believe in revenge. Somebody gets the best of me, I tip my hat to them. I have my interests and I pretty much just stick to those." He stroked his cheek, which hadn't been shaved in a few days. "Not that I'm self-righteous. I know people got their problems. Sometimes things get out of hand. I'm fully aware about that phenomenon. Sometimes you think you're heading for a good time and then you realize you got on some other road, and it's too late."

Pauline wondered where this guy was from. He could be from Virginia or Texas or from a mile down the road. She felt the familiar alarm she'd always depended on droning in the back of her mind, but it wasn't difficult to ignore.

"You want another light beer?" he asked. "Or you want a margarita or something, like when in Rome? What's a gal like you drink? We could get a bottle of wine. I don't reckon they have an extensive cellar, but they'll have something made out of grapes."

"Not wine," Pauline said. "I'll order something, though. Let me think about it."

"I'm going to pee and you think about it, but if you get anything, put it on my tab."

"It's all right," Pauline said. "I have a tab of my own."

"No, I'm serious. Whatever you get, it's on me. Well, it's actually on the magazine."

"Gotcha," said Pauline.

"I'm not messing around now."

"Message received. Not messing around."

"Look here, if you get something else to drink and don't let me pay for it, I'll make a scene. I'll embarrass us both."

"You're pretty much doing that now."

Herbie chuckled. He arose from his stool, patted a couple of his shorts pockets, then disappeared down a hallway that led to the bathrooms.

Pauline set her empty beer bottle down on the bar, and the bartender approached her immediately. She asked him for a shot of whiskey. The bartender asked her what kind and she said whatever was the most expensive. He nodded and pulled down an ornate round bottle with a cork in it, filled a shot glass, and set it in front of Pauline. "Put it on his tab," she said, motioning toward the empty stool beside her. "Put my beer on there too." She hadn't done a shot in a long time but she remembered that the wrong approach was thinking about the shot or smelling it or staring at it. She threw the whiskey back with her eyes closed, swallowing through the burn, and managed to get it down and keep it down.

She'd performed well in her encounter with Herbie and she thought the thing to do now was make a striking exit, to preserve some mystery. She asked for a pen and wrote her phone number on a drink napkin, then instructed the bartender to give the napkin to Herbie. "Tell him I had something better to do, but if he wants to call me sometime he can feel free."

The bartender bowed toward Pauline, his face hinting at a smile. Pauline gathered herself and began moving toward the front doors of the restaurant, wanting to slip out before Herbie returned from the bathroom. She sidestepped a waitress carrying a tray of full plates and then went around a huge party that had pushed some tables together, a celebration of some kind. She was steps from the door when she glanced down toward a little alcove of the waiting area and saw Herbie jabbing his finger huffily at an old man. They were standing in front of a cigarette machine. Herbie was doing the talking, the old man's posture recalcitrant but resigned. The old man, about half the size of Herbie, had on worn-out sneakers and a corduroy shirt. He was shaking his head stubbornly and Herbie was hissing at him, his left hand clenched in a fist by his side. Pauline found the handle of the door and pushed on outside before one of them could turn and notice her. She had no idea what there was to yell at an old man in a Mexican restaurant about, not the first inkling. She hurried down the front walk, eyes searching out her car in the lot.

Pauline had logged a few more fruitless phone calls, but eventually she returned to the police station in person. Bulletins had gone out. The car had been impounded, she was told, but she already knew that. The case file had been activated, but wasn't being investigated currently, whatever that meant. The police force was understaffed and underpaid, Pauline was told. A cop with the rank of sergeant who looked fresh out of high school told Pauline that in cases like this the missing person was usually missing on purpose.

"Everybody keeps telling me that," Pauline said. "I've heard that one roughly a dozen times."

"She'll turn up. Trust me. Sometimes people don't call because they're embarrassed, or they don't want to be judged or whatever. They don't want to have to apologize. But she'll turn up."

"She'll turn up?" Pauline said. "She'll turn up? That's the plan when a bottle opener is lost. Or tweezers or something. You just wait for them to turn up."

The sergeant gripped her gently by the arm for a moment, forbearing and sympathetic, and then left her in the lobby. He was wearing sneakers instead of boots and Pauline heard the squeak of the soles against the floor until a door closed behind him.

She sat down. On the wall was a board full of wanted men—some sneering, some blank-faced, some genuinely concerned about the course their lives had taken. Pauline had no idea what else she was supposed to do about Mal. She was sitting in a dingy, one-story police station, staring at the walls. Next to all the wanted men was another corkboard, this one crowded with articles confirming Palatka's status as a famous speed trap. Beyond that was a gumball machine covered in dust.

By now the balcony was entirely off-limits, as if it didn't exist. Pauline kept the back blinds closed tight at all times—the ones over the regular windows and the ones over the small window in the door. She didn't want to see the wind chimes out there—though she often heard them—or the spot on the banister where Mal always used to sit. She didn't want to contemplate the still undone deadbolt. Sometimes Pauline heard birds pecking around out there, looting what was left in the feeder, and sometimes the birds' noises suggested something more alarming, fracases and fighting, cries of surrender. When this happened, she had no recourse except to turn on music and move to the front room.

It had been a few days since she'd talked to Herbie. Their conversation already seemed unreal, like it might not have happened at all. She might not have seen him harassing that old man. She might not have done that whiskey shot.

She wanted to exercise, or at least she thought it would be good for her. There was no decent health club in Palatka, of course. She owned no weights or workout mats. She spread a blanket on the floor and dropped to her stomach. She did three pushups and then a pain shot from her wrist to her elbow. She flipped and stretched her hamstrings. She could hear the tapping of raindrops starting on the roof. She did some yoga poses she remembered, difficult ones that were hard to hold for very long.

When she needed a break she got up and checked her email, knowing there would be something from the company she was freelancing for, and sure enough. The subject heading was DEADLINE 2??? Pauline stared at the computer screen for a long minute, wondering whether she wanted to open the email. She had wanted to be chastised, but now she was thinking better of it. She heard a sound, a small gust of wind finding its way in from outside, a hinge creaking, and when she looked up Herbie was standing in the front doorway grasping a single hibiscus. He was standing right there, clean-shaven now, looking bigger in her doorway than he'd looked in the bar, holding the flower by its long woody stem. He'd somehow found out where she lived. He hadn't even knocked. Pauline had made an exit, and now he was making an entrance.

She didn't feel particularly startled. Not like she should've. He had the flower in one hand and the other hand he'd placed on his hip, like he was modeling his clothes—those same shorts with all the pockets, his wire-frame glasses. She felt equal to the idea of this strange man showing up in her living room. She'd been forcing herself to act like someone she wasn't, but now she didn't feel like she was playing a part. This moment felt real. She'd been invaded and she could deal with it.

"Are you taking guests?" he asked.

"I thought of something I should've said to you," said Pauline. "In the bar, when you said you could observe me with your five senses, I should've said, 'You'll be lucky to use two or three.'"

"That would've been clever," Herbie agreed. "But anybody can think of that stuff after they get home."

"I want you to take me jogging. That's how you can be of use."

He looked behind him, at the rain, and pursed his lips. "Yeah, let's go jogging. I can't think of any reason why not."

He stayed where he was but reached the hibiscus out toward Pauline, and she stepped over and took it from him. She found a tall, thin water glass in the kitchen to put it in. Herbie told her he'd stolen it from an old lady's sun porch. He said if there was one thing he couldn't tolerate, it was old ladies.

Pauline knew she didn't have the upper hand in here. She wanted to get them outside. She yanked on running shoes and led Herbie out the door and down the stairs. She told him to run in front so she could keep an eye on him, and he winked at her and set a pace, leading them out onto the road. There were no sidewalks, so when cars came they ran in the weeds, their shins whipped red. Pauline heaved and spat for a time and then she settled in. They weren't getting all that wet because of the oak branches that wound overhead. Only their shoes got soaked, pounding into the clay-colored puddles. Herbie was bowlegged. He maintained his pace faultlessly. Pauline focused on the back of his bobbing head. He was wearing a sleeveless T-shirt, and Pauline could see marks on his neck that could've been scratches from a person or could've been made by running through prickly foliage. Pauline wasn't going to ask about the scratches. She wasn't going to ask about the old guy at the Mexican restaurant because she'd never get a straight answer anyway. She wasn't even going to ask how Herbie's magazine story was coming. It would somehow be a display of weakness at this point, would somehow cost her leverage, to forsake spontaneity and put her focus on the mining of facts.

They loped past a parked cop car and the cop stared at them from inside, his expression both intense and vague. She had no idea how long they'd been running, but it was going to be night soon. Her hamstrings were itching with use; her calves were tight as balls of twine. They passed a pecan grove, then a hill of smoldering tires, the sky lightening and darkening. Pauline hadn't paid attention to the turns they'd made and was surprised when the back of her apartment building came into view. They cut through the swamp on a berm of dry ground and bounded up the stairs. Herbie went in and collapsed on the blanket that was still spread on the floor. He slipped a couple soft glasses cases out of his pockets and chose a pair. They'd been in his pockets the whole jog, however many pairs of glasses and a case for each. Then he peeled his shirt off over his head, pried off his shoes. There was something bullying and presumptuous about how comfortable he was acting in her place, but now she enjoyed it. The smell of him. The space he occupied. His body without a shirt looked good. The muscles of his torso all showed but he didn't seem like somebody who went to a gym.

She hung his shirt and socks over the back of a chair and set his shoes on a mat in the kitchen. "Hey, I have something for you," she said. "I have something to give you."

She hurried to the closet in her bedroom, plucked the boots from the outlet mall off the floor, and carried them out to Herbie. She felt lucky, competent even. Herbie rubbed the leather on his cheek and sniffed it, just as she had in the store, then he set the boots gingerly aside without trying them on.

"Who'd those things belong to?"

"No one. I bought them as an investment and it paid off."

"They'll lose a lot of resale value the second I put them on. That's the bitch of it."

Pauline laughed. It sounded strange to her.

"Kind of a forward gift, don't you think?" Herbie said. "A fellow could get the wrong idea."

He was flat on his back. He started emptying more stuff out of his pockets—a shiny little fold-up knife, a book of matches, a fifty-dollar bill. He stuck one arm up in the air and started signing what looked like the alphabet.

"I just quit my job," she said. "Well, I'm in the process of forcing them to fire me. Same difference."

"Sometimes I wish I had a normal job. It seems like it would help you stay grounded, having a boss and rules. Help a person master their vices. Also sometimes when I'm writing, I need to tell how my character hates their crappy job. I got no concept how that feels. You know, firsthand."

"Why do you know sign language?"

"People don't classify it as a foreign language because you don't produce it in your throat. They don't consider me bilingual. You believe that shit?"

"There's no region for it," Pauline said.

"There's a people."

Herbie took off the glasses he was wearing and didn't put on another pair. He looked more calculating with his face bare. He looked less happy-go-lucky.

"Two people knowing it," he said. "That makes it a living language."

He did the sign from the bar again, cupping his temple and then drawing a line to his chin.

"What does that one mean?" Pauline asked.

"That's an old expression," he said. "It means nothing is beautiful to the ugly eye. Or something in that ballpark."

Pauline had been crouching near Herbie, and now she rose and went to her room to change out of her wet clothes. She'd never finished the Goodwill project in her closet. She flicked through the hangers and found an apricot sundress she'd had since high school. She slipped it on and put a brush through her hair. She was perfectly aware that Herbie could be anyone, that whatever he planned to do to Pauline, good or evil, he was going to do. Maybe he'd slaughter her and leave her posing on a high dive. Or maybe he'd get a phone call and leave town and she'd never see him again. Maybe he was going to be the love of her life. That's how the world gave out prizes and abuse to its women; you had to accept the box before you knew what was in it.

When she came back out, Herbie wasn't in the living room anymore. Neither were the boots. Pauline held still a moment, and then she could hear something from back in the kitchen—just an alteration in the acoustics at first, and then the distinct clink of cheap blinds banging against a window. It could only be the little window in her back door. When she reached the kitchen it was empty, the door to the balcony swung open, the musty swamp air washing in. She stood where she was and listened. She could hear the soles of the boots scuffing out there on the wood, and then the sound stopped. She couldn't see Herbie from where she was standing, but something told her that he was peering into Mal's apartment. She wanted to know what his next move would be. Through the doorway she could see the dense, vine-bound jungle—the gray-brown cypresses with their great trunks and puny limbs, the lusty ferns crowding each other off patches of high ground. She stayed still and quiet for what felt like a long time. If he was going to open Mal's door she wanted to make sure she could hear it. A plank creaked, and she could feel the tension in her limbs as she held herself motionless. But the silence returned, and stretched out. No other sound came. A new silence, like he wasn't breathing. Like he'd vanished.

The next thing she heard from the balcony was whistling, faint for a moment and then less so, finding the right inflection. Herbie was whistling something for the birds, a keen, pithy strain that could just as easily have been a warning or a greeting.

PROSPECTUS

Marky Sessions was a slick-fielding second baseman who couldn't hit a lick. His last season of Little League was winding down, and he missed it already. Judd Farmer, a fat pitcher from Dade City, was overpowering Marky's team. There'd been whispers of some coaches from the fancy prep school showing up to check Farmer out, but Marky didn't notice anyone in the stands who fit that description. Same crowd as usual—the players' siblings, women who owned stores near the diamond, old folks relieved at having a place to go. Nelson Greer was way up in the bleachers, alone like always, huddled in a tan windbreaker. He could somehow eat the same pretzel the entire game. Nelson had been a hotshot financial adviser when he was barely old enough to drink, the toast of Tampa, then he'd gotten busted for some kind of favor-trading that people in that racket did all the time. He'd been a scapegoat. He'd gone to prison for three years, then bought a hopeless villa in the sticks and became a hermit. He only left home for sandwiches and liquor and to watch Little League.

Marky's team finished off their half of the inning without a hit. He trotted out of the dugout and readied himself at the edge of the infield. He watched his pitcher loop a knuckleball over the batter, watched the ball find its way under the backstop, watched the catcher crawling beneath the bleachers to sniff it out. Marky felt himself losing focus, and did not fight it. He was used to it—this wistful tide that left him feeling rooted into a too-particular spot on earth, a spot where something forgotten but important had occurred, where someone from another century had appealed to the gods or invented a joke. He wished they could go back to the first inning. He wished they could start the whole season over, wished the yolky midday sun would get stuck up in the sky, that the hot breath of summer would never cool.

The ping of the bat snapped him out of it. A pitch had been smoked back at the mound. Marky caught sight of the ball as it glanced off the pitcher's shin. It was skipping right toward him. He barehanded it, exhaled, and flung it to first for the out.

In the final inning, Marky came up to bat again. The infielders crept in a few steps, making him feel crowded, and a plan occurred to him. He held his bat out over the plate in a check-swing pose and kept it there. He held it as still as he could, and it became clear that he wasn't going to put it back on his shoulder. The catcher stared up at him quizzically. The umpire spoke but Marky shook him off, provoking Farmer to step off the mound and paw the rosin. Marky held stiff, gazing down fixedly at the glimmering barrel of his bat instead of facing the mound, looking like a mid-swing statue of some anonymous youth sportsman of yore. Farmer let rip a fastball that zipped past Marky's bat and was called a strike.

"I'm considering this bunting," the umpire told Marky. "He could roll the ball in and I'd call a strike, if you keep standing like that."

Marky did not flinch or reset, though his forearms were beginning to tremble. Farmer's next pitch left his huge hand and chinked off Marky's wavering, offered bat in the same instant. It took everyone a moment to locate the ball, which had blooped over the drawn-in first baseman and trickled onto the outfield grass. Marky pulled up with a comfortable single and peered at Nelson Greer, hoping for any reaction at all.

* * *

After the game had been lost, Marky mounted his scooter—a wood-framed chopper with angry bees painted all over it—and whined out of the swampland and away from the diamond. Marky had found the scooter near the railroad tracks and had it overhauled by the trade school mechanics, who'd made it too powerful for its own good. He stayed in third gear all the way to Hurley's house.

Hurley was in the custom musical instrument trade, among other things, and Marky needed a one-of-a-kind bass drum for a band he wanted to manage. He had known the guys in the band awhile; they were a few years older than him, upperclassmen at the local high school. Their band was called Some Cars Are Trucks; it featured a genius on harmonica but suffered from a dearth of thump and an even more alarming dearth of gimmick. Marky figured the absurd drum would get the band noticed, make them memorable, and from there talent could take over. The vast majority of bands wound up fizzling and breaking up, Marky knew, but he thought he might as well try to jumpstart these guys and if anything happened he'd be in for ten percent. The harmonica player really was amazing, and the band's songs were sad but not too sad.

He stepped high through some weeds and then scaled the manmade hill Hurley's house perched atop. He knocked on Hurley's door and it opened instantly. The man seemed older than Marky remembered—bearded, wearing a tennis outfit, snapping his fingers in thought.

"Marky," Marky said.

"Oh, I know. I like to see how people say their own names. Are you a Scotch drinker?"

"No, not really," Marky admitted.

"I know. I'm kidding with you. You're a teenager, you probably only drink beer."

"Nothing right now, thanks. I'm kind of on a schedule today."

Marky got a look at the living room, cluttered with record players and stacked terrariums, then Hurley ushered him down to the basement, which was twice the size of the house and was divided here and there by hung tablecloths. Basements were rare in Florida, and being in this one made

Marky a little nervous. It held racquet-stringing equipment, painted steel barrels, and plain tables to which vices clung. Marky was still wearing his cleats, and he stepped gingerly on the concrete floor.

"Can't light up down here," Hurley said.

"That's okay, I don't smoke."

"Don't drink, don't smoke. You sure you're a teenager?"

"Basically," said Marky. "I'm on deck to be a teenager."

"Hey, before I forget to tell you, I'm getting a bunch of books in next week. You should come back and take a look. I'm going to price them at a penny a page."

"Where are they from?"

"They were trying to start a college over in Redleg, but the money fell through."

"Oh, I heard about that," Marky said. "That Bible college."

"A couple of them I'm keeping. There's one all about how kings used to blind architects so they couldn't build the same castle for anyone else. Or cathedral or whatever. And there's one on carnivorous plants. Now that's a poker face—a hunter that has to have the prey *land* on him."

Marky nodded, holding an appreciative look on his face. After a moment he said, "Anyway, that bass drum. We talked about it at the pancake breakfast."

Hurley bared his teeth, as if for inspection.

"Twelve foot across," said Marky.

"Now if it's too big, you won't be able to hear it."

"Really?" Marky asked. "Why, too low a register?"

Hurley looked off, skeptical of his own assertion. "Well, no. I guess you'd hear it. You're going to hear it and also feel it."

"Ever make one that big?"

"No, I made a pretty big one for some people holding a parade once, but not twelve foot. Made a lot of stuff for those guys. Parades used to be much better than they are now."

"The ones I've seen have been lame," Marky agreed.

"You missed out on a lot of Golden Ages, and the Golden Age of parades is one of them."

Marky tried to think of something that was enjoying its Golden Age right now. There had to be something. He had the sensation, in this basement, that he was being filmed.

"I ever tell you about the radio station I used to own?" asked Hurley.

"Yeah," Marky answered. Maybe Hurley had told him about the radio station and maybe he hadn't. Marky couldn't remember. "I don't mean to be in a rush, but I was hoping to get a price from you and scoot on."

"Oh, for sure," Hurley said. "On the run. I know." He ducked behind a curtain then reappeared with a form, which read:

CUSTOM TANK

CUSTOM RACKET

CUSTOM INSTRUMENT*

If _____ cannot be delivered by _____ ,
the sum of _____ will be refunded in full
to _____.

X _____
X _____

*First LP or EP in which instrument appears will feature photography
by Hurley Simms in cover art.

"Waterproofing's extra," Hurley said. He pulled a calculator from somewhere.

"Let's just skip that."

"Moisture can kill a drum. Getting caught out in the rain. Or just the humidity on a porch, even. It can totally dull the sound."

"Yeah, I think I'll do without it, though," said Marky. "These guys rehearse at the community college. They should be fine."

"You may regret that, little dude. I don't sell insurance for these things."

"I don't buy insurance. I'm not sure I believe in it, actually."

Hurley took a retreating step, then for effect he took another. "That's badass," he said. "Tattoos and gangster rap, those are just products. Refusing insurance is badass shit."

Marky leaned his scooter in his uncle's garage, removed his cleats, and went in for a bowl of cereal. It was his uncle's naptime so he turned the TV on low, to a program about the strange things people ate in Asia. Marky's uncle collected antique pornography and had stacks of calendars and prints all over the coffee table. These pale, resigned, full-bodied ladies were more nurturing than seductive. Marky could imagine them eating peanut butter right out of the jar with spoons as big as hairbrushes, carrying hefty pens around in their hands all day, no intention of writing. His uncle collected all sorts of things. They lived among chili recipes and old car phones.

Marky knew that the man wasn't a loved figure up at the warehouse where he worked the evening shift. His uncle carried on a handful of feuds with various coworkers and called in sick the maximum it was allowed. The warehouse, which stored mainly hair products, was going to be bought out—according to the gossip it was all but a done deal—and no one expected Marky's uncle to survive the changeover. He wasn't skilled, didn't have a forklift license or anything. He'd only gotten the job in the first place because one of the shift supervisors had been an old friend of Marky's uncle's mother, before she died. Marky's uncle never stayed at a job more than a year or two, but it was getting harder for him to get hired anywhere—the economy, and the fact that he had a reputation by now.

The topic of Marky's uncle's precarious employment wasn't spoken of in the house, but there was a tension all could feel. The factory could be bought out next week, next month. Marky's uncle, on principle, wouldn't accept unemployment checks. He'd wind up in the temporary labor line, most probably, with the convicts and community college washouts, and the thought of that sank Marky's heart.

A shot was fired and Marky dropped the hosiery calendar he'd been holding into a splay on the rug. His cousin was shooting.

Marky went out the back, toward the little range his cousin had cut near the fill dunes. His cousin was seventeen and even less suited for this world than the uncle. Marky's cousin was a poet who spent most of his time observing birds and practicing with weapons. He was shooting cans of powdered barbecue sauce with a gun called a Mini-14. The concentrated powder, infused with calcium and ginkgo biloba, had been a science project of Marky's. Marky didn't want to startle his cousin, so he sat on a shellacked stump and watched can after can become dust in the breeze.

When his cousin was finished he set the gun down, shook his arms out, and removed a yellow plug from each ear. He came and stood near Marky.

"Those rounds cost a buck apiece," he said. "I just shot forty dollars."

"Does it seem like it was worth it?"

"It's worrisome how much I enjoy shooting things."

Marky's cousin interlaced his fingers and brought his hands to his chest, a gesture he'd performed ever since Marky could remember. It often meant he was about to say something that didn't quite make sense.

"Not enjoying anything for a full day is pretty satisfying too, though. If you don't fake it, at least." He paused. He had a look on his face like he was tasting something exotic. "Take that Nelson guy. Nelson Greer. He's made an art out of not enjoying anything. He seems miserable, but I think there's a sense in which he's happier than most. I saw him at the deli yesterday. He was staring at the lunchmeats with this flat, flat expression, but he was intensely in the moment. His case interests me."

"He was at my game again."

"Oh, yeah? I should try that. I should try watching sports. I used to watch basketball when I was a kid, but when my team lost I would cry and cry. I'm talking wracking sobs. I could probably handle it a lot better now. The vicarious losing."

"I'm going to try and meet him," Marky said. "I think he could help me with some of my ideas."

"You should bring a gift."

"Yeah, I should, huh?"

"You don't want to show up empty-handed."

"I should bring him some liquor or something. Do you have any to spare inside?"

"I think I can dig something out."

A plump bird on a low branch started chittering sharply. It seemed to be laying down the law, maybe to Marky and his cousin and maybe to other birds. They watched it until it was finished.

Marky's cousin looked at him. "I know that bird. He's here every year. He's a little insane. I see him pecking at his own feet sometimes. He ate an eraser once."

"Where'd he get an eraser from?"

"I was out here writing. I actually put it in the villanelle I was working on—how he kept trying to break it with his beak and then he finally gave up and swallowed it whole."

Marky had always admired his cousin, but he worried about him more and more. He didn't act in his own interests. The cousin and the uncle were his only family. His uncle, despite his occupational difficulties, was a good guy; he'd taken Marky in after Marky's mother had died. His uncle hadn't had to adopt him, but he had done it anyway. The man wasn't really suited to being a father in the first place, and he'd agreed to look after another child, another boy who was considered strange, though in a different way than Marky's cousin was strange. Marky could remember his uncle doing his level best as a parent when Marky was little. He could remember him helping with history homework, driving Marky to Pee Wee practice, making him breakfasts. And Marky's cousin had never resented his presence. He'd always treated him as an equal, the way he treated everyone as an equal. He'd liked having an audience, if not a playmate. But what Marky knew about the present version of his cousin, this almost-adult version, was that he would never survive in the world on his own. He lived in a bubble in this house Marky's uncle had inherited, and he wouldn't fare well if he ever had to leave it.

"I meant to tell you not to worry about all those books in my room," Marky's cousin said. "In case you got a peek at them, that's just academic reading. A poet not acquainted with suicide is like a shark with nothing but molars."

Marky waited.

"Suicide is for chumps," his cousin said. "And in my case, there's the fun of getting to witness whatever happens with your life down the line. Ultimately, I'm going to be very proud of you. You're a natural's natural. You'll swim the black waters, your stroke even and true."

"I'll do my best," said Marky.

Marky's cousin reached into a pocket of his shorts and pulled out an individually wrapped fig. He chewed it once or twice and swallowed hard. "Hell, I'm proud of you already."

As evening fell, Marky grew antsy. He filled a thermos with apple juice and carried it around as he straightened his room. He watched a political debate while solving his Rubik's cube. He was sick of giving away his ingenuity. Just last month he'd consulted with the new owner of the Big Spring Jungle Park, who was his baseball coach's brother. He had advised him to produce laminated bird-watching pamphlets, and to solicit field trips. He advised a dual ticket with the drag racing museum. Koi in the gift shop fountain. An old man who played the banjo. Already the Jungle Park had taken on new employees. It was the talk of the district. Marky knew that guys in big cities got paid obscenely for that sort of consulting, and Marky didn't have more than a few hundred bucks to his name. He knew it was a matter of time, and maybe not a long time, before he'd have to support his uncle and cousin. What Marky wanted was to start a business he could bring the two of them into, something where they could contribute however they felt like contributing, where they could find a way to utilize their talents.

He had been building up his courage to go speak to Nelson Greer, getting his ducks in a row as to what he would say, and now was the time. The ducks would never be in one tight row and there would always be more courage to build, but it was time to see Nelson. He had the address. He had a gift. He checked himself in the mirror, not sure what he was checking for. He put on a belt. Scarfed a granola bar. He went to the garage and gassed up his scooter, fetched the bottle of liquor his cousin had left for him and secured it under his shirtfront.

Marky puttered down to the Hart Road stop sign and made a left, then steered himself onto thinner and thinner lanes, his headlight flashing over stoic possums. There was a paring of moon way off at the edge of the sky, pale and shy, like the night's first little thought. Whenever he heard a car approaching he would downshift and veer off into the high weeds. Soon the air smelled different, foreign, like wet clay. Marky was heading generally inland. At one point he was chased halfheartedly by a light-colored dog. He saw a man repairing a hammock by lamplight, an old woman under a carport painting something on sawhorses.

Finally he steered between a pair of gateposts with no gate. This was the place. Nelson's villa was in a row of about a dozen, all the same. There was nobody in the courtyard. There were no pets about, no life to be seen or heard. Marky found the correct door and knocked.

After a moment Nelson peered out a window with clumps of dirt stuck to it. He came outside, checking something in the treetops before regarding Marky. If he was puzzled about his late visitor, he didn't care to express it. His jeans were unbuttoned, and he seemed to have a cold.

"You're on my tree," he said.

Marky tipped his head, not understanding.

"An avocado tree's trying to grow right there. I buried a pit. Wasn't that optimistic of me?"

Marky backed his scooter off the patch of weeds in question and eased it onto its side. He untucked his shirt and held out the rectangular bottle of George Dickel. Nelson took the bottle and held it like a remote control, reading each word on the label. When he turned to go inside Marky followed him in, uninvited, and sat on a loveseat. Nelson went to the kitchen and came back with two cups of whiskey on ice. Marky said, "God, no," so Nelson poured one cup in the other. The coffee table was laden with dumbbells, sharply folded T-shirts, a tray of dusty silverware, and a newspaper from Connecticut.

"They must charge a ton to deliver that paper, huh?"

"Comrade, there are measures I must take to keep sane on this tundra."

The line sounded rehearsed. It made Marky think of the Jack London he'd been given in school. He removed his hat and rested it on the Arts & Leisure section.

"You play second for the yellow team," Nelson said.

"That's right," said Marky. "That's me."

"Don't get flattered. I know where everybody on every team plays."

"What position did you used to play?"

"I pitched." Nelson chuckled hollowly then, apparently accessing some amusing memory.

"What did you throw?" Marky asked him.

"I threw a spitter, a Vaseline ball, and a scuff ball." Nelson paused to drink some of his whiskey, enduring the taste with a stiff, distressed expression. "You can tell a lot about a person by how they play baseball."

"Is that right?" Marky said. He was happy Nelson didn't seem crazy. He seemed out of sorts, but not crazy.

"That little trick you pulled against Farmer, that wasn't half bad. You used his skill against him. You gave him a target, and he couldn't help but hit it."

"I had to improvise. The kid weighs 230 pounds."

"You had nothing to lose," Nelson said. "It's easy to pull shit like that when you have nothing to lose."

"I would've done it in the first inning if I'd thought of it."

Nelson saluted Marky with his glass. "The best kind of loneliness," he said.

"How's that?"

"Pitching. It's the best kind of loneliness. It feels lonely but in a good way, out there on the mound."

Marky didn't want to let this meeting get away from him. He straightened his back and leaned toward Nelson. "I'm here because I need you," he said. "I'm a businessman and I need a partner. I know that sounds strange coming from a guy my age, but I think you and I could make a heck of a team." Marky was stuck a moment. Then he said, "I've paid my dues in the minors and now I'm ready for the big leagues. And for you, it's time for a comeback."

"I know who you are," Nelson said. "You're the little entrepreneur. Everybody knows who you are."

"I'm committed," Marky said. "I'm ready to put everything into turning some profits. I'm ready to focus."

"You don't have to sell yourself to me," Nelson said. He set his whiskey down, one big swallow left in the bottom of the glass. "I'll save you some time here, because I'm guessing you have the wrong idea about what I'm planning to do with the remainder of my life." Nelson's boxy old television, though it wasn't on, started making a buzzing sound. He leaned unhurriedly and slapped the thing hard on its side, then rested his eyes back on Marky. "I have a very average car with a very, very expensive stereo system in it, and I drive that car to baseball games. That's what I do. It's working for me."

Marky refused to give Nelson the smile he thought he was earning. He knew Nelson wanted back in the action. People always did. It was just a matter of who would pull him out of his funk. If not Marky, someone else would come along and court him and win him. Nelson's skill set complemented Marky's. Marky would generate ideas and Nelson would know what to do with them. Nelson could never turn that part of himself off completely. And he would need to make money eventually. Liquor wasn't free. Neither was gas.

"I'm going to help you get revenge," Marky told him. "On those people who sold you out. And we're going to have fun doing it."

"I don't need to get revenge on anyone. Nothing happened to me that I shouldn't have seen coming. Nobody forced me to do a thing."

"Maybe you need to get revenge on this person you've become. This person who's been wasting your time, not to mention your abilities."

Nelson raised an eyebrow. "You'd hate me after a month. Maybe quicker. We're not going to find out, but that's what would happen. I'm not easy to work with."

"You're not lazy. This recluse thing is..."

"Is what?"

"Lame. It's beneath you."

Nelson wiped his hand on his jeans like he'd picked up something sticky. "That's enough of the tough-love bit, kid." He sniffed sharply. "Look, I never appreciated when people wasted my time by letting me go on and on, so let me be clear. The answer is leave me alone. I want everyone to leave me the fuck alone."

"Okay, fine," Marky said. "I'll respect your wishes, but I'll just ask you to listen a minute first. Hear me out and then I'll leave."

As Nelson methodically crunched ice and massaged his elbow, Marky told him he had a dozen ideas for businesses drawn up in detail, each in a clasped brown folder, and he offered Nelson executive command of any of them he wanted to partner in. The startup for most of them was under twenty thousand dollars. Thirty for sure. A chain of shops where parents and their children made homemade ice cream with exotic ingredients—a snack and a learning experience for the kids, and mom takes home a tub of fig with black sesame to serve at the dinner party. Start in South Tampa. The places would be booked a year in advance for rich-kid birthday parties. A website where people punch a bunch of info in and then receive a list of unique gifts they could give someone. They put in the location where they live, and what they are to the person they're buying for—boyfriend or former karate student or whatever—and what they got the person last year and all, then out comes a menu of thoughtful presents. A service that pairs someone with money up with a poor kid who wants to be a musician. The patron furnishes instruments and lessons, on the condition the poor kid does well in school. It would be an investment for the patron. If the kid hit it big on the charts one day, the patron's family would get a piece.

"I haven't figured that part out yet," said Marky. "Maybe it would work best as a nonprofit. The way I figure it, nonprofit can lead to profit. A dating club that—"

Nelson had held up his hand.

"Here's my advice," he said. "Switch to right field and do all the daydreaming you can."

Marky almost went on with more business ideas, but stopped himself. The particular plans weren't important, and Marky knew Nelson realized that. Marky could think of a hundred more plans.

"I'm not going to give up, you know. I said I'd leave and I will, but I'll just come back. I'll come back again and again and again."

"I sure wish you wouldn't."

"The only way to stop me is by accepting the offer," Marky said. "Look, don't you want to be in business with somebody who needs you? Don't you want to start from the ground up? I'll be grateful to you for the rest of my life. Some random guys in an office building could never say that. You'll have an ally forever with me. We'll *be* something."

Nelson nodded at Marky, letting out a weak little whistle. He got his feet under him and stood laboriously. He picked up Marky's hat from the table and squeezed it onto his own head.

"Tell you what," he said. "You can come back over here, but when you do, bring a couple of mitts and a ball. I'm going to put you through the hard-to-get dance, and it's going to include playing catch. That's going to be the main element of it, in fact. No promises about anything else, but I'll play catch with you." Nelson had that same deadwood expression on his face. "And now, it's my dinnertime."

Marky stood up, feeling for some reason that it would be unseemly for him to smile, that it would be presumptuous or something, and Nelson handed him his hat. Then the man opened the front door and ushered Marky out into the yard. It was hot and humid out but Nelson shuddered. Marky wanted to shake his hand, but Nelson was already drifting off underneath a live oak tree. The meeting was over. Nelson had already given plenty and he wasn't going to give more. "Later," he called, his voice issuing thinly in the dark.

Marky went to his scooter, making a show of sidestepping the area where Nelson had buried the avocado pit. He fired up his little chopper and hopped on and rolled over the weeds and onto the road. He got up to speed, motoring around a gradual curve through a cloud of pollen. Marky was advancing with reserved dignity through this little moment, but he saw the big picture. He knew that the hurdles before him were petty, that the troubles behind him held no sway.

.

FURTHER JOY

One girl locked her bedroom door after soccer games—the lost breath and slick tanned limbs, the push of opposition, the spiked shoes. One girl came within a week of perfect attendance and then to avoid recognition for the feat stayed home from school doing nothing, a bit lonesome, nibbling pastries and watching old high school movies full of outdated, luxurious clichés. One of the girls' fathers owned a fast food joint that did wine pairings. One of the girls' fathers did not trust his documents in the trash, even if shredded, and he saved them all up and conducted a backyard fire every few months, no matter how torrid the weather. The neighbors would complain but by the time someone from the county appeared the fire would be all but over, the sky hazed with secret finances. A few of the girls enjoyed the zoo, but they didn't go there together. The zoo required a bus ride. The zoo was a place to be alone and not feel lonely. The girls did not imagine themselves old like their fathers; they imagined themselves as young adults in unknown gray cities, wearing coats that swallowed them up and coats snug to their figures, living in spare apartments nestled unknown distances above unknown streets. They imagined young men in loosened ties, with shy smiles and excellent manners. One of the girls locked her bedroom door after long days at the beach—the smell of the oil, the baking limbs, the bare feet. The girls had what they considered a common-sense policy regarding marijuana: they would not purchase it, but would accept it for free from people they knew, and only if another of the girls was present. The girls were fifteen. They lived in the middle-class section of a town known for wealth, and went to a brand-new high school where nothing was decided. The girls knew that their soccer coach was gay and resolved to keep his secret. He wore sunglasses and polo shirts like every other guy and spoke slowly and without accent like every other guy, but the girls knew. There was no charge when he touched their shoulders, no slight tension. At the end of practice when they got down to sports bras and chugged near the water cooler, spilling down their fronts, he could look at them with casual eyes and they felt no need to pose. One of the girls' fathers worked at a nuclear power plant in the next county, and every morning he was out of the house before the girl awoke. The girls had little preference where they went to college. They would move away from home, but were not in a big rush about it. The girls hated to be asked what their talents were, their interests and strong points. The girls had at one time or another boycotted espresso, celebrity perfumes, movies that involved outer space, the Internet, the classics of literature, bikinis, appetizers, music featuring electric guitars. One of the girls' fathers owned a restaurant named 6TABLE that served six parties per night, Thursday through Sunday. For a time, this girl had waited tables. One evening a lady had raised her voice at the girl and the girl's father had thrown the lady out. Like most of the customers, the lady was rich and bored and so after being thrown out she had dedicated herself to making trouble for the restaurant. Reviews soured, the health inspector appeared repeatedly, an annual gala turned elsewhere for its catering needs. Eventually, and not because her father asked her to, the girl wrote a letter apologizing to the lady, and then showed up at her home and apologized in person. It was hard to know what to apologize for, but the girl managed, leaning on the dictum that the customer was always right. Boredom was the woman's problem, the girl knew, not wealth. The poor grew bored too and labored at evil. None of the girls would ever run for a student government office. They didn't despise student government as some did, but the idea of losing an election was sobering. They were thought of as free spirits and could do most anything, *most* anything—they couldn't run for treasurer and lose. They couldn't run for vice president of the student council and draw posters and distribute lollipops and give speeches and then fail to win the election without also somehow losing prestige in the eyes of the rest of the school. One of the girls, cold turkey, stopped locking her bedroom door. She wanted to save up the thrill, bottle it. She didn't know if it worked this way, but maybe it did. One of the girls had once hated her freckles, and now was proud of them. She relished sitting under her parasol at the beach. It was glamorous, not being tan. It was original. She wore black; she blushed and bruised. The girls' fathers had stopped giving them actual gifts on their birthdays. Instead, each father would take his daughter and all the other girls to dinner. The girls missed the wrapped physical objects. They missed imagining their fathers wracking their brains, bumbling from store to store asking advice. The girls sometimes stayed up all Friday night making bracelets and then sold the bracelets the next day at the Saturday market. They were often given a stand next to a bunch of country boys who sold jerky. The boys were from out in the swamps but were not poor or stupid. They were cocky in a way that was fun rather than despicable. The girls could hardly understand their accents but they could talk about anything—hot rod engines, the local tax system, cities in Australia. If these boys pressed hard enough they could get somewhere with the girls, but they didn't press. These boys took it as it came. Returning home from the market, the girls would find themselves full of a diffuse yet pulsing frustration. Their fathers, the girls noticed, never entered the girls' bedrooms. The girls would come up the hallway and catch their fathers peering in, looking skeptical yet fascinated, like nonbelievers peeking into a dim cathedral. One of the girls had been marginally fondled by a shoe salesman. No more than three or four years separated the girl and the shoe salesman, yet he'd been a different element. He had veined forearms and jaw muscles and an accent that didn't come from the swamps but from some other lesser place. He'd been talking to her but then he stopped. Something lifeless and determined came into his eyes. The girl was the only customer in the store; she had gotten her hair done that day, and had gotten a pedicure. The shoe salesman had taken her bare feet in his hands in a way that was gentle but certain. The shoes sat in their box, impartial. He touched only her ankles and toes, at first, looking into her eyes, knowing all he needed back from her was nothing. And she gave it—a flat look, a look not only empty of protest but as determined as his. They felt like someone else's feet, to her; they felt like part of a beautiful woman who would never run out of stunts to pull. He let one of his hands wander quick to her hip and then the other hand caught up slowly, tracing its way up the skin of her other leg. When he had an equal grip, dug in close to the bone, the girl could feel very definitely that she was being possessed. When his fingertips ventured under the elastic of her underwear, she heard herself gasp. A bony, pinch-faced old lady came in then, toting a pert baggie that probably contained new sunglasses. The girl knew that if her father ever found out, he would hurt the shoe salesman. The shoe salesman was basically a man, but not like her father was a man. The girl would never have been able to explain to her father that nothing had really happened, and that if anything had it was only because she'd wanted it to. That wouldn't have been important. Each girl already appreciated her father. Each girl appreciated that her father was soft-spoken on the sidelines of soccer fields, that her father allowed her to try anything she wanted and allowed her to quit those things if she wanted to try something else. The very land, the streets of the neighborhood the girls lived in, possessed a flatness that often felt more than merely topographical. The girls recognized their home terrain instantly in photographs and movies. This literal lack of relief added an air of invincibility to the diffuse and pulsing frustration the girls often fell prey to.

One of the fathers followed a Mexican soap opera. The women were huge-eyed and single-minded, and the story would never end. It would outlive the father and maybe even his daughter.

To the fathers' wonder, their daughters drank like thirty-five-year-old women—a glass of wine with dinner, a cold beer at the end of a long hot week. They ate whatever was presented, whatever was handy, with equal zest, whether braised veal or a frozen cheese pizza.

The fathers could not discern the status their daughters held among their peers. It did not seem to matter that they were not wealthy. It did not seem to matter one way or the other whether they played sports. They were free to earn high grades if they wished. Their daughters were a clique, but took no pride in this. Exclusivity and welcome occurred naturally and were accepted without fuss. It seemed nerds no longer existed as they once had, or sluts. There was peer pressure to do such things as recycle and volunteer.

Each father understood that he could not tell how attractive his daughter was. Each assumed his daughter was beautiful because she looked similar to the other girls she hung around with, who were without doubt beautiful.

The fathers did not pal around with one another.

One of the fathers' daughters had a suitor, a white boy named Tyrone. The father did not know if the boy's parents had named him for a joke or a statement or if somehow Tyrone was a family name for them or what.

One of the fathers was in debt. He'd sold his crepe shop but no one knew at how great a loss. Now he cooked at an upscale breakfast place, folding mushrooms and lobster into omelets. He didn't know what people thought—that he'd gotten weary of the responsibility of owning, maybe, or that he wanted to stay in shape in the kitchen. He hadn't allowed his daughter to notice he was broke. He took her out for sushi and then, on his days off, he ate peanut butter sandwiches alone. He had begun secretly rooting against his daughter's impeccable grades, knowing everything would be easier for him if she didn't get into a prestigious far-off school. He had sold things out of the back of his garage, exercise equipment and a stately, attic-smelling grandfather clock. He had sold his bottles of fine California red. He had never decided what occasion might prompt him to uncork one of the wines, what sort of joyous triumph he was waiting for, and now he'd never find out. Good things had happened and he'd let them pass, occasionally handling and dusting the bottles but never celebrating with them. His daughter was the sharpest of the girls. She was a math whiz and a shrewd judge of character. He could not stand the thought of her being disappointed in him, of letting her down.

One of the fathers' daughters spoke four languages. Fluent Spanish, of course. Enough French to hold a conversation. Also, they had hosted a girl from Zimbabwe for several summers and the daughter had picked up enough of some African tongue to continue learning it on her own. The high school had brought in a tutor for her, a linguist from the university. Though public, it was that kind of high school.

One of the fathers, years ago, had bought his daughter a boxy antique camera. Later he found it in a spare closet and tracked down film for it on the computer and used it to take pictures of the stagnant canals that snaked through their part of town. He tried to catch the canals at low tide, when clans of exposed crabs lined the oyster beds.

The fathers depended on their daughters to keep them in the correct shoes.

When in doubt, the fathers encouraged their daughters to get enough rest and eat vegetables and to tell the truth—timeless, tried-and-true directives.

The fathers were aware of how far things were going in some quarters. It wasn't just nose jobs and breast augmentation anymore. Girls were getting their lips plumped. Girls were having their toes worked on, so their feet would look cute in sandals and flip-flops. None of the fathers' daughters had mentioned any of this nonsense yet, but that didn't mean they never would.

One of the fathers hired an escort every few months, an available reward to himself for how far he'd risen in life, and against what odds. The older his daughter got, the less purely he was able to enjoy this practice.

The era the girls were growing up in had no texture. The music betrayed nothing. The generation preceding the fathers' had been wild, and the fathers themselves had learned to be jaded, but the girls were past all that. Jadedness, for them, was an old stale religion not worth its costumes. Rebellion, to them, was quaint.

One of the fathers thought of the afternoon his daughter's braces had been removed as the moment he'd lost her.

One of the fathers wished he could work on cars. He wished he could prop his hood in the driveway and hang that competent and hopeful lantern and take a look at a belt or hose and then straighten up to his full height while wiping his hands on a torn green rag. Men like himself, driving by on the street, would notice him and feel lost.

One of the fathers thought of one of his daughter's friends while he lay awake at night. He thought of her during slow moments in the day, too, but in the day he only felt fond of the way she walked and the way she carefully formed words with her lips. At night it was something worse. He didn't think in terms of being in love. He had, apparently, been in love twice before. He knew there was no dependable advantage, when smitten, to doing something about it. There were numerous disadvantages. The father had never been addicted to anything, had never been unable to control himself. He would weather this, just another secret to keep. In so many ways, he was lucky. His daughter was lucky. Her friend, with her feline face and muscled calves and shabby fingernails, was lucky—lucky to be desired by a man who did not act on his wanton fixations. When the father picked all the girls up from somewhere in his restored classic Jeep, he hoped the girl he thought about at night would sit in the passenger seat. He had no way to encourage this. When it happened, when she hopped up beside him and the rest piled in back, he felt overcome, dizzy, like he'd had whiskey and a rich dessert. Her teeth were gleaming and slightly crooked and her skin was the color of honey when the sunlight shines through it. On the inside of her ankle was a pale beauty mark in the shape of a tropical fish. Her tummy sometimes peeked out. There were soft depressions behind her ears. She regarded the father with a comfortable sort of formality. There was no chance she understood him, but she trusted him. When she was in the front seat she didn't lean back toward the others to join the gabbing. She listened, an amused outsider, same as the father. He wondered what she would do if she ever noticed how he looked at her, but she would never notice. Or she already had. This was the father's problem alone, not the girl's. It was best to keep his visions plain, he knew, but the nights were soundless and aimless and in the dark he would imagine the two of them living on a meadowy ranch out west or holing up down in Central America, local children running into town to fetch them produce and rum. He imagined teaching the girl how to cook, imagined going on weekend excursions for the purpose of buying hats. He even imagined scolding her coarse etiquette, imagined her taking up cigarettes. They would buy a horse. They would read the longest novels ever written. He imagined her coming down with a swift and exotic illness, and nursing her back to health, giving her medicines with his palm cupped underneath a spoon, placing cold rags on her forehead, leading her on leisurely walks over mild hills until the gold color returned to her limbs. He imagined her desire returning as she became hale. He wouldn't rush her, he would wait until they were lying on the humid porch during the hottest part of the day and she sighed and pushed the tiny soft arch of her foot into his hand. He even allowed himself to imagine the fallout. His own daughter's injury. The other father's rage. A fistfight. The law. The shame. Except that nothing was going to happen. He was unfamiliar with the abandon that caused people to commit murder or rape or break into houses over a fix, that made gamblers end up homeless, that caused old ladies to hoard knickknacks and canned goods and small pets until their houses were condemned, that turned the upbeat overweight into the grotesque obese who couldn't leave their apartments. No, his mind was like his lawn; it could grow unruly, but there was a snug, irresistible pride in trudging out into the heat and mowing and clipping and raking. He had seen the girl in sundresses. He had seen her in men's-style pajamas. He had seen her in a soccer uniform. He had seen her in a thin, stiff coat and high boots. He had seen her in a faded clay-colored towel almost the same shade as her skin. He had seen her in a ball gown and in a middle school graduation gown. He had seen her in a beat-up sweatshirt, eager to paint houses for the less fortunate.

The fathers knew it was important to have meals with their daughters. For one father, breakfast was convenient. For another, dinner. One of the fathers regularly picked his daughter up from school and took her for salads in the quaint town center of their neighborhood. One of the fathers was only free on Sundays and he took his daughter to brunch on the water, and he'd recently begun to feel, sitting there just the two of them in the midst of so many hungover, sated couples and sprawling wedding parties, oyster shells and champagne everywhere, that something was not quite natural about his and his daughter's lingering over this sunny midmorning luxury, that this familiar indulgence had curdled.

The fathers remembered their own childhoods lovingly, remembered that first summer they were allowed to walk down to the old pier without any adults and fish an afternoon away, many years younger than their daughters were now. They remembered the storm beginning to assemble on the horizon as they pulled lunch out of a plastic grocery bag—a sandwich of whatever pastrami had been left after their father's work week, a peach, a warm can of ginger ale. They remembered taking their shoes off and setting them in an out-of-the-way spot where they wouldn't get knocked down into the swells. They remembered getting their bait stolen by pinfish, getting their lines tangled. They remembered the clouds rising, advancing, snuffing out the sun. They remembered pointing at the lightning in the distance and tasting a metallic tang on the breeze. Soon everyone else on the pier began reeling in and packing up and shuffling toward land, throwing in the towel—first the young professionals on a day off, wearing bright ball caps and expensive deck shoes, then those women of indeterminate age that had always frightened and interested the fathers when they were boys, with their platinum hair and harsh laughs and sculpted manly arms, and finally the pier hounds, their mustaches unkempt and shorts ratty, who fished for their dinners most days. The storm had been racing in, aimed directly at the pier, and then it seemed to hold itself in place a moment, offering a fair chance to anyone who'd not yet fled. The fathers found their shoes then. They remembered the sky growing dark as night, the thunder seeming to come from beneath them. That was when the snook finally started hitting, forced landward by the storm. They remembered throwing the wriggling creatures back, too small to keep anyway, and slicing a finger while dislodging a hook, knowing that this moment, with fish caught and the line up and blood dripping onto the planks of the pier and the lightning close enough to blind them, was when they should run for cover. But they didn't run. Something inside them wanted this danger. If the storm washed them off the pier, they would drown. The lightning could fry them crisp. Yet they baited and dropped their hooks once again. They remembered being fascinated at being alone, remembered turning and looking back at the beach, which was abandoned and which seemed itself to be bracing for a siege. They remembered the first fat drops of rain hitting the backs of their hands. The angry front was now hanging over them like a cliff. They remembered not being able to account for their stubbornness, not understanding why the thing that ought to chase them off was holding them still. The gusts rocking the pier. The surf pounding the pilings below. They remembered those days and prayed, knowing it wouldn't be so, that whatever fates their daughters were testing were as wholesome as rough weather.

THE INLAND NEWS

I t was breakfast time, and Sofia was in the kitchen with Uncle Tunsil. He was eating a lemon with sugar and had a glass of milk waiting for him. Sofia was working on a bowl of colorful cereal meant for children, crunching it down in the quiet morning. Uncle Tunsil gazed out the front window. The lemon tree was out there, and also a colossal nut tree that had been struck by lightning and rendered half dead. The branches that shot out over the house were pale and bare, while the branches over the road hung lush in their own shade.

Uncle Tunsil took down his milk in one steady draft, then looked toward Sofia. "I'll be right on the other side of the glass, and I'll make sure he's aware of that. We'll just see how this goes. I'm a long sight from comfortable with it."

"I'm pretty tough," Sofia said. "That's something you might have noticed about me."

Uncle Tunsil had already spent too much energy making sure Sofia wasn't frightened, telling her she could back out anytime she wanted, squaring what he was going to allow her to do with his conscience. When she'd first offered her help, her uncle had balked, and she'd had to remind him she was an adult who'd been through a lot in her life and could handle herself. She'd stayed on him two days straight about it. And she'd known he would relent. The two of them had gone years without any mention of the unexplained events of Sofia's childhood, but when Sofia finally brought up the topic, he hadn't shied away from it. Courage was a settled fact of Uncle Tunsil's makeup, and though he was charged with keeping order, there was something unaffiliated about him. He operated according to a reserved but staunch open-mindedness. He didn't care what people thought, didn't mind that some folks would snicker at his pursuing a case this way. And he understood this was important to her. There was a part of her she'd tamped down into a shadowy corner and she wanted to try to bring it out.

Sofia didn't know what to expect out of the experiment. She had warned her uncle that if she did in fact discover anything, it likely wouldn't be anything concrete, that she might only get a feeling, and probably not even that. Uncle Tunsil had tried to muster his familiar easy grin, and had told her a feeling would work fine. A feeling was exactly what they were lacking.

He started the faucet running and set his milk glass and lemon dish in the sink. There were some other dishes in there from last night. Sofia was finished with her cereal and he took her bowl too. He found a rag and started washing, his forearms flexing. He had a beard like Abraham Lincoln's. It would've made someone else look like a fool.

"I keep thinking would your momma have let you do this," he said, raising his voice over the running water. "I suppose we know the answer to that. That's what I'm always thinking, what she would've said."

"If my mother were around, she wouldn't still be telling me what I could and couldn't do. I'm the boss now. I'm the boss of Sofia."

"Whether she'd let *me* do this, is maybe what I mean. You're the boss of Sofia but I'm the boss of the police station."

The salt and pepper shakers on the table were in the image of a farmer and his wife. Sofia touched the top of each one, then licked her finger. When she or her uncle mentioned Sofia's mother, it was usually to say they missed her on a holiday or to praise her cobbler or, most often, to admire what a hard worker she'd been. She'd been able to leave enough money for Sofia's college, no small accomplishment.

Sofia said, "Her way to deal with this, to deal with me, was to... not deal with it. And maybe that was the best thing for me back then. I'm sure it was."

Uncle Tunsil was nodding, putting some elbow grease into one of the dishes. "You want to find out about yourself and that's fine. You want some answers, like everyone wants. I'm still allowed to say this thing makes me nervous."

"Think of it this way," Sofia said. "It's just talking to some guys who might be lying. For girls, that's old hat."

Sofia was behind her uncle, so she couldn't see if he'd smiled at what she said. Wisps of steam were rising up from the sink and vanishing.

"A murder case," he said. "I reckon if there's a time to pull out the stops." Sofia saw her uncle's shoulders heave and then settle, but couldn't hear his sigh. A shaft of sunlight was finding its way in at a low angle, spotlighting a swath of the kitchen floor.

"I expect I ought to be tickled," he said. "You know, professionally. Analyzing crime scenes and supervising interviews instead of, I don't know, busting some poor guy for buying beer for the trade school kids."

The man who'd been killed was named Barn Renfro. It was an understatement to say no one in town had been fond of him, but the murder, the first in the city limits in over ten years, had people uneasy. Sofia's uncle wasn't one for a witch hunt, but he was going to be as thorough as he knew how. So far he didn't have much to go on. Sofia didn't know if he had any real hopes that she could help him, or if he was purely humoring her. If he held strong beliefs about anything—from the supernatural to politics to cornbread recipes—he kept them hidden.

"Who was buying beer for the trade school kids?" Sofia asked.

"Al Terry. This was near a couple weeks ago. Had to charge him, even though I don't think he did anything wrong. I don't make up the rules, I just enforce them. If they have beer, to my thinking, they might not wind up on something worse. Maybe that's misguided."

Uncle Tunsil cut the water off and Sofia hopped up and grabbed a clean hand towel. She started drying the dishes, leaving her uncle free to gather his wallet and badge and gun and phone. He combed his hair in front of a small mirror on the wall.

"There's a sheriff in Oklahoma has this woman he uses. I follow her on the computer. She's part Indian. Her specialty is *where*. She don't know what it's going to be or who put it there, but she'll say to check the alley behind so-and-so, and sure enough, they'll find a clue. It's not an uncommon move anymore. Anyway, having another look at each of them boys in a stressful situation couldn't hurt."

Uncle Tunsil had himself together. He shook his head at Sofia, like people did when they thought they'd been sold a bill of goods. "So up at the station say one-fifteen?"

"See you then," Sofia said.

He slipped his sunglasses on. Sofia followed him to the door like she always did, then waited as he got in the cruiser and bumped from the driveway up onto the straight two-lane road and out of sight. The road was blanketed in shade, but the front steps of the house were already in full morning sun. Sofia stepped out into the humidity.

She was thinking about her mother now, how wary she'd seemed of Sofia when she was young. The drastic looks her mother used to give her. She remembered the doctors, the tests, being handled like something break-able. Her mother had forbid anyone to talk about Sofia having a gift of any sort. Explanation or no, a gift was out of the question. Simple motherly concern was there, Sofia knew—worry over the terrible time Sofia would suffer in grade school, perhaps beyond grade school—but also her mother had been panic-stricken at the thought of scandal. Up north, for many bygone generations, Sofia's family had been part of the lowest class, poor and of ill repute, immigrants who couldn't adjust and then simple hustling riff-raff. Sofia's great-grandmother had moved south, about as south as one could move, and started fresh. She'd toiled her family to the fringe of blue-collar, taking any honest work she could find. Her daughter, Sofia's grandmother, the next in the line, had been a dependable hand and eventually a permanent office employee at a booming citrus concern. Sofia's mother had attended a trade school, and Sofia a real college. Uncle Tunsil wasn't sensitive to this striving history like Sofia's mother had been, but it was women who'd struggled the family upward, not men. Most of the men had taken their leave, thrown their lots elsewhere.

Sofia's mother must've harbored fears that had nothing to do with her recent ancestors, or even with Sofia's well-being. No one blamed a child when these sorts of rumors made the rounds—it was the mother's doing, the softheaded mother who wanted to think her child was extraordinary, reading into things. Sofia understood all this. She didn't blame her mother for a thing. But Sofia was done with college now and she needed to figure out who she was. The rest of her life was sitting in front of her, a shapeless pale hill to clamber up, and she didn't feel prepared to begin the trek. She'd denied a part of herself for so long, had kept herself convinced of what was real and unreal, but she'd been aware all the while of a nagging doubt. It was all doubt for her now, if she was honest, because she also doubted that there had ever been a wondrous talent in her at all. She doubted that anything had ever been afoot other than coincidence and potent imagination.

She looked up through the leafless half of the nut tree, at the green-tinted sky. A few tattered clouds were strewn about, and an osprey, black at this distance, soaring so high it appeared stuck in one spot. Sofia strolled out into the yard barefoot, to the trunk of the towering tree, tiny twigs snapping under the pads of her feet, the soil still possessed of a slight coolness. She rested her weight against the gnarled bark and looked back toward the house—the steep tin roof, the bed of azaleas blooming under the front windows, the stained-glass water birds her uncle had let her hang from the eaves of the little porch. The sight of the place made her feel cozy and moored.

Sofia had her own reasons to put herself in a room with these men, but she also wanted to help her uncle. She wanted to be of use, wanted for once to be able to repay some of her uncle's kindness. Sofia had lived with him through half of high school and all of college. Now she'd been done with school for over a year and he still hadn't made a single mention of her paying rent or even chipping in for bills. He didn't hassle her about having direction in life. He'd given her no rules, nothing but trust.

On the way to her preschool there'd been a state prison, a clutch of wind-blown barracks crouched behind lookout towers and razor wire, and each time her mother drove past it, Sofia would go woozy and bewildered in the back seat. Finally she'd lost consciousness one day, and her mother had pulled the car over and shaken her awake. That's when the tests started, the doctors. All that ceased as soon as her mother realized that every specialist at every clinic was going to keep saying the same thing, that there was nothing physically wrong with her daughter.

Sofia had driven back over to the prison just a few weeks ago, two towns to the east. It had looked smaller of course, still with its burnt, beaten grounds. She'd cruised past it on the soft-curving frontage road, trying not to steel herself, trying not to peer through the fences, and she'd felt nothing more than the hollow heartache anyone feels at the thought of so many men locked up with their guilt.

Sofia remembered the night terrors, but children had night terrors. She remembered the trances, remembered a man in a striped dress shirt and open white coat asking her what her middle name was, her address. And then Sofia's pen pal. The girl from Kentucky. Sofia had been seven years old, and her mother had found her in the corner of her bedroom, hand-written letters heaped on her lap, sobbing the front of her dress damp for no apparent reason. Another letter was due from the girl by the end of the week. When it didn't show, Sofia's mother called the girl's mother. Sofia's pen pal had drowned. Shannon Janicek was her name. She had slipped off an icy dock and hit her head on the hull of a boat. She had been at the park with the family of a new friend of hers, a family her mother had never met, and so her mother could not help but hold herself responsible. The regret Sofia had endured, she surmised later, was Shannon's mother's. No one had ever found out about that one, about Sofia crying with the letters. It had stayed between Sofia and her mother.

There were other episodes Sofia could remember, and, she was sure, a bunch more her mother had let her forget. On a drive across the state, stopped at a gas station, a woman had run screaming from Sofia. They'd both been browsing the candy aisle of the little store, Sofia's mother outside pumping gas. The woman spoke to Sofia and Sofia, as if under a spell, glazed over and began reciting the woman's past, every failing and indiscretion. The woman had cursed at Sofia and fled the store, and Sofia's mother had hustled her to the restroom at the back of the building and splashed water on her face until she answered to her name again. Neither of them had said a word for the rest of the drive. That's the part Sofia remembered so clearly, the wordless drive. She didn't remember, all these years later, what she'd said to the woman in the store, but she remembered the roar of the wind in the open windows of her mother's car, remembered the burdened look on her mother's face. After that she'd knotted up something inside herself, and eventually the woozy feelings went away.

Sofia worked four mornings a week, giving tours at the Thomas Edison House over on the coast. During her last tour, shortly before lunchtime, she noticed her on-and-off boyfriend loitering at the back of the crowd. His name was James. He wore work boots and had parted brown hair. Sofia tried not to look at him, not wanting to lose concentration and forget her spiel describing Edison's establishment of a newspaper aboard a working passenger train. Sofia broke up with James often. The most recent reason she'd found to part ways was that she didn't want to tie him down, didn't want to saddle him with a serious relationship at this stage of his life. The truth was an old, ordinary story, particularly in her family: she was afraid to lose him, and the best way to avoid that was to keep pushing him away. He was handsome enough and his mind was impressive, but it was the company of his kindred heart she couldn't stand the thought of losing for good. When she was around James, her soul was calm. That was the best way she could describe it.

Sofia led her group into the final exhibit, a gallery crowded with photos of Edison clasping shoulders with various famous people. James was still bringing up the rear. An old man in a thin sweater was speaking to him, and he was leaning in and nodding. Sofia revealed that Edison had invented paraffin paper and then gave out handfuls of wrapped candies to the kids. Four or five people walked up and tipped her, and she flattened out the bills and folded them and slipped them into her back pocket. She exited out a side door toward the parking lot, where she guessed James would be waiting.

And here he was. He came over to Sofia, crunching the broken white shells of the parking lot underfoot. He was carrying a book, which was probably about pirates or explorers. He was a public health major, but all he read about was romantic maritime adventure. Sofia had met him at college. He was a year younger, still a senior, finishing up his degree with a couple night classes.

"How come you came up here?" Sofia asked. "You could just stop by the house and knock on the door."

"You might not answer if I knocked on the door. That's happened, you know."

"Fair enough."

"And anyway, I've never been to this place. It's right here and I've never been. Well, it's not *right* here. It's pretty far out of the way, really."

"Yeah, it's a serious commute for a part-time job."

"You're really good at tour-guiding. You seem like yourself but more authoritative, like you probably know CPR and would enjoy debating. Spirited debating."

"People debate me about Edison all the time," Sofia said. "They're usually right. I usually give in."

She was walking toward her car and James was walking along with her, shortening his stride so it matched hers.

"I don't like coming to your house because your uncle feels sorry for me."

"That's better than him thinking you're a creep."

"I'm not so sure. It gets old, having people think you're nothing to worry about."

They rounded a thicket of bamboo and started down a long row of glinting chrome. All the disturbed dust of the morning was hanging static in the air. James knew about Sofia's past. She hadn't told him the details but he knew the gist. He seemed to regard it all as an exotic happenstance

136

of her formative years, like if she'd lived in Africa as a diplomat's daughter or something. Like Uncle Tunsil, he didn't speak of it unless she brought it up, and she rarely did. Sofia didn't feel like telling him about the interviews she was planning; she didn't want to know what he'd think about that. He'd find out soon enough, the way news spread.

James believed in things—in ghosts, in God, in spontaneous human combustion. He'd once said he didn't understand the point of *not* believing in things. He made a lot of declarations and they didn't all jibe.

"So this concern you have about the sowing of my wild oats," he said. "It's valid as a concept, but it doesn't really apply to me. I don't think I'd be breaking a big story, saying I'm not your average dude. If I have any wild oats, I'd just as soon sow them with you. *In* you? I don't think I have a mastery of that metaphor."

"Of course you'd say that," Sofia said. "But I'm only the second girlfriend you've ever had. There could be plenty of girls out there you'd like better than me and you'd have no way of knowing it."

James scoffed. "First off, I'm not going to dignify that with a response. Second, isn't it my choice whether I want to date any other girls? Isn't that sort of up to me?"

"We have no brakes. We wind up spending every minute together. It can't be healthy."

"You need breaks from me?"

"No brakes. *B-r-a-k-e*."

James gently brushed a moth away from his pant leg, then watched it zip up toward the treetops. "I guess I don't see the problem. I guess that sounds like an ideal situation, spending every minute together."

Sofia tried not to feel flattered, tried not to feel like she was fishing for loyalty. They reached her car, an old Datsun the color of sweet-potato flesh, and she fished around in her purse for her keys. Her purse was tiny and she still could never find anything in it. She could see the cover of James's book now. It said THE BRITISH ROYAL NAVY. He started walking around to the passenger side of the Datsun.

"What are you doing?" Sofia said.

"What? Getting in the car."

"No way, James."

"But I need a ride."

"What about *your* car?"

"It's back at my apartment. There's something not right with it. The intake or something."

"How did you get here?"

"Rode the bus."

"From Lower Grove?"

"Rode like four buses."

"You rode the bus here thinking I would be forced to give you a ride back."

"You sure make things black and white."

"I'm not giving you a ride. It's not fair what you did."

James ticked one eyebrow up and then released a shallow sigh. "Honestly?"

"Honestly."

He pressed the corner of his eye with his fingertip, blinking. "So I guess that means I'll take the bus again," he said. "No, it's okay. It'll be good. I'm interested in buses. Bus routes. Bus transfers. Stuff like that. Interesting people who smell like gas stations."

James came back over to Sofia's side of the car. He kept his distance. His hair was a completely different hue in the sun than it was in the shade.

"You'll let us be happy one day," he said. "I just hope I'm not bitter by then."

Before Sofia could answer, James turned on his boot heel. "Bus to catch," he called over his shoulder.

Sofia watched him walk off and then lowered herself into the driver's seat, the vinyl warm on her back and legs. She was staring into a swath of jungle. She wound down her window and then leaned over and wound down the passenger window too, hoping for a cross breeze that wasn't to be.

* * *

She sensed nothing out of the ordinary, felt nothing, face to face in the interrogation room with this wiry guy wearing a brand-new T-shirt and brand-new ball cap. They were conversing stiffly, like distant acquaintances who had bumped into each other at the grocery store. His name was Spencer. Sofia couldn't tell where he was from, whether he had hidden scars. She couldn't sense anything more than what she'd known coming in.

Spencer was a half-brother of Barn Renfro, the murdered man. When they were younger, the two of them had inherited a boat repair shop on a small lake. Barn had bought Spencer's share with money he'd made dealing pot and Spencer had blown through that money in the span of several months. Barn had run the business for the past twenty years, while his brother shuffled from odd job to odd job.

Spencer told Sofia that he'd found Jesus a few months ago, that in his old life he got depressed if he didn't get into a fight every couple weeks. There'd been only so long he could march knees high with the program before he needed to get punched in the face. That was his old self, he said. Sofia knew all this. Everyone in town did. Spencer had been a prize for the congregation that had tamed him, a feather in the cap of Lower Grove Church of Christ. He sat at the table with his back straight and his shoulders loose, his fists resting on the dull metal surface. His nose leaned to one side, which had the effect of giving his face character. Sofia's uncle was watching from behind the mirror, along with his lone deputy. The session was being taped. The floor was linoleum, but for some reason the air smelled of old carpet. Sofia was hoping for any flash into the life of this man before her, a glance at anything incriminating. She was getting flat nothing.

"I finally started wishing Barn well, then he goes and gets himself shot," said Spencer. "I really was. I was hoping prosperity and peace on him. That's the lesson of my life: if I'm betting against you, you can feel pretty optimistic. If I'm rooting for you, you better watch your ass."

"I guess we all feel that way sometimes," Sofia said.

"Now God is supposed to tell me what to want and not want, so that simplifies things."

"Do you think God wanted Barn dead?"

"I got no idea." Spencer took a moment. He was tapping a spot on the tabletop with his finger. "I have a hard time seeing why He wants *me* alive. They say He loves me, though. They keep telling me that." Spencer closed his eyes as tightly as he could, then opened them and refocused on Sofia. "I can't believe in your ability," he said. "The Church of Christ doesn't acknowledge any of that as valid."

"Well," Sofia said. "Policy is policy."

She ran her fingernail along the edge of the table. There was a whiteboard in the room but no markers. And a smoke detector on the ceiling, its green light pulsing tirelessly. When she looked at Spencer again, he had drawn inward, into his own mires and impasses. Sofia wasn't supposed to feel let down at the futility of the interview, she knew. She was supposed to be a disinterested party, awaiting truth about the crime and about herself.

Uncle Tunsil took a paring knife to a couple of lemons, whistling softly while he worked, then got out the little pot of sugar and miniature spoon. Sofia was nibbling at some peach yogurt. Her uncle hadn't acted a bit discouraged yesterday after she'd yielded nothing at the station. In fact, he'd seemed relieved. He hadn't thought Spencer was guilty, she knew. He had made sure Sofia still wanted to go through with the other interviews, giving her an out while not openly pushing her in either direction. He probably didn't know what to think. If she kept coming up empty it would be bad for the investigation, which seemed to be stalled or close to it. But if she hit on something, that would be a whole other can of worms. Sofia knew it was him who was helping her, as usual, not the other way around. He wouldn't admit to that. He would insist he was running a thorough operation, utilizing all resources.

The plan was to meet for the second interview later that day, at one-fifteen again. Sofia had to go to the Edison House and her uncle had to meet with a state investigator at a hotel over near the interstate. He had his good boots on, and a shiny watch he didn't wear often.

"It just *looks* hot out there," he said, bending at the waist to peer outside.

The state of Florida was reaching the time of year when the nights were as hot as the days. Everything was still as a painting out the window.

"What time do you get up in the morning?" Sofia asked her uncle. "You always stay up later than me, then you're up earlier."

"I'm a fast sleeper. I don't dream. I don't even roll over. I don't get up and use the bathroom. I can sleep twice as quick as your average person." He was sitting now. He dug his spoon into a lemon. He had a way of maneuvering around the seeds, of getting the meat out without squirting the juice.

After a moment he set the spoon down on the table and his face clouded over, his brow creasing. He sat still, making no move for his milk.

"What is it?" Sofia said.

"Some boys up in Sumter County barbecued a manatee," he said. "Came over my radio this morning. You heard me right. They netted a manatee and drug it on land and cooked it like a hog in one of them brick pits."

Sofia had some yogurt on her spoon but she put it back in the cup. "Maybe they were broke."

"I hope so, because these days there's no place in Florida you're not a couple miles from a Publix."

Sofia watched her uncle's face. It wasn't often that righteousness showed on it.

"Sometimes you start wondering if *you're* a redneck," he said, "because the folks over on the beach think you are. But something always happens to put things back in order."

The second person of interest was JP. He was wearing a clingy long-sleeve athletic shirt. His shorts had numerous pockets and on his calf was a tattoo of an angel with dripping fangs. JP wasn't much older than Sofia, mid-twenties. He'd almost been a big deal in baseball, had been drafted out of the local high school and made it to the majors for a stint. Sofia's uncle said JP wasn't satisfied with his right share of screwing up. He was going for the record. He'd bungled a baseball career, had a divorce and bankruptcy behind him already, and was on parole for DUIs. He was at the station because he had a boat up at Barn Renfro's shop that Barn had refused to give back to him. Evidently, there'd been a misunderstanding over the fee. JP didn't even want the boat anymore, and he and Barn had wound up agreeing to sell it, Barn entitled to a consignment share that would square them. The deal to sell the boat was unsubstantiated, since Barn wasn't around to comment on it.

The very second JP settled in and leveled his disdainful glare at Sofia, she didn't feel right. She was taken by surprise, but kept a neutral expression on her face. Her limbs were leaden, her mind flustered. It came over her like a dry wind. She had a grip on her own knee under the table, and her sinuses burned the way they did before she cried. Was this it? Is this what it would feel like, after all this time? She took in a full breath and released it slowly. It could be the beginning of a flu, this feeling, or the product of nerves or bad sleep. She didn't believe that, though. She raised her arm off the table, trying to be casual, and dabbed her temples with the back of her hand. JP was sneering at her. She swallowed hard. Part of her was unhinged but part of her, deeper, was blessed with calm.

She was seeing a Sunday. The ancient pale sky and the black marl and the creatures in between that wanted to survive. A lie told. A boy sick and staying home from church—so yes, a Sunday—and then she saw a pistol. It was being looked at, but not yet held. Breathed upon. Sofia's fingers felt stiffened, as if with cold. She could feel surly boredom, but that's what JP was radiating right now. She saw a happy school bus on a country road. But Sunday? Little airplanes buzzing overhead, anonymous and joyriding. Buses and airplanes and pistols and church—the commonest of memories. Then she saw the egret, taking a high retreating step, puzzled at someone sloshing so close in the reeds of the drainage ditch. She could hear toads, the distant revving of an engine. JP was openly glaring at Sofia across the table, scratching his shoulder. She was still in the present, enough. Even scratching his shoulder, he was defiant. He still thought life was winning and losing, and he was claiming scorekeeper error and false starts. She heard the toneless echoing crack, saw the elegant white neck jerking, flung back and forth, an animal's desperation and outrage. Sofia saw the body stagger forward, dragging the barely attached head, blood already blackening the feathers. She saw the bird topple over in the stagnant water, instantly a sodden ugly pile, instantly a meal for buzzards and nothing greater. And then all of it began to dissolve, her consciousness becoming whole again. She had no say in it, as far as she could tell—the wind dying out at once.

"I told your uncle I got five minutes," JP said. "I hope I didn't come up here to compete in a staring contest."

Sofia sat up straight, giving her hair a shake. She quit squeezing her knee and crossed her arms in front of her, regaining her footing in the moment. She had no idea how to tack toward useful information, which was her duty here. She wouldn't have imagined JP capable of guilt, but everyone was. The more you had, the deeper you kept it buried.

"I don't have anything against you, JP."

His face didn't change. It lost no impatience.

"You're scowling at me," Sofia said. "I have no idea why."

JP absently reached down to one of his pockets, a smoker's habit. His pockets had been emptied. "I don't mind telling you, if you got to know. The reason is because you think you're better than everyone else. You always have, ever since you showed up here. And don't say it ain't true."

"What a boring reason," Sofia said. "Besides being wrong."

"See, like that. That face you just made. Everybody's always nice to you because your uncle's the law, but people don't appreciate you playing the little princess. I know, he's right there watching. He'll be mad at me now, but he's always mad at me anyway."

Sofia heard the air conditioner kick on in the room. She hoped the draft from the vent would find the back of her neck. Whatever had come over her was fully gone now, and she felt worn and hot. She was holding the egret in her mind's eye.

"I think the person you're mad at is yourself," she said. "That's probably not front-page news to you."

"I guess you aced your intro to psychology class at the college. You showed up here and held your nose through a couple years of high school and then off to get some bullshit degree so you can tell me who I'm mad at. Or is it *whom* I'm mad at. I'm glad you did that. I'm glad you went to school."

"You've never even spoken to me before."

"I am now, and it's going about how I expected."

"You could go to college, you know."

"Some of us got life to live," JP said. "Some of us don't have a benefactor." He looked over toward the mirror, toward where Sofia's uncle was. Sofia was staying composed. She'd told her uncle not to come in unless she asked him to, but that would go out the window the instant she seemed upset.

She wasn't going to see anything else, nothing connecting JP to Barn Renfro's death. She could tell. Just the egret, if the egret was real. She guessed he probably wasn't guilty, or he wouldn't be goading Sofia's uncle. Of course, some people goaded everyone all the time; that was their program.

"So how'd old Spencer do on this exam?" JP asked. "He pass with flying colors, like me?"

"I don't think I'm allowed to say."

"He's kind of a hothead, huh? Or he used to be."

"He's trying to be happier," Sofia admitted.

"I always liked him. I guess I have to raise twice as much hell now that he turned over a new leaf. I need to pull some doubles."

Sofia clasped her hands in front of her. They looked feeble under the fluorescent lights. She had no pen or barrette to fidget with. She could feel herself smirking.

"What?" said JP. "Whatever it is, say it."

"You and Spencer were never the same."

"Oh, no?"

"Spencer liked giving *and* getting. You, you're cut more from the bully cloth. Am I wrong? Tell me if I'm wrong."

JP laughed. It seemed genuine. "Is five minutes up? I'm a man of my word and I said five minutes. I got things to do today. I know you can't relate to that. I told your uncle my whole alibi and all. Do I need to walk you through it again? I will. I just want to satisfy the powers that be so I can go about my business."

"No," Sofia said. "The powers are satisfied."

"Your uncle must have nothing plus nothing on this, bringing in the... you know, the family circus." JP cackled ostentatiously, like people did who were used to laughing alone.

"When you were a kid," Sofia said.

JP nodded. He steered his attention back to her, bringing himself back to order. "Yeah?" he said. "When I was a kid what?"

"Did you stay home from church service one day and kill an egret? A white egret in a ditch?"

JP's face turned stony, and Sofia could tell his mind was working. "The hell you talking about?" he said.

She looked at him solemnly.

"An *egret*? When I was twelve?" He tugged at one of his sleeves. "Are you serious?"

Sofia couldn't tell what he was thinking. Maybe he was flipping through the catalog of cruel acts he'd perpetrated during his lifetime, or maybe he was thinking of something else mean he could say right now. He huffed and let his posture go jangly, pitching to one side in his chair. There was curiosity in his face, competing with the scorn. Sofia knew she wouldn't get an answer out of him, that there was no way to prove that she hadn't invented the egret and killed it herself.

"Nope, I didn't shoot no water birds," he told Sofia. "Sorry to disappoint you." He sniffed sharply into the back of his hand. "Think of it, I didn't shoot no bald eagle neither. And I didn't kill no redheaded woodpecker with a slingshot."

That afternoon Sofia ran into James at the coffee shop. He was sitting along the far wall under a painting of a dove, absorbed in a book, and he didn't notice her until she walked up to his table with her mug cradled in her hands. He lifted his feet off the chair across from him—grudgingly, Sofia noticed—and she sat down. It always seemed odd, during the periods when they were broken up, to not kiss when they saw each other. It left a sad void to be pressed through.

"I've always liked watching you read," Sofia said.

James looked at what was left in his cup and threw it back, then closed his book, using an old receipt to mark the page. Sofia's coffee was too hot to drink. She asked James what his book was about and he looked down and made a face at it.

"It covers a good bit of ground," he said, his voice flat but chafed.

"Give me a highlight," said Sofia.

"How about a lowlight? Lowlights are easier to come by, I find."

"I'll make do with a lowlight, if that's all I can get."

James let his eyes drift to the ceiling, his lips tight, as if selecting just one downbeat tale out of so many was a chore. After a moment, he clucked his tongue. "Okay, how about this? I'll tell you about this dude named Pánfilo de Narváez." James shifted in his chair and cleared his throat. "I can't get a ride from you but you can come talk to me if you feel like it. I don't quite see how those rules are fair, but I'll go ahead and give you one little morsel of woe." He began, not looking at Sofia, speaking quickly as if to get the story out and done with. "He's a B-list explorer, this guy. He comes over to Florida with a small army, the intention being to defeat Cortez. But after he lands, he decides to go on a little side mission to look for gold. Cortez can wait a couple weeks. So de Narváez starts interrogating whatever Indians he can find, asking them where all the treasure is, poking them in the ribs. Pretty standard stuff."

"Okay," said Sofia. James still wasn't looking at her.

"Lo and behold, he can't find any rich stuff. The Indians are sending him on goose chases. He's getting bit up by mosquitoes, has diarrhea. He's fed up. What he does then is arrest the chief of this particular tribe and start questioning him in a more persuasive way. Enhanced interrogation, we call it now. Chief won't say a word. He's a statue. You could put him in the cigar store. De Narváez keeps threatening him, beating him up—he just cannot scare this Indian. What ends up happening is de Narváez orders the chief's nose cut off. Cuts off the guy's damn nose. Bloody mess. Some of his men are embarrassed, a few of them walk away from his command. After that, the guy *really* won't talk."

James's eyes had widened, a sign of life in his face. His expression conveyed bemusement. Sofia wasn't sure if he'd come to the end of the story.

"He crossed a line between men," James said. "He was cursed after that, they say. When he finally got around to confronting Cortez, he got slaughtered."

James slid his book toward the edge of the table, pinning a saltshaker against the wall.

"Is there supposed to be a moral in that?" Sofia asked him.

James snorted. "The moral? There's a moral in anything if you want there to be."

Sofia was accustomed to James carrying a certain resigned disappointment in the world, but he'd never seemed cold before. Especially not toward her.

"I guess you heard about what I'm doing for my uncle," she said.

He brought his gaze up to her face. "Yeah, as a matter of fact I did catch wind of that."

Sofia blew into her mug. The coffee was still too hot. "And?"

"I was kind of wondering why you didn't tell me yourself."

"I wanted to," Sofia said. "I would've. But we were broken up and all."

"What did you think I was going to say?"

"I don't know. I just didn't want any discouragement, I guess."

James looked provoked. "Is that what you've ever gotten from me?"

There was no need for Sofia to answer the question. They both knew the answer. "I'm sorry," she said. "What *do* you think about it? Will you tell me now?"

"I think it sounds like an interesting thing to do is what I think. And something you might be good at." James stopped and patiently rolled each of his sleeves to the elbow, making sure they were even. Then he took a breath. "What I'm skeptical about is the idea that you can make the future easier by parsing out the past. That's what concerns me. You're trying to find out what to do next, but you're facing in the wrong direction." He shrugged, as if to suggest that his opinion wasn't necessarily important. "The only thing to do next is be a good person and let the moments unfold. I know you don't want to hear that. My part in the play is to tell you everything will be peachy and yours is to say there's heartbreak on the horizon, but honestly, neither of us knows."

Sofia leaned forward. She wasn't going to argue. Her discussions with James were always full of opposing truths. She was thinking about Pánfilo de Narváez. He had been asking the wrong questions. He had been worrying about gold when he should've been worrying about Cortez. James was right— you could tease morals out of anything if you had a mind to.

She touched James's book with her fingertips, searching for something yielding in his eyes. The smudgy dove was above them, taking flight before a lavender sky. The coffee shop had gotten quiet, it seemed.

James rested his hand on his book and pulled it away from her, out of her reach. "If you don't mind," he said, "I'd like to get back to my reading now."

"Eight months," Reeve answered.

Three interviews in, Sofia already felt experienced, on home turf in this interrogation room. Her subject was wearing a canary shirt and a beige sport coat, and looked nowhere near perspiring.

"Why here?"

Sofia looked Reeve in the face and waited for his answer. He seemed intrigued by his surroundings and by Sofia herself, like this interview was a life experience he was gaining.

"I was ready to get away from things, away from the city—well, if Jacksonville is a city, which compared to Lower Grove it is."

"What about Idaho, some place like that?"

"In hindsight I did insufficient research."

"But why here?"

Reeve adjusted the collar of his coat. He made no move to take it off. His legs were crossed and he folded his hands atop his knee.

"My family used to vacation over in Labelle, when I was a little guy," he said. "This one-story motel with a pool. Next door was a field full of donkeys. My dad would grill. I guess I have a positive association with this area." Reeve cleared his throat. "I drove over there a couple weeks ago. Motel's still there; no sign of the donkeys."

"What do you do, that you can move to the economic middle of nowhere?"

"I was a pretty good businessman in my day," Reeve said.

"Past tense."

"I built up a chain of high-end health clubs, nine of them. Took fifteen years. When the time was right I sold them. I had commercials on TV and billboards and everything."

"And now you don't have to work?"

"Not if I live somewhere like this."

"I see," said Sofia.

Reeve was intending to convey openness and full cooperation. His act seemed too flawless.

"Do you have any experience with the spiritually adept?" Sofia asked him.

"Actually I do. By marriage," said Reeve. "My ex-wife's aunt was a medium in St. Augustine. People used to fly in to see her. Some of them came once a year, like a checkup."

"But you never sat with her?"

"She wouldn't do family."

"You could go see her now. She's not family anymore."

Reeve frowned, not unhappily. "You could do it. You could give me a reading."

"No, I couldn't do that."

"Why not? My wife's aunt made pretty good dough."

"I don't think I'm nosy enough."

Now Reeve chuckled. "Work from home. Cash business."

"Your ex-wife's aunt," Sofia said. "She's mostly an actress. Not to say she doesn't have a talent, but she put herself in show business."

Reeve uncrossed his legs. He regarded Sofia wryly. "What about this here?" he said. "You're in business."

"This is pro bono. I'm not getting paid and I'm not taking advantage of anyone."

Reeve thought a second, picking something off his sleeve, and when he spoke again Sofia couldn't hear him. There was another sound in her ears. She was being flooded with exactly what she needed to know and not a thing more, the knowledge filling her abundant and organized. She felt like her mind was being held at the bottom of a fast-moving river, but it had all the air it could use. The feeling was serene yet bracing. It had nothing to do with her body, asked no physical effort, nor even surrender.

Barn Renfro had made a bad investment, sure enough, an illegal one. He'd been planning on selling a bunch of the boats at his shop and slipping away, going into hiding. Barn's debt had nothing to do with Reeve, but it was the reason Barn had a loaded gun in arm's reach when Reeve came over in search of his dog. Sofia had all this intelligence and she didn't feel a bit strained, just very awake. She was breathing easily. She wasn't losing any time. It was all here before her, like a light had been switched on in a dark room.

Reeve lived on the opposite side of the lake from Barn, which was the reason he was being questioned. He was Barn's only neighbor and his alibi, according to Uncle Tunsil, was nothing special. Sofia saw why. Reeve had been carrying on a feud with Barn since the day he'd moved in, a feud he hadn't mentioned to Sofia's uncle. There'd been a dispute over the property line, and Reeve was hoping the paperwork from that dispute was buried by now. Reeve was *not* pleased to be attending this interview. He was *not* being open. Like so many, like his wife's aunt, he was a great actor.

When it became clear that Reeve was going to win the property dispute, Barn had cut down a pair of sprawling live oaks that, in another forty-eight hours, would've belonged to Reeve. Reeve had called the county once about Barn dumping his shop waste in the lake, and after that Barn had begun dumping everything in there—even grass clippings and bacon grease. Now there were no fish in the lake and the live oaks were history. Barn had called the fire marshal when Reeve's family had visited and were roasting marshmallows in the backyard. Reeve's young nephew had wandered over to Barn's side of the lake early one morning, curiously examining all the dry-docked boats, and Barn had come around the corner with a filet knife in his hand, telling the boy exactly what happened to people who got caught sneaking around where they didn't belong.

And then there was Reeve's dog. The animal liked to wander. He'd never destroyed Barn's property or even growled at him, but Barn hated the dog. A couple times he'd yelled across the lake for Reeve to come and get his goddamn mutt before he carted him off to the pound. The day of Barn's death the dog had gone missing. That's why Reeve had gone over to the shop. He'd surprised the fear-racked Barn, who'd stayed awake the whole night before on alert against his creditors, and who had been subsisting on pork rinds and beer. Reeve had been prepared for a confrontation. He had begun, in the hour before he'd strode around the mucky lake, to consider the prospect that Barn had killed his dog, that his pet was dead by the hand of this stupid backwoods grease monkey, this man who was a scourge of Reeve's well-earned early retirement. If Barn had pushed the feud to a new height, Reeve would need to push back or be less than a man.

Barn could've killed the dog or he could've driven him out to the middle of nowhere and left him. Reeve had been breathing raggedly when he'd barged into the dim shop out of the blaring sun and stopped short at the gathering sight of Barn pointing a gun at him. He couldn't even see Barn's face, except the bulging, bloodshot eyes. Then the barrel of the gun was advancing, Barn's fingers squeezed fat around the handle, his face coming into focus, merciless but full of something like, it seemed to Reeve, relief. Reeve could smell the man when he came close, could almost make out the curses and oaths he was reciting.

When Reeve thought back on the ungainly grunting struggle that followed, as he was doing right now, sitting across from Sofia, he thought of how the gun had felt once he had it in his hand, the foreign coolness of the grip soothing him in that steamy shop in the wilds of this steamy county, the gun's perfect balanced weight and perfect incuriosity. Barn was slobbering, vanquished and separated from his pistol, gathering himself as well as he could, staggering, spitting. Reeve watched him read the situation, injured and beyond all reason, watched him grab an outsize wrench off his worktable and lumber forward, grinning now, saying Reeve would never do it. Reeve remembered wondering if Barn was right, the man raising the wrench overhead into the dusty air of the shop, his intent simple and evil, and then there was a bright roar all around them, a shudder running through the walls.

Reeve had regretted the act immediately. He'd regretted the entire feud, regretted leaving Jacksonville, regretted letting his wife walk away. His entire past was a mess. He could smell blood through the sour gunsmoke. He should've gotten the hell out of the shop the second he had possession of the gun. But he hadn't. He'd wanted to be dared, had wanted to stand the ground he'd gained, to push his advantage. Reeve had stalked onto another man's property, a native's property, half expecting an altercation, and that man had wound up dead.

He wiped off the weapon as he'd seen done in a thousand movies and returned home and scrubbed his kitchen. He dusted every piece of furniture in his house and swept his garage. He kept washing his hands, he didn't know why. He started a commonplace grocery list—eggs, milk, bread.

Now he had to hope the animosity between himself and Barn was not unearthed. He'd been asked nothing about his dog, Salvatore, who was still missing. Reeve wasn't aware that Barn was mixed up with criminals. He could easily get away with this, but he didn't know that. His mind was a stew of worry but he looked to Sofia like a man on a demanding vacation, a man who'd ordered a complicated drink and was awaiting its arrival. He was a murderer, this guy across the table. He'd taken a man's life.

After the interview, Sofia drove out along the Hargreaves Trail, toward Barn Renfro's place. She'd driven past it before, maybe a half-dozen times—the nondescript boat shop that was twice the size of the house it sat next to, the lake you barely caught a glimpse of as you passed. There was a wide spot in the gravel just past Barn's spread, and Sofia parked her Datsun and got out. The air was laden with the odor of burnweed and the only animal life present was the many varieties of small dark birds—on the fences and power lines and pecking about like chickens near the road. Sofia could feel the heat from the gravel right through the soles of her shoes, her keys jingling in her hand. She turned up Barn's drive and headed straight for the shop. The front of it was hung with a single orange ribbon, across the regular door and the big bay doors. The structure was very tall now that Sofia was close to it, to accommodate the boats Barn worked on in there. Used to work on. Sofia figured the door was locked. She didn't want to try the knob. She just needed to see inside, so she kept on around the side of the shop, looking for a window, and when she saw one she went up and rested her fingertips on it.

The surprise would've been if this wasn't the place she'd seen in the interrogation room, but when she pressed her nose to the glass it was all there. Right on the other side of the window was the table where Barn had grabbed the wrench. Same table. It was covered with iron files and sockets and screwdrivers and pliers. Beside the table was some sort of press—Sofia couldn't tell what it was for but she remembered it. She kept her face where it was and after a minute she could see more, a familiar red toolbox, and a miniature fridge. A bookshelf full of manuals. A rack of fishing rods suspended from the rafters. She turned her head and checked behind her. Everything was quiet. The pines that marked the other edge of Barn's property were perfectly still. She imagined Reeve's dog running out of those pines, bounding toward her and barking lightheartedly. She had no clue what had happened to that dog. Maybe *Barn* had happened to the dog. Or maybe the world had simply taken it away.

She turned and peered again into the shop, more familiar details coming into focus. This was the place she'd seen in her vision, and she ought to have been feeling satisfaction over that. Her ability had been proven, the question answered—the reason she'd gotten involved in all this in the first place. Reeve, composed and accomplished, in good shoes and a sport coat, a recent retiree, was a killer. This was a fact. But satisfaction wasn't coming. There was a corkboard on the far wall where a half-dozen boat keys were hanging. Beneath that, an air compressor. There was a big clean spot in the middle of the dusty floor, Sofia saw. It had to be where Barn had fallen dead, where his blood had been mopped up. No, satisfaction was nowhere close.

That evening, Sofia sat with Uncle Tunsil on the front steps. He had a glass of whiskey resting on his leg. Through the branches of the nut tree the sky was pink.

"The smart money's on an out-of-towner." Uncle Tunsil straightened his back until it produced one hollow crack. "Smart money's been on an out-of-towner from the start. Bookie or dealer or something. Oh, well. Poor old Barn."

Sofia nodded.

Uncle Tunsil took a nip from his glass and his face tightened. "I should get better bourbon. I go through about a bottle a year."

Moments earlier, Sofia had looked her uncle in the face and lied to him about Reeve, had said she'd gotten nothing. She had lied to her uncle and now was finding it hard to speak to him. She couldn't be responsible for Reeve getting punished, couldn't be the one to decide a man be tried for murder. She had a talent, but that didn't make her anyone's judge. If anything, she'd seen how far from black and white these matters could be, how presumptuous it was to think she ought to intervene, how presumptuous, even, to think that anyone ever really got away with anything.

Sofia looked over at her uncle, gently rocking the liquor in his glass, squinting into the thick-aired evening. Sofia felt she was sparing him something too, by keeping quiet. He wasn't cut out for nailing unfortunate people to the wall. He was a big, tough innocent. Still, she felt disloyal. She'd wanted to help him and now she was working against him. Lying to him. He'd hear grumblings in town, might even lose some respect in some people's estimation. He might not care about that, but Sofia did. There was a foul nagging in her chest.

She wasn't going to worry him anymore about her gift. That was for sure. He didn't deserve a psychic in his house. She was going to let him think the matter had been resolved.

"I got more to look into before I shelve the case," he said. "The guy the state sent is heading back to Tallahassee. He can't wait to get out of here. He told me when he runs over his hundredth snake he's going back home, and he's got about a dozen to go."

Sofia wanted to ask her uncle for a pull of his whiskey, but she knew she would hate the taste. Her stomach was roiling gently. There was still no breeze, no cars on the road that ran past the house. The only sound was the rising chant of insects. Sofia thought she could smell the lemons on the little tree in the yard.

"You know," her uncle said. "You should quit giving that boy of yours a hard time."

Uncle Tunsil hadn't been looking at her and now he was. It was out of the ordinary for him to say anything to her about James.

"Yeah, I know."

"Do you?" he said. His voice was stern, but his eyes weren't.

"Of course I do."

"You got your gifts and I got mine. I can detect a good dude when I see one. In these parts, they're about three per thousand."

Sofia gazed ahead, past the road, at a huddle of weary myrtles.

"That's a good dude wants to treat you nice. Your best policy with that kind of customer is stay open for business. Sometimes you young people think too much. You can think yourself into the loser's bracket."

Sofia felt inert. She didn't expect to speak, but then she did, like she wanted to confess something. She told Uncle Tunsil what she had been telling herself all along, that she was scared of what came after the chase, scared that James would get tired of her once he knew he had her. It sounded flimsy in her ears.

Uncle Tunsil looked unimpressed too. "History repeating itself, huh?" he said. There was a gnat or something in his drink, and he fished it out with his finger and flicked it away. "I'm not the lecturing type. I'll just say it isn't always an advantage thinking you're a step ahead. Because here's the thing: you never are."

A lone gull flew overhead, seeming lost, piping its peppy, shrill call.

It zigzagged over the house and out of sight. Of course Sofia's uncle was right about this. She should tell James all of it. She should open the whole book to him. The interviews. Driving past the prison as a child. Shannon Janicek. She should spend every minute with him, give him everything he wanted. She'd felt all along it was foolish not to.

Uncle Tunsil finished his last spill of whiskey and didn't seem to know what to do with the glass. A few minutes remained before it was night.

"The kid's lucky in a way, despite the treatment you lay on him. To love something the way he does you. It's not everybody who finds that. Not the real thing, like he has."

Sofia and Uncle Tunsil were quiet then. They weren't happy or unhappy. The hunting birds were swooping now, nighthawks and the like. Something seemed different in the known little world of the front yard, and they realized a breeze was sweeping over them. It rustled the leaves of the good half of the nut tree and lisped against the roof of the house. It wasn't going to keep blowing for long. It was going to die out any moment and leave Lower Grove to deal with the real summer.

NAPLES. NOT ITALY.

On TV is a painting show. It's like the show that guy Ross used to do. This new guy is more Ross-like than Ross, dreamier. His clothes are astounding. What he's painting looks like a flowerpot until it looks like an oaken bucket. He starts filling the bucket with something, his brushstrokes precise yet whimsical. Wheat. Soon the bucket is on a table, outside. We wait to see what he'll do with the sky, what kind of weather is on the way.

For us, it rains the whole weekend and on into the week, sometimes barely drizzling and sometimes resembling a monsoon. Our friend is down for a visit, a woman our age who's newly single and rankled. After a few hours, she softens. She needs my wife and me in order to be herself, or a version of herself she can live with. In the old days, in the desert and in a lot of other places, we showed her that she didn't have to volunteer for anything, that she didn't have to smile at strangers or defend her opinions. We forced her to learn how to prepare lots of dinners. And now she has returned to us, to this shabby old condo we're renting.

*   *   *

The TV in the sunroom stays on, muted, day after day. None of us have what it takes to turn it off or to sit and listen to a program. The TV is as big as a booth, an old-fashioned big-screen from before they started flattening TVs out and pinning them to walls. You could collect tolls from inside this TV, or dispense pills. The TV is our connection to the fresh disasters of the world. We watch earthquakes soundlessly topple buildings in Asia. We see Alabama leveled by tornadoes, hollow-eyed couples gazing at rubble. Naples is due for a hurricane, the weather experts say, but it won't much matter; the retirees here are rich and have deluxe insurance policies and houses on concrete stilts. And if someone dies, well, they were getting ready to die anyway.

The TV shows us which priests and congressmen and starlets can't stop doing the wrong things. We make a point not to root against them, to remember that everyone needs to make a living. The ways these people make theirs come with extraordinary demands.

The TV shows us the world of the young, too, and they're the sorriest young people yet—empty of righteous hatred, casual in their loves, seeking a thousand shallow alliances. The young are easy to make fun of, but this fact does not comfort us in the least. They still have youth, regardless of what they do with it, and so we envy them.

Lara, our visitor, owns a near-empty condo in another part of the state. She doesn't want to return to it. Two dozen acres around Lara's condo are clear-cut, a vast tract of dingy sand. Her building was the only one completed before the whole development project was halted. It looks lost, her building, like it arrived at a ball field on the wrong day. When you drive up Lara's street, you see just how flat Florida is, and how exhausted. At night, at Lara's condo, it's like living on the moon.

In the mornings, before we're awake, she runs in the rain until her feet hurt. A desperate practice, but one that earns a person a certain seriousness.

She makes lunch soups full of beans and organic herbs. She spends hours mending torn clothes or writing letters to her aunts—the types of womanly tasks my wife no longer finds the energy for.

We play a game, out under the roof of the front porch, called 20-Point Turn. All you do is sit with your drink, hidden among fronds, and watch the old folks try to park. The rules of 20-Point Turn can be changed on the spot. Every time a wife gets out and directs her husband—that's two points. If she does it decently, without squawking, she gets points too.

When I go to the mailboxes, the old men think I'm mocking them. I've done something to my back, something involving a disc. There's never anything out there except coupon booklets, but I carry those inside so we can check if there's anything funny about them, anything ridiculous about this week's discounts.

We talk about nicknames. That's the type of thing we try to talk about, so Lara won't cry. You can always talk about nicknames. Other types of inside jokes spoil, but not nicknames. If any of us ever have children, the first thing we'll do is nickname them.

My wife wants Lara's nickname to be Dwayne for a while. My wife says she wants to leave notes for Lara and address them to Dwayne.

What kind of pill is best for a backache is a topic. Whether to keep doing our own taxes is a topic. The yoga Lara does every day after lunch is a topic. Computer brands. Libertarians. The various ways movies can be made. I tell the gals about how Florida used to be, since I'm the one who's from here— how there used to be orange groves everywhere you looked and now there's Home Depots and chain bakeries. I tell them it used to be pleasant to drive on 41—people did it for fun—and now it's a traffic jam of senile Long Islanders. You used to be able to camp on the beach, with a fire and everything; it was safe to be out there overnight and the authorities wouldn't hassle you. There was a family-owned pecan grove right down the street from my childhood home, and my brother and I would walk over there every Saturday and get free pecan logs from the old lady. Now, I tell them, that plot of land is a used-car dealership. The trees are long gone, not a matchbook of shade on the whole lot.

My wife bangs her tea mug down on a glass end table and walks out of the room, leaving an airless quiet in her wake. I know what the problem is. She's tired of my complaining. She's heard it all before.

Lara picks up the abandoned cup and takes a sip from it, a breezy look on her face, as if to dismiss my wife's behavior. We've both noticed her sour moods, but it's not something we could talk about. My wife has made no effort to commiserate with Lara about her breakup. In the old days, she would've, but now it's as if she's unwilling to acknowledge that she's in a position to pity anyone, to hand down aid or wisdom.

Lara and I look over toward the TV. It feels like we're allies, yet we avoid each other's gaze. There's a press conference on the screen. A black man in a three-piece suit is slouching against a podium. He could be talking about anything. Next to him, a stone-faced woman scans the crowd.

There's a spot on the edge of town where you can pull off the roadside and view alligators from the safety of your car. My wife and I haven't made our way over there, and now Lara has started campaigning that we go, that we pack some sandwiches and find a radio station and stare at the huge languorous reptiles for an hour or two. She thinks it'll cheer us up. I tell her maybe we'll go tomorrow, if the rain stops. Then, because I can tell my wife has no interest in this field trip, I try to talk Lara out of it altogether.

What the alligators do nowadays, I say, is wait for old ladies to walk their pooches too close to a drainage ditch. They collect indigestible collars in their guts. That shouldn't cheer anyone up. I tell her there's wildlife right outside the window, and it's true—a tall white bird is out there in the drizzle, stabbing the soft ground with more urgency than seems necessary. The bird is in the rough and beyond the bird is the fairway. Beyond that, peering out from screened lanais, are pairs of dismayed old folks. They promised themselves they'd die in lovely weather, and now that they're here it's just raining and raining and raining.

The note on my car says: HOW ABOUT GIVING US A BREAK, WE CANNOT GET IN AND OUT WITH OUR BIKES AND BUNDLES. It's been taped to the driver-side window inside a plastic baggie. It's not signed. Whoever left the note wants me to believe I'm blocking the front walk by parking where I've parked, in the closest space, but he and I both know why he doesn't want me there. That space is bigger than the others. It's wider. I park my little Honda there on purpose for the good of our game. My wife suggests we put a new note on my car window, one that will read: IF YOU WANT A BREAK, GO BREAK YOUR FUCKING HIP.

We won't do it, though. We're not sure why, but we won't do something like that. It's the teenagers and old folks who do whatever they please. And there's no one else in this town, just teenagers by the hundreds and old folks by the thousands.

Each evening, we go to a restaurant in the ritzy downtown, our only outing of the day, jogging in the rain from the car to the closest awnings. I limp when I jog, but still, I can jog. The restaurants are too expensive for us, but we can't let the old folks win. If they're going to have red snapper in a tangerine and rum sauce, so are we.

We enjoy food more than they do. And we know the wines from when we were out west. We hope, each of us silently, that when the old folks see us sighing and cooing and letting our jaws roll luxuriantly, they'll think about the sex they once had.

* * *

The condo we rent still has all the landlady's figurines in it. The day we moved in, we piled them all in the spare room, enough ceramic and porcelain to fill a grave. Except one, a foot-and-a-half statue of a dark-haired angel in a tuxedo. That one we move from room to room with us. We take it out to the porch, and on car rides. The angel's chest is puffed, his waist petite. He looks sort of like an exasperated maître d' and sort of like he's about to break into song. His hands are empty, his wings folded against his back. He stands sunk to his shins in a cloud, like someone in quicksand.

The condo complex is immense. You could claim it's ten square miles and no one could argue. The pool, which we have yet to walk over to, is the largest in this region of the state. The deepest it gets is four feet.

The last night of her visit, Lara wins 20-Point Turn. She's got a Nissan she's taken great care of, that she takes religiously for waxes and transmission flushes and new tires even when it doesn't need them, and an old man trying to park runs right into it. Now her Nissan has a dent in the quarter panel. Lara decides not to care. She decides that her incessant car upkeep is getting sad. The dent is a blessing. It's worth a dent to win the game, because she could really use a win.

When the guy finally gets into the space and rises up out of his Grand Marquis, the three of us stand and cheer. I hold the angel statue up like a trophy. It seems like the old days for a moment—Lara is genuinely giddy and my wife's smile is full, unfettered. She's not withholding a part of herself, not acting reluctant in order to make some point. And I feel I'm partly responsible for getting us here, having been a steady, buoyant presence in our little home.

The next morning my wife gets up early. That's not unusual; most nights, one of the two of us slips out, sleepless, to watch the wee-hour newsfeeds.

An hour or so later I get up, too, and make a full pot of coffee. The night is just subsiding; by the time the coffee is done brewing, I can see out the windows. I pour myself a mug and carry it to the back of the condo to check out the birds on the golf course. As I pass through the living room, I see that my wife isn't on the couch.

I can hear now how quiet the condo is. I walk to the front end and ease Lara's door open a couple inches, sensing that her room is empty. I set my coffee down on the Formica table in the kitchen. Maybe the two of them went running together, though that would surprise me. Out the front window I can see that Lara's car isn't there.

I decide to forgo a bowl of cereal, in case they went out to pick up something for breakfast. I head back to the rear windows and lean on the sill. A mismatched gang of water birds is advancing up the fairway. It's like they've fanned out to look for something one of them dropped. There's a blue heron and an ibis and a snowy egret—a few distracted gulls, not helping with the search, nestle on the clipped grass like it's a calm bay.

When I'm too hungry to wait any longer and my coffee is cold, I return to the kitchen. The angel statue catches my eye, proud-looking, planted over on the white sideboard. And then I see the note pinned underneath it. The stationery bears the logo of a hospital, and the hurried writing tells me that my wife and Lara drove up near Sarasota for the day, to hang out on Lara's friend's boat. And that they may stay the night. It's my wife's handwriting. She didn't put her name at the bottom, or put my name at the top—didn't sign off with the word *love*. She's being petty, Lord knows to what end.

I dump my coffee and pour a fresh mug. No name for this friend of Lara's? *Near* Sarasota? I suppose I should be happy the girls are reconnecting, returning to one another's favor, but happiness isn't the feeling that's arriving. The note didn't say whether they were going to sit at the dock or take the boat out, but I assume it's raining in Sarasota too. It feels like the whole state has been under these clouds.

I sit in the kitchen until my coffee is lukewarm again, then I grab my keys and head down the front steps. I'm not sure where I'm driving until

I pull into the grocery store. I fill a hand basket with fruit and grab a sixer of cheap beer. I can already envision the apples and limes in bowls in the kitchen, already feel how they'll help the condo, and I can see the forthright, cheerful cans of beer on a shelf in the refrigerator. At the checkout I take a newspaper too.

Back at the condo, I spread the paper out. There's an article revealing the best places to use a metal detector. An article about a wild boar that startled some beachgoers. A girl in Fort Myers was shot while sitting in her car. I read every word. I'm trying to lose track of time, and it's working. A soldier went berserk in a post office. A new podiatry clinic is opening.

When I fold the paper back up, it's the middle of the afternoon. The coffee pot has been on all day, and I finally shut it off. I shouldn't call my wife's phone, but I know it's only a matter of time before I do. I take a shower and eat something, then I open a beer and go to the front porch. 20-Point Turn is no good all alone. It's just people parking and nothing more, people coming back from dinner before it's even nighttime. I can hear the card games from the other porches—outdated games I don't know the rules to. There are silences, murmurs, peals of laughter. Lara's space is taken now, by a long, gray Lincoln. I find myself doubting very much that Lara has a friend in Sarasota, or that that friend has a boat, or that my wife would want to be on that boat.

I pull out my phone, as I knew I would, and when I call my wife it goes straight to voicemail. Lara's phone gives me the same treatment. It's possible they're offshore, out of cell range. I have no way of knowing.

At lunchtime the next day, they still haven't surfaced. What I understand is that my wife hasn't been my ally for some time. It's true we love each other. It's true that eventually she'll return from wherever she is and all this will pass. But we're not allies.

I wonder what to do next. There's a mammoth sporting goods store nearby that I wouldn't mind walking around in. Doubtless there's a coupon booklet in the mailbox. On the muted TV there will be sobering news from

Africa, from the Pacific Rim, from everywhere. The rain is going to cease soon—later today, tomorrow—and the thought worries me. All the old people will rejoice, beaming in their tennis clothes and grilling steaks and rubbing down their long automobiles to prevent water spots. They will cherish those little duties. Our neighbors are finished with the tasks they toiled away at in life; they know what it is to be finished, to have worked a lifetime toward a satisfaction that begins rotting after a week.

THE DIFFERING VIEWS

The man did not offer to buy Mitchell a coffee. He described the job as a sales position but managed to avoid saying exactly what Mitchell would sell. Mitchell found he could not get a word in, and after a while he quit trying. The man seemed like he'd been to prison, something about how cloudy and expressionless his eyes looked. His pinstripe suit was like a disguise. He had made several allusions to a payment of $300 and Mitchell finally understood that the man wanted *him* to pay $300. The man made wisecracks about some starving-artist types that were haunting the coffee shop, making fun of what they did with their time and also making fun of their clothes. He was holding a laminated graph. It showed a steep increase in something. Mitchell's mind went to the gas he'd wasted driving into Albuquerque. His mind went to all the things he'd at one time or another studied in depth—the history of Paris, North American hummingbirds. He'd once known the entire Book of Psalms by heart. To buy himself an espresso drink would be, at this point, an extravagant expenditure.

* * *

Mitchell had spent six years with Bet. Bet had family money and fancied herself a writer and moved every few months, on whims. Mitchell had met her when she'd passed through Chattanooga. He'd agreed to tag along with her, had left his crappy adjunct job at a branch of the state college to drive the open parts of the country with the windows down. That was the kind of thing he'd always been able to do—make his escape when others were afraid to. He'd come to know Bet better than he'd ever known another person, and perhaps they'd grown *too* close. This last move they'd wound up in some bleached, dusty town out east of Albuquerque, and after only two days Bet had said she wanted to pack back up and move again. She'd said she had complaints, but they weren't really about New Mexico. There'd been a convoluted fight during which Bet had used the term "curdled" to what she believed was great effect, and then she'd left. Six years. She'd driven away in her tasteful little SUV, crying in sharp breathy yips. It was the same way she cried at anything—the death of an animal, songs. She produced these high-pitched whimpers and her nose got stuffed up, but only a tear or two would fall. It was one of the only things Mitchell didn't like about her, her crying, and he was glad that this was the last image he'd had of her as she left. If she'd driven off with one of her resigned frowns, it would've crushed him. If she'd flashed him that look of distanced amusement, the one cheek bunched up and her eyes barely squinting, he'd probably still be standing out there, frozen at the edge of the parking lot like a cactus.

Mitchell had been alone for a week now. He could see that he was worn out too, though not of Bet. He was tired of the road, of packing and unpacking, of learning new streets and new restaurants and new neighbors and new weather and suffering new allergies and not knowing the name of the county he lived in. He was tired of looking for work.

He had a two-bedroom condo all to himself and the first month and security deposit were paid. He had a last-legs Isuzu Stylus he'd bought cheap a couple stops ago, when the only job he could find was twenty miles outside of town. He was a bachelor. That was the situation. Big clean appliances. He had nothing to put in the second bedroom but a folding chair and a lamp. He had $4,100.

Left to his own devices, he ate twice a day, all his meals working out to about $7. Sandwich and potato salad and a Coke. Burritos and a Coke. Three stiff slices of pizza and a Coke. Chicken fingers and cheap beer. He knew his crappy diet was one of the reasons he felt sluggish. He and Bet had always gone out to good restaurants, usually on her dime, or if they ate in they had salads and expensive cheese.

Bet had taken her laptop, which they'd used to read articles or listen to the radio. Mitchell had an old box TV, but they'd never used it as a TV. It hadn't been plugged in since Chattanooga, and had become an ornamental artifact. At a villa he and Bet had rented in Maine, they'd used the TV as a centerpiece for their dining room table. In Baltimore, they'd taped a tropical beach scene over the screen, something to look at during the winter weather. This condo Mitchell was in now didn't have cable hooked up, but he doubted the TV would work anyway.

Before Mitchell and Bet had driven to New Mexico, they had planned a number of desert outings, and now Mitchell couldn't find the gusto to undertake any of the outings alone. One of the places they'd planned to visit was a farm of gargantuan satellite dishes that monitored the webby corners of the galaxy for sonic anomalies. They'd planned to hike out into White Sands. Tour the pistachio groves. All these places had seemed foreign and enchanting before, but now, as a guy alone, they were just radio apparatus, just a wash of pale dirt, some nut trees.

Mitchell bought a package of heavy paper and drove to a small library the color of tired earth. He obtained a library card and sat down at a computer and typed an up-to-date version of his work history. He put his fancy paper in the library printer and came away with a purposeful stack of résumés. It was eerie to look at his new résumé, to see all the places he'd been with Bet, all the things he'd done with his hands for money, to think at one time of all the warehouses and mills and machine shops where he'd logged a month or two, all these places he hadn't been suited for and that had already forgotten him. And teaching hadn't suited him either, if he was honest. He could remember clearly, even all these years later, feeling like an impostor in front of the students. He could remember acting like he cared about whether they learned, could remember drumming up just enough enthusiasm within himself before each class meeting.

Mitchell looked at job listings on the Internet, ads for general labor. Some wanted his résumé emailed to them. Some jumped Mitchell to other sites, seemingly unrelated, where he was supposed to fill in questionnaires and compose statements about loyalty and tolerance. Mitchell's time on the computer ran out and he logged off and wrote his name on the sheet again. He spent a half hour reading a science fiction novel and then looked up numbers for every temp agency in Albuquerque and called them all and made appointments to come in and drop off his résumé and do whatever else they had people do. He called three different numbers advertising "environmental jobs" and got no answer. He went and sat in a squeaky chair and scanned the want ads in the newspaper. People wanted HVAC technicians and exotic dancers.

It wasn't uncommon for men in a predicament like Mitchell's to turn to hard drinking or worse, but Mitchell couldn't find the impetus. He didn't want liquor. It didn't really make you forget anything—nothing you *wanted* to forget. He sipped at his beers from the corner store and they perhaps dulled his bitterness. He would open the kitchen window for the wash of dry air and drink three or four watery cans of Budweiser at a spell, and what he would miss most about Bet, he admitted, was walking down an unfamiliar street with her, holding her hand, watching her face to gauge her reactions to whatever they encountered. Some days they'd keep to themselves and some days they'd talk to fifty strangers. Bet would always have a superb coat on, and superb shoes, and Mitchell always had the sense that she belonged to the rest of the world as much as she belonged to him. It was what had kept him fascinated by her, the fact that her heart could never be pinned down.

* * *

Mitchell awoke on the couch in the living room, where he'd been sleeping since Bet left. He could sense that something had occurred. Something about the condo was odd. Something was different. He felt like he'd been robbed, except nothing was missing. There was nothing *to* rob. The TV maybe, but there it was in front of him, dark and mute. He shuffled into the kitchen, which looked the same as always. He yanked his jeans straight and stretched his back until it cracked. He could hear something innocuous and steady from outside, a distant tractor-trailer or maybe only the wind with nothing to whistle against. He went over to the bathroom. Everything looked normal there too. He peeked in the shower. Square-cornered bar of soap. Tiny hotel shampoo. He came out into the hall and paused in front of the spare room. He was listening, he still didn't know for what. He pushed back the door and leaned his head into the room and there on the floor were six or seven brains. Seven. Human, as best he could tell. Mitchell blinked hard a few times. He could feel himself breathing, his chest rising and falling gently as ever. He was lightheaded but not at all dizzy. They looked like brains and that's exactly what they were—sleek, oyster-colored lobes, firm yet vulnerable. Those perfect hemispheres. They weren't moving, but Mitchell could tell they were alive. If they were dead he'd have known it, the way you know anything is dead. He was outside himself, watching himself stare. The blinds were closed against the morning but the room wasn't dim. The light hitting each brain seemed to hide it rather than illuminate it. Mitchell felt like a child who'd walked in on something shameful. There was no humor in the room, no humor in Mitchell.

He retreated clumsily to the kitchen, using his hand against the wall, and sat on his stool at the high, round kitchen table. He spoke aloud in the third person, a tactic he'd used since he was a child to ground himself. He said his name, then recited what season it was, and what day of the week. "It's morning," he said. "Or depending when you woke up, late morning." His voice sounded fine, maybe a touch reedy. Everything else was normal. Everything else looked the same. It was cold outside but he was sitting in a patch of sunlight from the window. He drummed his fingers rather than doing nothing at all with them. He found himself almost savoring his shock, fully aware that his shock was irrelevant. He looked at the calendar and it seemed like the wrong year, like it was marking time that had already passed.

Mitchell smoothed his T-shirt and made his way back across the condo to the spare room. They were still in there, all seven of them. He went ahead and entered the room this time, cautious where he stepped. He sat down in the chair and clicked on the lamp, and in the artificial light the brains were translucent. Mitchell turned the lamp off and unscrewed the bulb and held it in his palm. The brains were not veiny. They were not in distress. Mitchell could not find it in himself to disbelieve what he was seeing, to dismiss his senses out of hand, and he knew that that was the wrong way to think. He knew he shouldn't give that kind of thinking an inch.

He sat silent in the spare room for a long time. His back hurt but he ignored it. He was thinking a hundred miles an hour. Here were plain facts, seven in number. Why seven? So neutral, seeming not to care about Mitchell a bit. They had no ill will in them, no kindness. These brains weren't possible, yet he felt he'd been awaiting them or something like them for some time. A memory came to him of those summer afternoons when he would steal an hour from the fun everyone else was having and sit by himself in a culvert or under the public dock at the river, taking a rest from the blustery cheer of his neighborhood. He remembered being hidden in the cool. He remembered the tirades of the birds above, who weren't used to trespassers in their out-of-the-way dominions.

It turned out they *were* moving, the brains, just very slowly. He had to close his eyes for several minutes in order to mark their advancement across the hardwood. Mitchell gathered the courage to crouch down and touch one with his thumb, feeling ludicrous and fearful, and it didn't seem to bother the brain a bit. The brain felt like a snake, smooth and muscled and dense. The brains smelled like wet peanut shells. They produced a dull hum that never grew louder.

Mitchell put on his sneakers and locked his door and drove slower than the speed limit in the approximate direction of town. The sky was a fault-less, inscrutable blue. In a featureless area of the desert he passed a vagrant wearing a beret. The man was limping down the roadside with no hope of catching a ride, and after Mitchell had passed him, the man turned around and started walking the other direction, doubling back toward wherever he'd come from. Mitchell watched the man until he disappeared from the rearview. He passed a clinic for animals, with a thirty-foot ironwood in its front yard and an array of colorful garbage bins lining the drive. He passed some low, isolated settlements, and then a vast car dealership loomed up, festooned with pennants, some of the vehicles displayed on ramps, some of them with their doors thrown open in welcome. Mitchell had reached the outskirts. He pulled into the near-empty parking lot of a movie theater. He went in and selected a movie and sat in the dark. Passive jazz music played over the speakers. Mitchell wasn't doing great—people who were doing great, who were doing fantastic at the moment, didn't see vital organs living in their spare rooms. But maybe he wasn't doing that badly either. Maybe no worse than a lot of people. He was unemployed, but that was common nowadays. He'd probably wasted the prime of his life, but who didn't? Aside from athletes and rock stars, who used their primes proudly? Mitchell remembered certain weekends with Bet, how he'd felt pleasantly disconnected from everything, how the two of them could be their own slow little city, losing whole days in naps, getting the world's bad news long after the worst was already over, insulated from the failing economy by Bet's money.

He'd forgotten to get any candy or popcorn, but now the trailers had begun. He hadn't been in a movie theater in a couple of years. Bet had come up with the idea of doing all the worst things they could think of in a single day, once—they'd had breakfast in an Arby's and attended a boat show, listened to right-wing radio and read about Jessica Simpson online for a full hour. In the evening, they'd gone to see whatever Vin Diesel car-chase movie had been playing, filing in with packs of teenagers. Toward the climax of the film, Bet had started making out with Mitchell, showily tongue-kissing him as nearby adolescents stared. He could remember other trips, before that—times when he himself was in high school, driving into Chattanooga from his sleepy town and slumping alone in an art house matinee, feeling tragic and uncommon, then drifting outside afterward into the broad daylight, the world exactly as he'd left it.

The movie Mitchell had bought a ticket for was about a high-end catering company in Los Angeles. It was a comedy where all the characters sabotage each other, but at the end a guy gets fired and all his rival coworkers quit the company in solidarity. When Mitchell walked outside his hands were cold and bloodless, and he stood in the parking lot for several minutes holding them out in the sun. He could tell the brains were still in his condo; his mind felt the same as when he'd entered the theater. They were still there, and Mitchell didn't want to drive home and see them.

He headed up the frontage road, the shopping strips growing larger and cleaner, until a proper mall materialized. Being around people might help, he thought. He strolled up and down the vaulted corridors, both floors, at an even pace, considering the stores, considering the young couples and old men, smelling the pretzels and Chinese food. He'd bought a suit in the last mall he'd visited, in Sacramento; he'd gone to a department store with Bet because an uncle of hers was getting married.

He sat down on a bench in front of a fountain, across from a straight-backed kindergarten-age boy with no parents to be seen. The mall was not helping. He knew when he got back to his condo he would see the brains. Mitchell couldn't see his way to a reasonable outlook on this fact. Sometimes in life, denial was the sound policy; sometimes there was nothing to do but continue on with blinders. But how reasonable was it to contradict your own senses, to start arguing with yourself about what was sitting right in front of you?

Mitchell drove across the Eastern basin as slowly as the other cars would allow, and didn't return home until past dark. He didn't stall, after that. He strode over and looked in the spare room and they were indeed still in there, unchanged, unconcerned. He came back to the living room and sat on the sofa. His hands were still chilled but his back was soaked. He'd been sweating all day, he gathered. He pulled off his shirt and draped it over the arm of the sofa. He thought there was a chance the brains would disappear at midnight, a one-day affliction. That was something to hope for. If they stayed past midnight, into tomorrow, then there was no telling how long they'd be in there. But then, midnight wasn't even real. Midnight was a contrivance. Mitchell was tired and he wasn't going to have any correct thoughts. He hadn't had any all day.

The next morning the brains were no less real. Mitchell forced himself to drink some water, then drove in the opposite direction he'd driven the day before, out into the empty wilderness. The sky was hazy, an adulterated white. He'd never come out here before. The road was straight as a high wire. Snatches from the wee hours of the previous night came to Mitchell, glimpses from his troubled sleep. He'd had a dream in which he told someone about the brains—he couldn't recall whom now, but knew it wouldn't have been Bet—and when he'd awakened and realized it was only a dream, that no one knew what was going on with him, he hadn't been sure how to feel. He'd known relief wasn't the appropriate emotion.

He came to a hairpin curve that made him slow way down, and it seemed as good a place as any to pull off. He turned off his engine, picked his way out through the spiny shrubs, and sat on a flat warm rock. He could hardly open his eyes against the glare. He was out here with the lizards now, the hardscrabble reptiles, all the way off the grid. Solitude was something he'd craved and romanticized most of his life, but maybe he was out of practice at it. He heard birds but he didn't know where they were.

The ideal resolution to what was happening was to let it run its course. People had put up with a lot worse. He could manage for a few days, even longer if necessary. The brains would leave when it was time for them to leave.

He spent the rest of the day in the condo. It was where he lived, he decided, and he wasn't going to be chased out of it. He kept drinking water, roaming from room to room to compare the differing views out the windows. He couldn't help but peek in on the brains every so often, taking a careful step into the spare room, into the close fleshy scent, moving his eyes from one identical brain to the next.

He scrubbed the shelves of his refrigerator. He wiped down the windowsills, disinfected the sink. Everything was clean already and he made it cleaner. He neatened the bedroom closet, then he sat in the living room and stared at his dead TV.

The next day Mitchell got called into an agency named ATN Staffing that needed to make a copy of his social security card and his driver's license. This was the world giving him something productive to do, and he was grateful. The agency was run by two gay men who were clean-shaven and wore polo shirts and boots. While Mitchell waited in the lobby, contemplating having a monetary value again assigned to the hours of his life, he heard the gay men responding to phone call after phone call from friends of theirs. It was Friday afternoon and apparently the men were throwing a party that evening. Their agency specialized in seasonal retail help, but even with the holidays approaching, they finally admitted, they had no work to offer. He was at the top of their list, but there wasn't a single thing right now.

Mitchell still had his same backpack from college, and he fished it out from under the bed and removed a stout blue book from it. This was a Russian novel Bet had bought him over a year ago in a bookstore in Kansas City, an ornate edition with silver embossing on the cover. In the course of a conversation he'd admitted he had never read this particular work, and Bet had treated this as a meaningful, terrible shortcoming, a situation to be swiftly rectified. She'd found a bookstore on her phone and dragged Mitchell away from his lunch.

Mitchell had read a dozen of these fat tomes when he was young, but for the last decade they had seemed like too much to deal with. He knew what he would find in the book. Each character would adhere to a different philosophy of life; there would be vodka and epaulettes and peasants. But the story would get him out of his own mind, which had to be good right now.

Mitchell got on the couch and read the biographical information about the author. There was a timeline, noting when this author had met other authors, and in what cities the meetings had taken place. The introduction, written by a scholar whose name Mitchell vaguely recognized, was forty pages long. He figured he'd get through that today. After a few minutes he began reading aloud, preferring the way his voice sounded in the air to how it sounded in his head. The scholar admired the author's vision, but was wryly skeptical of any declarations the man made about his own work.

When Mitchell reached a stopping point in the introduction, he set the book on the floor, using a hair ribbon Bet had left in the bathroom as a bookmark. He drank a glass of water and then went over to the spare room. These things were his doing, his creation. He'd never believed in the supernatural, and he still didn't. He wasn't going to change his beliefs because it might be convenient. *He'd* put these things in here. Their scent had come from him. The way they hovered slightly above the floor and moved incrementally, never colliding, was his doing. He crouched down and put his eye close to one of them, thinking he might be able to see the workings within its translucent flesh, but he could see nothing. It was like trying to peer to the bottom of a muddy pond. The brains weren't something to solve. Trying to figure them out would only make things worse. He went back out to the couch and read a little more of the introduction. There were things the author had claimed to love, but didn't. Things he'd claimed to hate that he couldn't have hated. Mitchell let the book slip back to the floor and fell asleep, hoping for uninvolved dreams.

He didn't know how long he'd been napping when a sharp knock at his front door awoke him. He eased himself upright and rubbed his eyes clear. One of his arms was half asleep. He got to his feet and padded quietly to the front of the condo. What he could see through the smudgy peephole was a tall figure in uniform, cradling something. Mitchell looked back toward the spare room. He dragged a breath in through his nostrils and pulled the door open enough to stick his head out. It was a delivery guy holding a box. The delivery guy said Bet's name and held out a clipboard and a pen and then Mitchell was alone again and now *he* was holding the box. The box had once been white, but had been battered in a way that didn't seem like ordinary shipping wear and tear. The return address was worn off. VA, Mitchell could make out.

Nothing had come to the condo since he'd been there. No one had even knocked on the door. The box wasn't light or heavy, and when he shook it there was a scratchy, papery sound. Mitchell thought of a pound of feathers and a pound of rocks—how they weighed the same amount. He set the box down gingerly and stepped back outside. The delivery guy was gone. It was the middle of the afternoon, not a person to be seen anywhere in the condo complex. A car was in a driveway here and there. A deflated basketball sat in a yard across the street. The air smelled of concrete and seeds. Mitchell had never paid attention, but he saw now that there was a flowerbed along his front wall, with a row of low, pale shrubs in it.

A mail truck rounded the corner and advanced up the street. Mitchell watched as it got closer, the little doors opening and closing, the bundles being deposited. Mitchell didn't get mail. He didn't know many people anymore; the only person who had this address was Bet. He'd walked down and looked in the mailbox once, and there hadn't even been anything to throw away.

There were three boxes banked together there, at the bottom of the walk, and Mitchell watched as the mailman slipped something into the first, then the second, and then, to his surprise, into Mitchell's. The white flash of a letter. The mailman noticed him and gave a quick friendly wave, then motored on.

Mitchell stalled a moment, letting the mailman get out of sight, then strode down and yanked the letter from the box. It was from Bet. As it had to be. It didn't have a return address but the postmark said Tucson. Mitchell had never been to Tucson. The envelope was crisp and Bet's hand-writing on it betrayed nothing.

Mitchell took the envelope inside and sat down on the couch with it. He brought it to his face and inhaled, but it didn't smell like anything other than an envelope. He looked at the back, where it was sealed tight. After a while he understood that he was not going to open it, not yet. Whatever it was, he wasn't ready now. He was rattled and he could admit that.

So now he had something *to* Bet and something *from* Bet. He went toward the spare room, walking softly but not being sneaky, and eased the door open. The brains and now the package and the letter—his privacy felt invaded from within and without, like things were happening to him that were none of his business. He didn't know what any of it meant, didn't know what he was being told.

Over the next couple days, Mitchell started leaving the door to the spare room wide open, but the brains made no move to wander. He read sections of the Russian novel aloud, but they did not acknowledge his voice. At times he stood at the threshold of the spare room and observed them, like a rich man watching his exotic pets. There was absolutely no way to tell them apart. He wondered if the brains all knew the same things or if their knowledge was complementary. He wondered whether they were accruing new information or working with what they had.

One evening, Mitchell skipped dinner. He sat in the folding chair and as night fell, the light behind the blinds blooming with sunset and then hushing to blue, he confided in the brains. He was talking to himself, he knew, but in a way he never did when he was truly alone. He spoke of his travels. He told the brains how Bet had always rented their places sight-unseen because she liked to be surprised, liked to adapt. In Colorado they'd lived in what amounted to a shantytown, their neighbors all Mexican illegals. In Oregon they'd enjoyed a luxurious studio overlooking a quiet cove. In Florida they'd dwelled in the villa of a deceased old woman, hastily rented out by her children, the place packed to the gills with figurines and discount-brand canned goods and crowding fake trees. They'd driven through Kansas, the sunflowers leaning to face them. In California they'd rolled around in a vineyard. Mitchell could still see the clusters of heavy late-harvest fruit outlined against the sun, barely hanging on.

Mitchell told the brains about the letter he still had not opened, and the package that had just preceded it. He had left the letter unopened on his kitchen table, sitting there at a casual, haphazard angle, and now he glanced at it each time he passed. The box he had put in the corner.

Bet might've had a change of heart, Mitchell told the brains. Bet could've begun to miss old Mitch. She could be moving again and could want him to rejoin her. She could be heading on to Flagstaff and wanting someone to pal around with for ski season. Maybe she was regretting the way she'd left, acting like it was so obvious she and Mitchell were bad for each other, were holding each other back, like if he didn't recognize that there was something wrong with him. Throwing all her things back into her fancy luggage after two days, but of course not roughly enough that anything might break—her ivory ink pens and handmade bracelets and a pair of engraved teacups someone had given her as a gift. Everyone bickered, Mitchell had told her. Bickering didn't mean anything. Bet had put Mitchell in the position of begging her to stay, and maybe now she saw how low that had been, how degrading to them both. Mitchell had made the mistake of being honest. He and Bet had agreed, back in the early days, never to start saying they loved each other. As soon as you started saying that, it was a matter of time before you were forced to say it, before you were saying it without meaning it, before you resented saying it. They'd both seen what happened when you went down the love road. Mitchell had followed the agreement all those years, but in the heat of Bet saying she needed a change he'd lost track of himself. When he'd uttered the forbidden phrase, Bet had seemed frightened. She'd packed up the rest of her things as hastily as she could and had driven off. She'd abandoned him, Mitchell proclaimed into the fusty air of the spare room. She'd abandoned the only person in the world who truly cared about her, but maybe now she'd come to her senses. Maybe that was what the letter was about.

*   *   *

Nestor Employment called. This was an outfit in the tangled middle of Albuquerque where Mitchell had filled out a cursory application and left it with a man who had acted like Mitchell was interrupting his day by looking for work, like Mitchell's lack of a job was acutely inconvenient for him. The man was calling because Nestor was switching to an all-electronic system. He was entering Mitchell's information and couldn't read his handwriting. For a moment, Mitchell could not think of his address. When he finally came up with it, the man said, "You sure about that?" This guy thought he was the greatest thing ever because he had a stupid little job to go to. Mitchell wanted to tell him that anyone could do his job, that anyone who walked into that office could switch sides of the desk with him and no one would notice. Mitchell wanted to tell the man that he had no skills and no knowledge and that the universe had simply granted him the pity he was worthy of.

"I commend you on your temporary avoidance of failure," Mitchell said into the phone. "Foul luck is afoot in many quarters, and you seem to be evading it."

Mitchell caught himself considering the possibility that the brains were not his invention. He knew it couldn't be so, but if the brains were not products of his imagination, that would mean they'd chosen him. That he'd been deemed suitable. He was thinking about this predicament from all angles, which was inevitable and probably healthy. He caught himself in the thought that he would be the ideal person to be chosen, because for better or worse he was more decent, more possessed of discretion, more open of mind than anyone else he'd ever met. It didn't mean anything, but it was a fact: if there were fragile, unnatural beings looking for harbor, Mitchell would be the safest choice, the best choice. Mitchell didn't want to have thoughts like these, but when they came he couldn't chase them away. Beer didn't help. The Russian novel certainly didn't help. He knew the brains weren't real. He knew that.

He was watching a desert jay tinkering around industriously outside the window, and when the bird flitted away Mitchell walked across the living room and down the short hallway. He closed the spare room door, giving the brains the illusion of privacy, and then got down flat on his belly in the hall and spied through the little space underneath, his eye to the floor. He wanted to catch the brains doing something other than what they always did, but of course he discovered nothing. He wanted to catch them piling onto one another affectionately or huddling under the window and aspiring to the sky.

Mitchell went into Anchor Workforce Solutions and hung up his coat and a friendly woman in a blouse began giving him instructions. Her desk was as big as a barge. She told him all the skills he was going to be asked to exhibit and then pointed to a room where he could be by himself.

First Mitchell had to type. He had to read paragraphs out of a booklet and punch them into the computer as quickly as he could. He did this a minute at a time, no idea if he was typing fast, no idea if he was supposed to go back and correct his mistakes. He had to read a series of eighty statements and next to each had to mark either STRONGLY AGREE, AGREE, DISAGREE, or STRONGLY DISAGREE. The questions were concerned with work ethic and being punctual, and most were meant to be strongly agreed or strongly disagreed with. There was a skills checklist, full of tasks Mitchell had never had occasion to perform but was sure he could if someone showed him how. There were math problems. There was a stack of policy statements Mitchell had to sign, about not doing drugs or harassing people.

By the time Mitchell was finished with all this, his shirt was sopping with sweat. He went in the bathroom and took a piss. He washed his hands and face, then dried off with the paper towels. Breathing deliberately, he fixed his gaze upon himself. He'd always thought he was building up character with all this temp work, with all this scrambling around for low-rung gigs, but where was all that character now? If he had it, where was it?

*   *   *

When he got home, Mitchell slid the beat-up box that had come for Bet onto the kitchen table, slit the tape, and began pulling everything out— papers and notebooks, folded letters and clipped documents. He set the empty box aside and began putting like with like, and then organizing chronologically. While he was poring over the contents of the box it became evening. They were the papers of a guy named Tom Spelher—only a fraction of his papers, it seemed. Vast stretches of time were missing in his correspondence. Contracts were unsigned, notebooks unrelated.

Bet had mentioned this guy. She had talked about writing his biography. The box hadn't been sent by a university or an auction house, but instead, Mitchell gathered, by Tom Spelher's sister. Spelher was dead now. There were letters of recommendation in the box for various grants Spelher had applied for and never gotten.

Mitchell went out to a colorless wash of earth a couple hundred yards behind his building, gathered a bunch of spiny dead shrubs, and started them on fire. He surrounded the fire with a circle of rocks. He arranged withered cactus paddles in the flames, a heavy cottonwood branch. He jogged back to his building and grabbed a lawn chair that had been in the condo when he and Bet had moved in, and he grabbed the beat-up box and shoved all of Tom Spelher's property back into it. He went out and sat in the lawn chair and burned the papers one by one. Tom Spelher, he decided, would remain a dignified unknown. Mitchell would do Tom Spelher that favor. He stood and looked around occasionally, but no one was going to say anything to him about his fire. Nobody was watching him except the stars.

Mitchell was nowhere near the leg of the Russian novel where people would begin getting what they deserved. He could only read about five pages at a time before he lost concentration. He was never going to finish the thing, he saw. It would be like his TV—another purposeless item to carry around for the rest of his life.

Sometimes Mitchell thought it would help him to break something but there was nothing in the condo to break, no china or anything. There was nothing in the condo but basic furniture and the TV and twice he picked the TV up to hurl it against the floorboards but was able to stop himself.

He ate a couple handfuls of stale granola and swept his kitchen and then shut the door to the spare room and sat in the living room with his phone in his hand. His tongue tasted like cardboard and his eyes were watery. He dialed the number of the woman who ran the complex, an almost-old lady with red hair named Ruby, and when she didn't answer he left a calm, clear message saying he wanted to switch condos as soon as possible. He said at her nearest convenience he wanted her to get him into another place. He didn't like the sun in the morning and preferred a west-facing unit, a one-bedroom if she had it.

Mitchell hung up and rested his chin on his fists. It would take him half an hour to fully move out of this condo. Half an hour tops and there wouldn't be a trace of him. He wanted a fresh start. Different walls. Something else out the window. There was nothing wrong with New Mexico. He just needed to hit the reset button. He reclined back on the couch, letting his shoulders go slack, and tried to trust the small spring of calm that was running through him.

When the call came back, just ten minutes later, Mitchell couldn't coerce himself to answer it. He was full of panic, staring at the thin black phone in his palm. He saw RUBY REYNOLDS on the screen and listened to each incurious ring until there wasn't a ring, until one of the silences in between drew out and no ring came. He went and set the phone on top of the TV, happy to get it out of his hand. This wasn't good, that he hadn't answered the phone. It was unwise, the wrong fork in the path. He could tell himself he didn't want to run away from his problems, but that wasn't true. He had no qualms about running from problems. Somewhere inside him he wanted to see how this was going to turn out. He was curious about the brains, about what end they might come to. If he had brought them into existence, he wanted to see how he was going to get rid of them. If he hadn't brought them into existence, which was unlikely but couldn't be totally dismissed, then he wanted to know their purpose, wanted to wait until he could learn something important about them. If he fled them, he'd have to wonder forever. He'd never be in his right mind again.

Ruby called back every few hours for the next couple days, forcing him to turn off his ringer, but he could still hear the phone vibrating against the kitchen counter or the floor or wherever he'd left it.

He never picked up the letter but he shifted it here and there into different positions on the high round table in the kitchen. The envelope was no longer flat, from getting baked by the morning sun over and over. It looked brittle, wizened.

Mitchell brought home another meatball sub. He slid Bet's letter out of the way and sat at his kitchen table and got down as much of the sandwich as he could, which wasn't a lot. He folded the whole mess up in its wrapping and, rising off the stool, caught sight of something over on the living room floor that shouldn't have been there, on the other side of the couch, looking at a glance like a bunch of loose slippers or something. Mitchell walked over there and stopped short before the spectacle. He felt himself nodding in appraisal. It was the brains. All seven of them. He was clutching the balled-up sub to his chest, the even ticking of the clock behind him somewhere. The brains, out of the spare room, arranged in a soft-pointed diamond, all of them still spaced equidistantly. This was a migration. It had taken them an hour to get this far. Maybe more. Several hours. Here they were, on the move, each one following the subdued hum of the others.

Mitchell returned to the kitchen and stuffed the sub in the trash can, then went around and closed all the blinds, twisting the clear plastic staffs. He washed his hands at the sink, came back to the living room and flipped the overhead light off. He'd begun to lose faith, but now something was happening. Mitchell was wearing a T-shirt with long sleeves and he tugged the sleeves up to his elbows. His hands were clammy, like that first day.

His mind's eye was so crowded it was blank. The brains looked the same as ever. There was no such thing as effort for them. They were all oriented in the same direction, advancing toward the front of the condo, aimed, in fact, straight at the front door. That had to be where they were going; there was nothing else over there but the door. They were leaving. Whatever they'd been doing here, they were finished. Dusk was taking hold outside. They would leave overnight—judging by the distance they still had to cross, sometime in the wee hours. Mitchell didn't know what he should think of this. He felt tired in his body but alert in his mind. He could smell the brains now. Their peanut musk was drowning out the odor of the meat-ball sub. Relieved, obviously. That's how he should feel and he did feel it. This problem of his was finally working itself out. He'd indeed handled it correctly. He'd kept it to himself and had kept his mind intact and now this trouble was taking its leave of him. He'd endured it. Mitchell sat on the arm of the couch and watched the brains for a few minutes. Of course, they moved too slowly for him to perceive it. That had always been the way. You had to leave them alone and come back later, like they said about getting water to boil.

He stood up and paced across the living room in a composed manner, ready to take some inventory, feeling tired in a welcome physical way rather than just feeling sick of himself, feeling weary in his legs but excited about the future. He went into his bedroom and raised the window, shimmying it around to get it unstuck. The temperature was dropping outside. Mitchell stuck his head out and the night sky looked familiar. He had been caught in a pernicious orbit but it was about to break apart. His eyes were dry and keen. He could see the puppetlike silhouettes of the desert birds perched on the cacti, could see their little beaks snapping open when they called. He could see the shadowy features of every rough hill, all the way to the flats where he'd conducted his fire.

Mitchell looked at his bed, made up with its sharp-cornered olive sheets as it had been since the day Bet left. He hadn't slept in it since she'd gone. He doubted he was going to sleep tonight, but if he did it was going to be here, in a bed like a normal person, on this perfectly good queen mattress.

Mitchell went over to the closet and slid the doors all the way open. Besides the sneakers he was wearing, he had two pairs of shoes—boots and dress shoes. He took the sneakers off and lined them up smartly with the other pairs on the closet floor. He organized the clothes he had on hangers, the two coats together, the handful of dress shirts together, a light pair of pants and a dark pair. Next he opened the top drawer of his dresser—a few balled-up pairs of socks, nail clippers, a receipt from a vegan coffee shop he and Bet had stopped at in Santa Fe, a travel-size bottle of leather conditioner. He left the socks where they were, and everything else he took out and set on top of the dresser. Mitchell looked forward to facing his life again. He knew he could do it; he could participate. He was going to iron his shirts and shine his dress shoes. He was going to pick out a day and finish that damn Russian novel in one go. He thought of the letter, still sitting out there on the kitchen table, almost smirking. He didn't care anymore what was in the letter. Mitchell felt now that he could throw the letter out, another bit of tidying on tomorrow's agenda. He didn't need to imagine good news in it anymore. No good news could come from Bet. She thought it was one-sided, that Mitchell needed her and she didn't need him, but she'd find out sooner or later that she wasn't going to find anyone better than Mitchell. And then it would be too late. Mitchell was going to move on with his life and she was going to keep avoiding hers, and by the time she saw the error of her ways it would be too late. Way too late.

Mitchell stepped lightly back into the main area of the condo. He circled around behind the brains, checking their position in relation to the couch, and they had definitely moved a little more toward the door. A couple inches, at least. Their formation had lost its shape, now more an oval than a diamond. It was happening, just as he'd thought. They were leaving. It was night now, the first act of the darkness. He only had to be patient.

Mitchell padded back to the bedroom. He kept his money under the bed, paper-clipped, and now he got it out and counted it. He counted it again, and a third time. It would be enough for another month. He was going to double his efforts to find a job. Triple them. If they wanted him to stack boxes and sweep floors, he'd be grateful to do it. If they wanted him to clean bathrooms, no problem. He was going to catch a break and find employment, and he was going to cook balanced dinners and exercise. Maybe he would ask a woman out on a date, a woman as different from Bet as possible, a woman who stayed in one place and wasn't afraid of being attached to someone—afraid at her own expense. He could get a job and a girlfriend and a dog from the pound. He could keep a hardy little cactus on his table. This was the United States. If you wanted to get with the program, they had to let you. Maybe Mitchell wasn't all that old. He could turn the spare room into a study. There was no telling what he could accomplish with all this peace and quiet. He would get a haircut, get his long-suffering little car washed, buy a comfortable pastel-colored patio chair for his front steps.

He waited another twenty minutes, then couldn't help checking on the brains again. They were still drifting in the right direction, however slowly. A couple more inches, getting past the couch now. He didn't want to hound them, didn't want to drive himself crazy checking on them, but he felt nowhere near sleepy. He went over to the front door and disengaged the deadbolt. He opened the door about halfway, wondering if a gust of wind was going to blow it closed. He needed to prop it open. He went and grabbed the Russian novel off the floor near the TV and rested it against the foot of the door. The chilly air was washing in slowly from outside, smelling as clean as glass, the darkness out there enormous and fair.

Mitchell awoke on the couch, staring at the ceiling, the silvery dawn everywhere in the high corners of the condo. He felt rushed, startled to have fallen asleep, and he stayed put until his pulse calmed. His throat was dry and his neck cramped, but he felt great. This was the first morning of whatever came next. He felt different, confident. He was better, he could tell. He got himself to a sitting position and then rose to his feet and wheeled around to face the front door. It was still open. The novel was sitting at a different angle than he'd left it, the door not even touching it, thrown all the way open against the outside wall. He walked through the doorway and out onto the steps and stood with a hand on his hip, looking up and down the road that wound through the complex. Nothing was amiss. The air was brisk. Cars were in driveways, newspapers lying here and there. The world could not have been in better order, could not have been more credible.

Mitchell picked up the big novel and took it back inside with him. He went into the kitchen and drank a glass of water. Bet's letter. He would throw it away later. He wanted to savor that moment, maybe make a little ceremony out of it. He knew what he would do, after he opened the spare room door wide and opened the window in there so it could air out. He was going to get in his car and zip over to Thewlis and buy a sleeve of bagels and some cream cheese and a jug of orange juice. And he was going to pick up a newspaper, not one of these outpost rags but the paper from Albuquerque. He was going to sit on the front steps and rattle the pages and find out what was going on in the world. He would find out what fun was to be had over in the city this week—bands playing, special exhibits at museums. All the things he'd gotten used to doing with Bet but that would probably be more fun without her. He would make a shopping list and pick up a cheap grill. He had a steamy shower ahead of him. Maybe he'd jog. Maybe he'd take a nap in the afternoon and then attend a happy hour downtown somewhere.

Mitchell strode down the hall toward the spare room, a man rightfully reclaiming a portion of his home. He would hang a couple pictures in this hallway, and he'd get mats for the bathroom and for in front of the kitchen sink. He filled his lungs easily and pushed the door all the way open and stood inside the moment, his body blocking the light from the hall. He was conscious of standing in the direct center of everything he knew, a divide of some sort.

First the smell hit him, the woody stench of protein. The hum was in his ears, but the world was full of such sounds—water in pipes, electricity in wires, the tunneling of insects. Mitchell could keep himself from looking directly down for only so long and when he did he saw them. The moment assumed its shape. The brains were without luster and stationary and very much alive, like always. Mitchell heard himself snort. He felt his throat tighten. He squeezed the doorknob until his forearm began to quiver and pain shot through his wrist. It felt like his soul was lost out at the bottom of a canyon somewhere, like anything could be happening to it. He knew by now he could expect no explanation. It wasn't simple blood that was coursing through his veins, and he thought he might not be able to stop himself from putting on his work boots and stomping the brains into a fucking puddle. He stood stiff, not moving a muscle, his fingernails cutting into his palms.

Mitchell staggered to the kitchen. He ripped open Bet's letter and yanked out what was inside. There were two items, neither, in fact, a letter. One was a photograph and one was an invoice Bet had printed up that showed Mitchell owed her half the first month's rent and security deposit she'd paid on the condo. Mitchell laughed aloud. It wasn't from a lawyer, wasn't anything official. She knew he'd never pay her; she wanted to make him feel small, wanted to have the last word. The photograph was a picture Bet had taken of Mitchell way back when they'd first met, back in Chattanooga that first weekend. Mitchell was hanging off the balcony of a downtown bistro, trying to pluck a blossom off a pear tree. The entire time they'd been together, Bet had used it for a bookmark. His hair was thick in the picture. His back was straight. He was trying his best to win an enchanting woman but he knew it was okay if he didn't. He had the look, in the photo, of a person in possession of a reserve of charm, a person who believed that if he was patient and alert he would get everything he needed.

Mitchell was called into another temp agency and an old lady who should've been retired told him there might be a position for him at a plant that processed raw paper into lunch bags. She couldn't guarantee anything. The old lady had to run his background check and he had to sign some forms.

"Where are you from originally?" she asked him.

"Tennessee," he said.

"Why don't you have an accent? I can tell people by their accents."

"Do I not have one?"

She shook her head. "What part of Tennessee exactly?"

"Chattanooga."

"You definitely ought to have an accent."

"I used to," Mitchell said. "I remember it. When I first moved away everybody said I had a drawl."

The lady looked at him warily. "That's bad news, losing your accent. That's an important part of a person."

Mitchell had been up most of the previous night. Keeping his wits about him and clinging to his generous spirit had not been the correct program, he'd decided—that much had been proven. Instead, under cover of darkness, stomach growling and eyes red, he'd carried six of the brains, stacked three on top of three in a plastic wash basin, off the rear of the complex's property, past the spot where he'd burned Tom Spelher's papers, and out to a modest, ragged ravine with a dusty arroyo at the bottom of it. He'd tossed the brains one by one into the dark drop, and heard the dismal, moist-sounding thud each made when it found the rocks. Then he'd thrown down the basin too.

"But I wouldn't trade the traveling I've done," Mitchell told the lady. His voice sounded poor and forceless, so he cleared his throat. "There's a cost, but you also learn about yourself. I wouldn't trade all the one-of-a-kind experiences for anything. I can't imagine what I'd... where I'd be without them."

The lady nodded. She'd begun flicking through a sheaf of forms.

One brain Mitchell had kept inside. It was still in the spare room, for now. He could participate in this tribulation, could have a say. He could put the thing in the freezer or cook it in a pot. He could lob it down into the ravine with its compatriots, to be feasted on by buzzards. He could just leave it be, his prisoner. The brain had to wait now, like he'd had to wait.

The light filling the windows of the temp agency was harsh. It glinted off a mug full of metallic pens on the old lady's desk. Mitchell still hadn't eaten. He felt mostly calm. He tried to sit up straight in his chair, tried to look eager and capable. He smiled at the lady, wondering what she thought of him, wondering what her hopes were for the days to come.

SKYBOUND

SAN JOAQUIN

He had sped westward in an access of instinct, fleeing to the far edge of the country and then backtracking a hundred miles. He was forty-five and had enough money to last him a few decades if he lived frugally. He could do that. He could live frugally. He was leaving a few friends behind, but he had often dreaded talking to them as their lives grew less manageable and more joyous. There was a sandwich place he'd miss on weekdays. A radio station he missed in the evenings that played all types of music, punk rock and Brahms. And an uncle he would begin missing at some point. He did not own a gun, was no more a criminal than most in his profession. It was a profession of using advantage, which he'd done to the last. He felt no rush of pride at beating the underworld bureaucracy and did not think of himself as cool. He was cool in that he didn't need other people the way most did, but he was uncool in that he felt able to put himself on a categorized budget and adhere to it for years to come. He chose for himself a dusty town which was a great shopping mall surrounded by farms.

After a week he attended a prayer group founded by a couple who'd won the lottery and then blown all the money. The prayer meetings were held in a building the couple had been unable to sell off, a farmhouse on a busy street. They'd adorned the inside of the place with paired photographs— pictures of places in different parts of the world that looked exactly alike. A sprawling mini-storage facility in front of a retention pond, low chain-link fencing snaking everywhere: India and Florida.

He attended a Catholic church for a time, returning to his heritage, and as before it didn't feel that anything was taking place at the masses that wanted his presence. He tried a Buddhist temple, and nearly tried a synagogue.

He lived across the street from an ignored tourist attraction, an estate once owned by a poet/statesman/farmer. He got the idea that this man was known more for the company he'd kept than for his deeds, that this man was adept at leisure in a way the rich no longer were.

He missed weather, which was nothing now but a breeze and a brush of clouds. There was no guarantee of winter. He had a fireplace and split wood and many copies of the local newspaper, and for all he knew they might just sit there and sit there.

He was wealthy, in the important way. He drove a seven-year-old Honda and subsisted on second-rate sandwiches, but he never again had to work. He had slipped from the machine, he who had oiled and exercised its sharp little parts since before he could drive a car. He who had of course come to depend on the machine.

The sky was splendid out here but it went on and on dumbly. He had succumbed to prayer as the handiest crutch. This is what he'd wanted—this escape. He still wanted it, but in the hollowing way you wanted something once you had it.

The members of the prayer group sat with exemplary posture around a big black table that seemed a few inches too high, and this made them seem like businesspeople at a meeting, like people from his old life, except that they were hammering out spiritual details instead of contract points. There were Bibles lying about in many translations. He could not discuss his situation, so when it was his turn to address the higher power he prayed in a general way for everyone he used to know, changing their names. He prayed for the men he'd ripped off, though they didn't need it.

II

THE MIGRATION

Men had taken back up the time-honored practice of stepping out for smokes and never returning home, and it seemed all these men were hiding in Oklahoma. Deadbeats from the Mississippi Delta, the Piedmont, even the bustling sarcastic northeastern cities, either resting here or losing heart for the road. And some from the West, unraveling the sorry destinies they'd manifested, punishing themselves, wanting a place whose recommendation was its very lack of recommenders. These men had wanton meanness to vent and many were out of cash. They had, in the only matter that matters, failed. The latest trouble was someone had stolen an ancient piano from Second Baptist—or not just some*one*, the thieved item weighing as much as a prize steer. The empty space in the congregation hall where the instrument used to sit now looked like a corner of some ghost town saloon, and the Sheriff couldn't push it to the side of his mind. He couldn't remember names lately, couldn't pick up melodies. The removal of the piano was a brazen and planned act, bordering on a pointed affront to his office. Before all the boarding houses had filled the Sheriff had always had a suspect mated to any crime, and then he could attempt to prove the suspect innocent and often he was successful and often happily so. He didn't know any of these new drifters from the Sultan of Brunei. He didn't know what they would or wouldn't conceive of in the name of fun, didn't know what profit-seeking enterprise they could or couldn't carry out.

The Sheriff had a pair of deputies, junior and senior, though the titles didn't indicate differing prowess or promotion due to merit. Gil had been in the job a year longer was all. Gil's daily talent was for brewing perfect coffee and Tommy was a former track star. They wrote tickets, maintained order weekend nights. Trivia junkies, the both of them. The Sheriff gave them a hard time, but they were decent deputies, loyal and even-handed. They could both grapple tolerably well. The Sheriff and his crew hadn't solved a consequential case in months, so at the end of June, to shake his outfit by the collar, he snatched the jar of cash off the shelf above the coffee pot and told them there'd be no dinner outing this month. This was the money that built up from swearing, from the meager wagers the deputies were always making, from the floors of their cruisers. The money wasn't going to a restaurant this month, the Sheriff told his men, but to old Teaford, the mystic who lived up in the driest corner of the county. Gil managed to betray no reaction at all and Tommy smirked. "We been running up the middle long enough," the Sheriff said. "It's time for a flea-flicker." The Sheriff was pulling a stunt, but in truth he had always believed in curses and ghosts and the like. He believed certain ranges lost, certain families luckless, certain women septic of soul from birth. They would ask Teaford about the piano. That was the play the Sheriff was calling.

Teaford had an austere stucco ranch house pinned down to the worst corner of the worst rangeland in the area. On one side of his house there was a struggling watermelon patch and on the other a lone oak tree. He emerged before they'd made it to the front door and led them around to a square of concrete at the back of the house that served as a patio. Teaford had a long braid resting on his chest and he clung to it with two hands like someone clinging to a rope. He was wiry of limb, of course, and his fingernails were longer than they ought to be. The Sheriff gave the pertinent information about the case and handed him the money that had been in the jar, upward of sixty dollars, and then Teaford donned a headband and slipped a vest and some gloves out of an ornately decorated leather sack. He provided paper and pencils and asked the Sheriff and his deputies to write down their full names and whether they were born during the day or the darkness and also the birthplace of their mothers. Teaford explained that his desperate-looking land was rich in its way—it contained a Breach, and this Breach provided the vision and he himself was a mere vessel. The Sheriff and his men already knew this part. There was a deep chasm out on the property somewhere and Teaford was going to lower himself into it—over fifty feet, he told them.

They walked over a few shallow yellow hills and along a dragged-down fence, and suddenly there it was: a deep quiet flue straight down into the prairie. It was blue inside and then black. It didn't look like the work of nature nor of man. Teaford had rigged a simple harness inside, something like people used for rock climbing, and he strapped himself into it and descended with little ceremony out of sight. He had uncapped the pipe he used for talking to people up on the surface and the Sheriff and his guys went and stood around it.

"What do you reckon he had us write that stuff down for?" Tommy said. He was leaning away from the pipe, whispering.

The truth was, the Sheriff hadn't appreciated that part, hadn't liked turning over personal details, but this excursion was his idea so he'd gone ahead and done what was asked. He'd put down correct information, and that now seemed an odd choice. "I expect we made his holiday card list," he whispered.

A wind kicked up and whistled in the pipe. The Sheriff tested the ground with his boot and it wasn't as hard as he'd expected. The sky was vacant and still. After a few minutes they heard noise coming from the pipe, Teaford jostling around in his harness. Then they heard him hemming and hawing, mulling something over, and then it was quiet again. Gil got out his cigarettes and the Sheriff shook his head, motioning for the deputy to put them away. But the Sheriff was feeling impatient himself. He felt a pang of regret about giving Teaford the dinner money. He had hoped to make a point, but the point already seemed labored, standing as they were in the middle of a remote field waiting for clues from a crazy person down in a well.

"Do you know who used to play it? The piano player at the church— was it a man or woman, young or old, or what?" Teaford's voice, resonating up through the metal pipe, was thinner and less grave than it had been up above ground, like he'd fallen out of character.

The Sheriff lowered his head toward the pipe and said usually it was the Parmalee gal. She was early twenties, a student at the junior college.

There was another silence, and the Sheriff wasn't sure whether he was rooting for or against Teaford.

Tommy yawned and Gil took a step away from the pipe and coughed, and then Teaford was speaking again. He told them the piano was in fine shape, though out of tune after its bumpy late-night ride, and that it was being housed in a red barn that was nearby an institution of learning.

The Sheriff tipped his head upward, a gesture of consideration. Off the top of his head, he could think of two such barns. Three, really. He looked back toward Teaford's house, the direction they'd walked from. The watermelon patch, even from this distance, was a sorry sight, a charred tangle. But the oak tree on the other side was immense and lording and seemed somehow disappointed with everything in its view.

III

THE CUSTOMS

Joyce had taken up smoking again. As a girl she'd smoked imported cigarettes that came in lavish tins, but now she smoked light American brands like everyone else. She was able to go to a street fair themed on berries and pick out a red ashtray shaped like an octagon, on which was printed the message: OH, GO AHEAD. She got to buy a lighter too. The lighter had a dolphin on it, and a sun of faded orange.

Outside a liquor store a kid stopped Joyce and handed her twenty dollars, wanting Joyce to bring him out some beer. The kid had two bony, bad-haired girls waiting in his car. They were in bikini tops. They were watching the kid open-mindedly, giving him every chance. Across the street was a driving range. People in thin sweaters kept smacking balls and losing sight of them.

Joyce asked the kid why he'd chosen her and he said he'd been waiting ten minutes and no one young had gone into the store. Not that she was old. He said there was one guy who was fairly young but he didn't look right.

"Why not?" Joyce asked.

"Just the attitude, I guess," the kid said. "He seemed… really sure about the day he was having."

Joyce shouldn't have known what he meant, but she did. She nodded toward the girls in the car. "Where are you going to take them?" she asked.

The kid was wearing a dress shirt, sleeves buttoned at the wrists. He took a moment deciding what to do with Joyce's question, realizing he had to answer whatever she asked if he wanted his beer.

"Way out in the woods," he admitted. "This place my dad took me fishing once."

"I hope it's still the way you remember it."

"Nobody would've built on it or anything," the kid said. "It'll be the same. It's just a scummy little pond."

"Well, maybe you'll make some new memories on it."

"Thanks," the kid said. He might've been blushing.

"My father never took me fishing. He only took me to rodeos."

The kid glanced inside the liquor store. "My dad is dead. He's been dead for years. I guess your dad's probably dead too."

"What did your dad die of?" Joyce asked.

"Liver troubles. Among other things."

"You should tell the girls he died last week. Or do they know you?"

"No, they don't know me. They don't know a damn thing about me. I live in Colorado now. I'm just back for the week."

Joyce smiled at the girls in the car. She had the kid's crisp bill folded and pinched between her thumb and forefinger. The multitude of low pings from across the street was mustering into some kind of crescendo.

The name of the lot was Coos Auto Brokers and the motto was Good Cars, Good People. The cab dropped her off under a huge concrete overhang, and she pushed inside through the glass doors. On the counter in the lobby sat a toaster-size television playing a British movie. After a minute, Joyce's salesman, Garrett, took her outside. Joyce had shared a car with her daughter for years, neither of them needing to drive very often. She'd gotten rid of that car, a modest Japanese errand-runner, but hadn't bought another one. She hadn't felt up to visiting a car lot until today.

Garrett looked like a Navy kid home for a holiday—crew cut, cloth tie. He pressed a button on the keychain then guided open the driver door of a Saab station wagon. The cars passing on the road were very close, mostly pickups.

Joyce said she wanted the car. She said she wasn't in the mood to do a test drive. Garrett looked into Joyce's eyes. He told her that test-driving the car wouldn't prove anything, anyway. He gave her his word that it ran as smooth as whatever simile she liked, that it handled as tight as whatever simile she liked, that the extra space in the back was as handy as any simile she liked. On the downside, the stereo was tricky. Also, the nearest Saab mechanic was up the coast in Florence.

In Garrett's wood-paneled closet of an office, Joyce filled out the paperwork. Garrett lit a cigarette and put his feet up on his flimsy desk. He had hung tiny stuffed fish on the walls, fish that looked like bait.

Garrett put his cigarette out; the room was too small. "Do you want to go see those carnivorous flowers with me? I'll tell them about this sale and they'll give me the afternoon off."

Joyce dialed her daughter's number and the recorder picked up. She listened to her daughter's voice, then she called back and listened to it again.

Her daughter had had about a hundred friends. She'd been on the verge of adopting a Korean child, an ordeal she'd reached the final stages of after three years of hustle. She'd been a steady, strong person, not feisty and impulsive like Joyce. Joyce had gotten pregnant young and had raised her daughter with everything she had, persistently, at times by example.

What Joyce remembered of her daughter's funeral was the wind. It had been born over some desert, worlds away, and had gotten lost—a sharp-gusting and dry wind that had left Joyce's coat crisp and wrinkled, her skin nipped. The sun had been out. People squinted and held down their dresses. Joyce hadn't known half the mourners. They'd been a crush of intelligent, light-colored eyes. They'd dressed so well, had removed their jewelry and done what they could to conceal their tattoos. It felt like they'd come from another country but knew the customs of Joyce's land better than she.

The utilities in Joyce's daughter's home had been shut down for months, but Joyce still paid the phone bill.

Joyce opened the blinds and saw a barge plowing tranquilly out to sea. A bunch of gulls tussled over something and then decided they didn't want it. Out in the surf, a dog chased a tall bird. Whenever the dog got close, the bird, with gawky effort, would beat itself into the air and glide farther down the beach, where it would resettle, regain its dignity, and put the chase out of its mind. And here came the dog again.

Joyce neatened her house, dusted, wiped down the mirrors without looking at herself, lined up the tumblers and flutes and shot glasses and highball glasses and martini glasses just so. She folded laundry, dumped the rest of the coffee down the sink.

She put on a long sweater with big, square pockets and stepped out onto the back porch with her cigarettes. There was enough breeze to carry the barking of a single sea lion. Joyce heard them all the time now, always sounding like they were protesting a loss, like they were calling helplessly toward the sky, refusing to be reasonable.

ESTUARY

You may remember that summer, the way it ground to a halt. The sun would get straight overhead where you could barely find it, and just stay lost up there. I kept leaving sunglasses all over town so I started buying the cheapest pairs I could find, six dollars and oversize and with lenses that turned the world gray. The baseball team down in Tampa was still in last place. There'd been repeated threats of shipping them to a bigger market where they could get a fresh start, but finally everyone understood it was a bluff. Tampa was stuck with them, as they were stuck with Tampa. Freaks roamed the beach, my favorite an old man who ate entire watermelons on demand. Children would approach him, lugging the outsize fruits in their frail arms, and the old man would whip out a machete and get to work and every trace of the pink flesh would disappear down his gullet in under a minute. And of course there were all the minor shark attacks, which were even more frequent that year. Everyone kept saying something was in the water, that some pollutant was turning the sharks even more ornery. The town I was living in was built on a shallow cove with two or three thin rivers pouring into it, and the sharks out there were mostly youngsters. The waters were a training ground—the school fish drowsy, the currents mild, the swimmers pale and off-guard and accustomed to chilly lakes.

It wasn't like I had nothing to do. I'd agreed to fix a restaurant space up for an old high school classmate and her girlfriend. The place was small but it was on the corner of a block right down by the beach and had windows you could sell out of hand-to-hand. It wasn't going to be a sit-down restaurant. Cammie, the brains of the operation, and the money, didn't want to deal with a wait staff. She was going to serve cold soups and pressed Cubans, one appetizer of salsa and plantain chips, key lime pie and coffee. I'd known Cammie since the old days. She'd used her real name then, Rachel. She looked exactly the same now, but with simpler hair. And she still had those same legs. She wore unmemorable white shorts and unmemorable white sneakers, but you remembered her legs. I'd never met her girlfriend, but I imagined she was on the brawny side because she worked security on a rundown casino boat.

Cammie's job, on the other hand, was orchestrating the dessert room at a pricy steakhouse down in Tampa. She was paying me $350 a week right out of her salary, and the deal was that when the restaurant opened I'd be in for a percentage and get a job with them—assistant manager in charge of sweeping or something. Chopping up the salsa. Didn't matter to me. When I pictured Cammie and her girlfriend I pictured them peaceful and whispering at the end of a day. Maybe they'd have a lamp on, and they'd each be reading a book, their legs tangled up on the couch. One of them would pass the other a cookie from a plate. They didn't *need* the restaurant. It was a venture that might make their nice life even nicer.

I had no deadline for getting the place ready and I always felt like I was working too fast. I wasn't used to getting paid by the day, wasn't used to being an employee, and I wondered if I was meant to be stretching the tasks instead of burning them up. After a couple weeks, I had the storeroom stripped and the ceiling repainted and the toilets installed and new screens in and the windows gliding up and down with a finger. Lighting fixtures and ceiling fans. Hot water heater. There were a couple steps just inside the door, and I bolted a handrail onto the wall alongside. I had most of the floor ripped up. I knew I needed to pace myself, so I began a slow morning habit of clearing all the breeze-fallen palm fronds off the front walk. I dragged them to the fence at the rear of the strip mall, where they rested in a brittle rising drift, dry as paper. I had the feeling, doing any of this, of going through motions, a dull, drained feeling, like if anything were going to work out for me it would've already happened.

A couple nights a week, tired from working and from trying not to work, I'd sit in my truck down on the stretch of beach where you could drive cars and I'd wait for people to get stuck. In the dark you could easily veer from the hard-packed strip into the loose sand. One night the dusk brought me this stand-up comedian and this woman twice his age. He was set to perform at a club I'd never heard of, opening for a sitcom actress I'd never heard of. He didn't come up with any funny remarks about being stuck in the sand and, in fact, acted kind of solemn while I hooked him up behind the 4x4. He and his middle-aged woman were in a rental, a late-model muscle car made to look like its classic predecessor. After I hauled the car loose, the comedian said he was eternally grateful, in those words. He'd never been late to a show in his life. The woman was drunk, or maybe she wasn't. Beads and feathers were dangling in her hair. She said this was the last summer she was going to be sexy. She was glad it was lasting forever.

The little city I was living in was a few towns north of Tampa and a few towns south of where I'd grown up. People wound up here because no one else would have them, because there were already too many lawyers in better towns or too many pharmacists in better towns, because they couldn't afford to retire in Naples, because, in rare instances, they were born here. In my case, a bunch of projects had fallen through at the same time. Normally my projects collapsed in a staggered fashion, which always left me with one or two irons in the fire, one or two reasons to be optimistic. Marketing was my area of schooling and I was also handy enough to help out on a construction site, but I'd tried to push into the foreclosures boom, had sought a patent for a lawn-care tool, founded a maid service, bought a slice of an on-demand storage company that went belly up. I'd taken a couple stabs at the forty-hour-a-week cubicle thing too—once I got laid off and once I hated it so much I wound up walking out in the middle of the morning.

My girlfriend finally had enough, and that's what left me fleeing south for shelter. We'd been together nine years, so "girlfriend" doesn't seem weighty enough a term. We'd always been happy, at least fairly so, until the last year or two. We were the couple who wouldn't split up—everyone else believed that and for a while we did too. It got to where I was rooting for her to leave me, wishing for it every afternoon once the profitless, drummed-up tasks of my day ran out. I had no idea if I was still in love with her or not. Once enough time passes, there's no way to tell. What I did know was that we'd stopped taking meals together, we'd stopped asking how the other's day went, and when we slept together it was like we were actors, like we were trying to convince each other how much passion was still between us. I honestly wanted better for her than what she was getting from me. I honestly wished her well.

So now I was living with Mike and Melanie. Freeloading, one might say. My girlfriend was up in Atlanta and my parents had retired to North Carolina. I had breathing room, at least. Before I left, I'd sold everything that was mine, that I couldn't imagine my girlfriend having use for, and left the proceeds pinned under the toaster for her on the kitchen counter. I only kept my big pretty 4x4. It was my lone significant possession. $350 a week, the fixing-up-the-restaurant money, wasn't enough that I wanted to try getting my own place. It was enough for tallboys and gas for the truck and it felt righteous, pathetic as it sounds, to sock some honest cash in a manila envelope for savings. My girlfriend and I had had some investment accounts together, and I'd taken my name off them. I hadn't wanted to mess with divvying any of that, and I have to say it was a free, clean feeling—not having a money market that inched sideways each month, not moving puny sums from here to there and trying to figure out if it made a difference, perking up or pouting with the rise or fall of the stock market.

Mike and Melanie were lawyers. They had too many rooms in their house so one was Mike's painting studio and one an exercise room. They were friends of ours, of my girlfriend and me, but somehow it didn't feel awkward that they'd taken me in. It didn't feel like they were taking sides or anything. I think my girlfriend, my *ex*-girlfriend, was happy to be able to talk to Melanie and keep tabs on me. And Mike had always enjoyed my company. I felt like I was using up some kind of capital living with them, all the credit I'd accrued by conducting myself decently. I thought I deserved a soft place to crash because I'd always been fair and forthright. I'd never cheated anyone. I didn't lie.

I didn't know how long I could stay with them—how long I wanted to, or was allowed to. Melanie went for protracted runs around the neighborhood and Mike came home late, usually holding up dinner, amazed and amused at how hard his firm worked him. Most days, they'd leave a bunch of ingredients out on the kitchen counter and I was supposed to cook. This was Melanie's idea. She was smart. She'd buy all these ingredients I couldn't afford, but by cooking I got to feel like I'd contributed. Lamb. Veal chops with rosemary. Steak tartare and mussels. Thai green curry fish.

One day, I was getting some braised pork belly and sweet potato fries underway and Melanie came home and presented me with a pair of sunglasses. They glinted in the dim kitchen lights. They had a case and then the case had a snug baggie it fit inside. I couldn't have made a guess at how much the sunglasses cost. I thanked her and set them up behind the sink, next to a potted bamboo plant.

Melanie hoisted herself onto the middle island to face me and watched as I rubbed fennel seed and allspice onto the meat.

"I decided I'm going to tell you if Dana starts dating anyone," she said. "And if you start dating someone, I'm going to tell her. I'm not getting into keeping secrets. It's something I decided about how to handle this situation, so I'm letting you know."

"What if I don't want to hear about her dating someone?" I said.

She picked up half a cabbage and held it in her hands, looking at me like I was playing a tiresome game. I perused the knife block and chose one and slid it out. They had a knife for every different food you could possibly want to cut.

"So?"

"So?" she said.

"Is she dating anyone?"

"No, not yet. I'm saying *if*. I'm just laying out my policy."

I pulled out a deep fryer and poured oil in it, then pushed a newspaper that was lying there to a safe distance, over near a decorative jug of chili peppers.

"Remember when we all went to Paso Robles?" Melanie said. "This is something I was thinking about."

I waited.

"The last place we went, we could barely walk. You ran over a rosebush with the rental car. You guys were taking big handfuls of the chocolates. The lady who worked there was getting all worked up, giving us tiny pours, and Mike asked her what kind of champagne she'd recommend for a toddler's funeral."

"I think I remember that."

"She kicked us out. She had the phone in her hand, like she might have to call the police."

"I remember that day," I said. "Most of it."

"You fell on the ground laughing," Melanie said. "I just stood there. I didn't see how it was funny. The look on the lady's face—she was afraid. She was shaking."

Melanie was wearing skimpy, strappy shoes. She had a lawyer job where she breezed around town to meetings and Mike had a lawyer job where they chained him to a desk.

"I think that's when I got my first glimpse of a side of Mike I see all the time now. The big, jovial bully. He hid that part of himself for years, but that was a glimpse of it. I was just thinking about it today."

"We were pretty drunk."

"Well, yeah," she said. "That's a given."

I watched her eyes get still and dark then, her thoughts drifting off somewhere, away from Paso Robles. She had a little nervous tic she did with her fingernails, and for a moment it seemed she forgot I was standing there. I picked up a hand towel and folded it into a square, then refolded it. When she finally looked up at me, she only asked how long till dinner.

"Two hours max," I said. I had the knife and a cutting board ready, and she handed me the cabbage.

"You couldn't fry an egg in college, and now you're like a chef."

"When we lived in that town in Tennessee there were no restaurants."

"You see that, you acquired a new skill. I haven't acquired a new skill in a long time."

"People who fail a lot wind up with a bunch of new skills," I said.

Melanie shrugged, not quite surrendering the point. She straightened some spice bottles, making it where all the labels showed, before easing herself down off the island and making toward the garage, plucking her running sneakers from the bottom of the stairs as she passed. I heard a door open and close, and then another, and then the hum of the air conditioner. I always felt relieved and anxious at the same time, alone in that cavernous house. I looked out the kitchen window, knowing there was nothing out there but the next lawn.

There'd been talk of polished concrete for the restaurant's floor, but that turned out to be a lot of hassle. I ended up putting down simple, smoke-gray tiles. They were cool and smooth, and I took my shoes off some days and padded back and forth in the long dim room of the future restaurant I would work in and slightly own. It was getting harder to kill time, so one afternoon I took a walk. I'd forgotten about walks. The city had posted new red signs along the beach warning of the fledgling blacktips. The most recent victim had been an elderly woman collecting shells. The shark had leapt from the shallows and beached itself, such had been its lust for the lady's bony, purple-veined ankle. They'd had to kill it to make it let go. It had been out of the water for ten minutes and was still holding fast. They'd gouged its eyes, tried to tempt it with a half-rotted squid, put a lighter to it. Finally, they'd sliced it open and bled it dry and it quit gasping.

* * *

Mike had told me he and Melanie were trying to get pregnant, and several nights in a row I heard them going at it from my room. Mostly I heard *her*. I'd be stretched out on top of the covers, staring at the ceiling, and suddenly I'd hear a noise and realize it was Melanie. It would get louder and then turn into these sharp, breathless chirps. I'd stay right where I was, frozen. It made me jealous, of course, but I also felt like I was doing something wrong, like I should've snuck outside and waited out there until they were done. The next afternoon I'd feel awkward when it was Melanie and I alone, chit-chatting while I cooked, but then Mike would come home and we'd all sit and chew our fork-tender meat and Melanie would have a glass of wine and there'd be earnest, decade-old music playing and all would be normal enough again.

The routine became that I would go out to the porch with Mike after dinner and hang out with him while he smoked, usually with gin drinks, talking sometimes about the pitiful baseball team but mostly about the assholes Mike dealt with every day. Mike hated his boss. He hated his clients. Hearing about all these lawyers and the slimy companies they defended, it was easy for me to believe in that good-guy capital I'd built up.

One evening, Mike clinked his ice cubes around and poured more gin. Then he looked me in the eye and said he envied me. His tie was loose, his eyes glassy. Melanie had gone to bed.

"Your life doesn't boss you around every second," he said. "Every once in a while you get to choose your next action. I don't remember what that's like."

"I choose my actions, but I usually don't choose them well," I told him.

"If I got turned loose on a Monday morning I'd probably wander around bashing into tree trunks, then drown in someone's pool. I'm a red-tape artist, is what I am. I do the devil's paperwork."

I looked upward and the sky was an empty screen. If Mike wanted a bunch of sympathy from me, that didn't strike me as fair. "What about coaching that football team?" I said.

"That's for the firm. We have to do shit in the community." He was chewing a mouthful of ice. "Everybody's claiming little pieces of me. You're like, a self. I know you think you're on hard times, but at least you're still whole."

My impulse was to run myself down, to convince him not to envy me, but I resisted it. Everybody had a self. Some people's selves had gainful employment and understanding wives from well-off families.

"I don't want to have a kid," he said. "That's why it's not working. My sperm have low morale."

"Still nothing?"

"I'll talk myself into it eventually. I'll talk myself into wanting a child, just like I talked myself into going to law school."

He lowered his drink and then raised it back up and finished the thing. I didn't know where his energy came from, if he was so unhappy.

"You're free, man," he said. "You could buy a crappy old boat and sail to Mexico if you wanted. You could hop in your truck and drive to Alaska."

I laughed, and even to my ears it sounded caustic.

"Fuck it," he said. He was out of cigarettes. He flipped the empty box off in the bushes and pocketed his lighter. "I need to start rolling my own is what I need to do."

He slipped his tie off, folded it neatly, and lifted the lid of his monumental barbecue grill. He rested the tie across the grates, the apple-green silk lustrous even against the polished heating elements. Then he brought the lid back down, grinning bleakly.

The next afternoon I hung around the restaurant while the guy from the air-conditioning company installed the new unit and inspected the ductwork and put in new filters. I decided to skip dinner at the house in favor of sitting in the cab of my truck with the radio turned down low, a six-pack of tallboys for company. I was down at the beach, waiting for people to get stuck again. Well past midnight, I watched a Japanese pickup flounder and then sink itself to the wheel wells—the tiny kind of truck they don't even make anymore. I went and said hello and hooked them to the hitch. A fresh Air Force cadet and his gal. They were so drunk, I felt I hadn't had a drop. The boy kept talking about his uncle, saying he was going to do precisely as his uncle had told him, saying his uncle had instructed him to take this girl out on a date and get to second base. The girl cackled. The boy said his uncle had told him to send the wine back at the restaurant and damn if he hadn't done it. He'd had one sip and sent it right back.

The next time the sharks struck, it was a little girl. She lost a finger right in the middle of the morning. I heard the ambulance siren from the restaurant and walked down and got the story third-hand from an old jogger. The girl had been told to stay out of the water, to stay where it was dry and build sand castles while her aunt tanned and trolled a romance novel, but the wind flung the girl's pail into the water's-edge foam and she went after it. She didn't know anything had happened, they said—it was a clean, almost surgical amputation—until she sat back down at her sand castle and saw blood running into the moat.

The next time I took the 4x4 down onto the beach, Mike came along. I found my accustomed spot on a shallow rise just north of the pier and shut off the engine and the headlights. Mike stripped down to his undershirt, shucked off his shoes and socks. He opened the glove box and tossed in his phone. "We'll leave the choke collar in here a little while," he said. I usually sat in the cab facing the pier, but Mike didn't want to be cooped up, so we got out and I let the tailgate down. No tallboys tonight. Mike had hauled out gin and a bottle of tonic and a thermos full of ice cubes. He even had slices of lime in a plastic baggie and some ginger cookies a client had sent to his office. The breeze kept kicking up, blowing sand on our shins. There was a volleyball court not far up the beach, and now and then we heard the dull thud of a spike.

"What now?" Mike said.

"Now we wait," I told him. "If we pull one out, that's a good night. If we get two, that's a great night. Three, historic."

"We'll probably get half a dozen," he said. "I'm something of a good-luck charm."

There was no moon yet. A jet passed overhead, trailing its roar behind it. We finished the first round of drinks and made another, drinking fast because of the heat. A bunch of people in matching red T-shirts hurried past, whispering urgently, participants in a scavenger hunt or some other whole-some mischief. Mike and I started talking about people we used to know in college, the successes and catastrophes. A guy we used to hang around with was running for Congress. Another was a professor at a school in Singapore. Another had his own show on the Weather Channel. A couple guys we knew had overdosed on drugs, and one had drowned in a river in Alaska.

Mike ate the last cookie. He crumpled the box and tossed it behind him, into the bed of the truck. "I'm not going to ask anything about Dana," he said. "If you're not upset about her, I'm glad. If you are upset still, talking to me isn't going to help. I just want to let you know, for whenever you want to take me up on it, that I'm acquainted with any number of legal secretaries who are having a hard time finding a decent guy. I'm not a matchmaker, but just so you know. My resources are at your disposal."

"So you'll tell them I'm a decent guy?"

"Well, I guess I have no idea about that. It's always the ones like you that turn out to be serial killers."

"Killing people isn't for me," I said. "I don't like secrets."

"Right," Mike said. "And the dry-cleaning bills."

He surveyed the makeshift bar he'd set up, then looked at my glass and at his own. "I didn't bring enough liquor, did I? I underestimated our thirsts."

"There's plenty," I said.

"Yeah, for now."

He took a pack of cigarettes out of his pants pocket. He peeled the plastic wrapper off and let it fall away onto the sand.

"I'm going to do something for you guys once I get some money saved up," I said. "I appreciate you letting me crash. I'm going to get you guys a weekend vacation somewhere."

Mike got his cigarette lit, shielding it from the breeze. He took a steadying drag. "I like having you around. It's a lot of house for two people. You could stay forever if it was up to me."

"If it was up to you? What, did Melanie say something?"

"No, she didn't say anything. When she wants you to go, you'll know it. She doesn't play any games, you have to give her that. When she wants you gone, she'll walk right up and tell you."

"She doesn't really go in for the passive-aggressive tactics, huh? The dirty looks and weird comments and whatnot."

"She's pretty special in a lot of ways." Mike was measuring his words now, like he didn't want to be misunderstood. "She can be pretty demanding about the big picture, but when it comes to the details, the day-to-day, she's surprisingly... lenient."

"Can I have one of those?" I said.

Mike held out his cigarettes and then handed over the lighter. He didn't make any comment about my wanting to smoke.

"Even though it's obvious she needs to lighten up—like, that's the first thing you notice about her—you can tell she's nowhere near the end of her rope," he said. "She'll never snap. She'll just stretch and stretch."

I took our glasses and poured a fresh round. The thermos was one of these super-expensive models for people who went trekking in the desert, and the ice cubes were still in good shape. We weren't getting a lot of traffic thus far. Maybe fifteen cars had driven by, among them a few compacts that were prime candidates for getting stuck, but they'd all motored in and out of sight without any trouble.

"This is like fishing," Mike said. "You hope nothing gets on your hook because then you'd have to put your drink down."

"Nobody's out tonight," I said. "It's eerie."

After a minute we heard the approaching racket of motorcycles up on the street, that crackling growl. There was a whole company of them, their helmets flashing as they passed under the streetlights.

Mike flicked his cigarette butt into the darkness. "They're probably all lawyers," he said. "They're accountants for an insurance company that insures insurance companies."

We were close to drunk, and soon Mike started outlining all the sordid events that had occurred in the area in recent years—the driver's education teacher who'd been fired for taking the school's car during his planning period and picking up hookers, the girls' high school soccer coach who'd taped himself getting a handjob from one of his players. Eventually I saw that he was building a case for not having children, for the unsuitability of the world.

Around midnight a bunch of people started coming by on foot, strolling in the meek surf. Several couples. A gaggle of teenagers. None of them acknowledged us, as if we were part of the scenery. A mother and daughter ambled by. A lone old man. A woman in fancy party attire, clutching her skirt up out of the water.

"I know what you're really waiting for out here," Mike said.

"What's that?" I asked.

"You want to be here when the next shark attack happens. You want to pull somebody out of the water and be a hero."

"Yup, that's my plan," I said. "I'm always out for the glory."

Mike put his hand on the back of my neck, rough but brotherly. The moon was still absent, but a scatter of bright low stars had fixed themselves where they belonged. Mike took his hand back and stood up from the tailgate and started walking toward the water, drink and cigarette in hand. He went out into the gentle slosh, his white undershirt seeming to glow. He went right in with his suit pants on, without looking back at me, up to his knees and then all the way up to his waist. Then he stopped and stood there, facing the whole unlit cove. I set my gin glass down. My throat was burning from the couple cigarettes I'd smoked. I started cleaning up our mess, capping the bottles and chucking the limes. I felt angry, I didn't know at what. I heard a strange noise on the breeze, and I could tell it was coming from the direction of the water. Then I heard it clearly. Mike was laughing. He was out there howling at full voice.

*   *   *

Cammie stopped by the restaurant. I was happy she caught me working. My head was all corners from the previous night's drinking, but I was used to ignoring that. I looked up from some molding I'd decided to replace and saw her legs first, which put me in mind of tennis in a bygone era. She approved of everything I'd done, thought the place looked great. I showed her the big framed black and whites of Bryson's Canal she'd ordered. I'd picked them up the day before, and I didn't know where she wanted them hung. Bryson's Canal was a local landmark. A hundred years ago, probably more, some guy got it in his head to cut a canal all the way across Florida. He made it a few miles inland before the government stopped him, but the part he'd dug was still there, straight as an arrow, lined with alligators.

Cammie hadn't come around sooner, she said, because she wanted to be stunned by the changes, like in a before-and-after photo. She'd been dropping my pay off at Mike and Melanie's, a stack of paper-clipped twenties with a ten on top, same every time.

"What's with the ashtray out front? You smoke now?"

"Trial basis," I said.

I asked about her girlfriend, just being polite, and Cammie sighed and said she was threatening to move to Las Vegas. Mini-mansions for a song out there. Real casinos to guard. Casinos that didn't have a bow and a stern. Cammie's girlfriend enjoyed hiking, apparently, which wasn't a thing to do in Florida.

"You think she's serious?" I said.

"Hard to say. Last summer she told me she was thinking about shaving her head, and I thought she was kidding because it was so hot out. I came home the next day and there she was, bald as anything."

"She's bald?"

"Not anymore. She's got the cheekbones and the eyes, so it doesn't really matter. But no, she let it grow back out."

I wiped my hands off on the front of my pants, mopped the sweat off my face with my T-shirt. I guess I'd been waiting for a shoe to drop, whether

I'd known it or not. Eager for it, in a way. "What would happen then, if she really wants to move?"

"Well, I guess she'll get a Nevada driver's license. Go see Hoover Dam. Wait for her furniture to arrive in the big truck."

"I meant what would happen with the restaurant. I guess I know the answer."

Cammie's eyes registered the question. "How do you know I'd go with her?" she asked.

I was straightening things on the steel countertop now, my hand tools and such. I normally just left them in a jumbled heap. "Because all towns are the same if you peel away a layer or two, so why not move? They all have frozen yogurt and a Target, right? But they don't all have a girl you love."

Cammie reached over and squeezed a drill bit with two fingers. "Yeah, I probably would," she said. "I'd probably go to Nova Scotia if she wanted me to. She's really good for me."

"It doesn't have to be Las Vegas. This is about the point where all my projects fall through. I can feel it. This is right about the time."

"This isn't really *your* project, so relax," said Cammie. "I said moving was mentioned. I didn't say it was happening. Who knows, she could be bringing up moving to leverage something else. It could be part of a strategy. Women, you know?"

"A big soup and sandwich chain will move in down the block. Or the licenses will get held up. It'll be something. Probably something we can't think of right now."

Cammie made an impressed face, like she'd been enlightened about something. "Wow, you can really make a hurricane out of a dark cloud, huh?"

"It's never just a dark cloud for me. I should've warned you about my luck before you hired me. It's truly not pessimism. It's just acknowledging a pattern. Scientific observation. I'm okay with it. Worse things happen to people than being snake-bit in financial endeavors. A lot worse things happen to people."

"Okay, so if this restaurant never opens, which no one is saying is remotely the case, you will have made money off the whole affair. It's me who loses money. If anybody should be doing community theater about that situation, it should be me. But I'm not, because there's no situation."

"Oh, it'll be something," I said, and I could hear stagey put-on wisdom in my voice. I felt comfortable and fortified, poor-mouthing the future.

"Geesh," she said, almost laughing. She was about to say something but she decided not to. She twisted her hair into a tight knot at the side of her head. "I'll tell you something. You sure did an awful nice job in here for somebody who doesn't think this restaurant is going to work out."

One especially still, humid evening I came home and the house was silent except for a faint whimpering sound. Mike was at some work function, I knew, a charity dinner. I followed the sound upstairs, to a room I'd never stepped foot in. The door was usually closed, and I'd always assumed it was another of the countless closets. I peeked my head in and saw wall-to-wall packages. Unopened gifts. It took me a second to figure out they were wedding gifts. Melanie was in among them, curled up. After a moment, she realized I was standing in the doorway. She didn't seem startled, but she stopped crying all at once. I asked if she was okay and she turned her face away from me, looking at nothing.

"What did you guys get us?" she asked.

I couldn't remember, of course. I hadn't had anything to do with picking out their gift. "Something monogrammed," I told her. "Like maybe some pillow cases."

Melanie shivered. I wanted to get down next to her, but I stayed put. What Mike had said about her being special was true. She never got onto anyone. She never nagged Mike. Not really. She never asked me any pointed questions about my plans. She never moaned that her talents were misused. When she cried, she did it in private.

"Why haven't you guys opened these?" I asked her.

She puffed up with a breath and then deflated. "Yeah, that," she said. "We went on the honeymoon, so we were going to wait until we got back.

When we got back Mike's mom was sick, then by the time she was better we were moving over here from the apartment. I've asked him to open them with me two or three times. At some point it became a thing, you know? He says he's too busy, which there's some truth to. I'm not going to force him to do it but I'm not going to open them by myself. I still haven't sent out thank-you cards. When you're a woman you have to send thank-you cards. There's pretty much nothing worse you can do in the world than not send thank-you cards."

She stopped talking so I said, "I get it." I said, "This stuff gets complicated, doesn't it?" It felt wrong that I wasn't getting down on the floor next to her, that I wasn't at least touching her shoulder.

"That it does," she said. "That it certainly does."

I watched her there breathing evenly, absently fingering the ribbon on one of the gifts.

"Dana still isn't dating anyone," she said.

Next the sharks got into a family of Canadians. They were way up the beach, so I didn't hear the sirens, but word traveled down the strip fast enough. One gang of preadolescent hammerheads had shimmied into the soundless surf behind the waist-deep Newfoundlanders, and another had advanced from the open water. Hundreds of stitches. The town council was making a plan already. When the family got released from the hospital, a bank of suites in the swankiest hotel on the beach would be waiting for them, if they could be convinced to stay.

The fronds kept falling and I kept lofting them onto the mound at the back fence. A dozen parking spots were unusable, including a handicapped one. I could hear critters scurrying around under the pile, I had no idea what kind. None of the other business owners had complained. I guess business wasn't brisk enough that it mattered.

There wasn't much else I could do for the restaurant. I decided to add a layer of insulation in the ceiling and put in decorative flashing in the areas where customers could see. It was going to be mostly a carryout place, but we needed at least a couple tables and a set of barstools, so I went with Cammie to the big hardware store and she made her choices and we scheduled a delivery. The barstools we took back to the strip mall ourselves, in the back of my truck. Cammie messed with the radio the whole time, stone-faced, flipping through all the oldies and Latin music and talk. She was wearing a stiff, buttony jacket, not sweating a bit, and of course a skirt.

Inside the restaurant, we positioned the stools and I settled onto one and watched Cammie walk around and touch all the fixtures. She ran water in the sinks, opened and closed cabinets. She gazed forlornly at the photos of Bryson's Canal for a minute, then went over and messed around with the lights and left them off. She walked over in her sneakers and closed the blinds. There was still plenty of light. I could see her coming toward me with a thin, frank look on her face, and she just kept advancing. I stayed on the stool and she stepped between my knees, washing in like a wave, arching her back so that our faces stayed apart. I was taken by surprise and suddenly wondering all sorts of unhelpful things. She touched my eyebrow with her thumb, smoothing it down. We were eye to eye, her standing and me stuck on the stool.

"You men wear me out," she said. "Every one of you thinks you're a one-of-a-kind." She grazed my ear with her thumb. It was like she was examining me for purchase. "You're good-looking, though. I won't deny that. Not you, just men in general. With your forearms and your stubble and all."

She looked down at herself, like she was wondering how I saw her. She rested one foot on the bottom rail of the stool.

"I don't think I'm one-of-a-kind," I said. "I'm a dime a dozen."

"You guys have some bad luck and you fall in love with it. It's just breakups and business. It's just divorces and shitty jobs."

"I won't be getting divorced any time soon," I said.

She put her hands flat against my chest and locked her elbows, making sure to keep me at arm's length. Her hands were tiny and certain. Whatever had her agitated, it probably had nothing to do with me.

"You're everybody's friend, aren't you?" she said.

Her scent was full in my nose now—an easy, natural smell, only a trace of sweetness.

"I can count my friends on one hand," I told her. "Even if I include you."

She leaned in and gathered my head to her chest, pressing my cheek against her jacket. She was hugging me like I was a child she was accustomed to worrying about. "You can count me if you like," she said.

She pulled my head up and found my eyes again. Her lashes were lush and her teeth gleaming. Her blunt fingernails were in the back of my neck. I felt cursed with hope. Then that quickly, she detached herself. She stepped backward and I was empty-handed, balancing there. Her jacket made brusque scuffing noises as she crossed the room, and then the door swung open with a rush of warm air and closed gently behind her.

I stayed perched right where I was, feeling like time had stopped. But it hadn't. It wouldn't. Next I would lock this place up and drive my truck down Charter Street and cook a delicious dinner in a well-appointed kitchen. I would have a stiff drink and a smoke and then lie in bed awake for hours and hours. But I was going to sit in this dark building for a few more minutes first.

The temperature that night in Mike and Melanie's house was going to be perfect, where you cover up with a sheet but you don't need a blanket. My bedclothes would be freshly laundered. My truck was running smooth as ever. The calluses on my fingers had returned. I lived in the United States, in Florida. I was healthy. Overnight, people would drive the length of the peninsula and get where they were going. The loose cats would fight each other and survive. When the sun came up tomorrow, children would learn math and go fishing and search for lost toys.

ABOUT THE AUTHOR

John Brandon's three novels are *Arkansas*, *Citrus County*, and *A Million Heavens*. He has spent time as the Grisham Fellow in Creative Writing at University of Mississippi, and the Tickner Writing Fellow at Gilman School, in Baltimore. His work has appeared in *Oxford American*, *GQ*, *Grantland*, *ESPN the Magazine*, the *New York Times Magazine*, *McSweeney's*, the *Believer*, and numerous literary journals. He now lives in St. Paul, and teaches at Hamline University. This is his first story collection.